The Old Spring

Also by Richard Francis

Novels

Blackpool Vanishes
Daggerman
The Enormous Dwarf
The Whispering Gallery
Swansong
The Land Where Lost Things Go
Taking Apart The Poco Poco
Fat Hen
Prospect Hill

Non-Fiction

Transcendental Utopias
Ann the Word
Judge Sewall's Apology

The Old Spring

Richard Francis

**Tindal
Street
Press**

First published in UK July 2010
by Tindal Street Press Ltd
217 The Custard Factory, Gibb Street,
Birmingham, B9 4AA
www.tindalstreet.co.uk

2 4 6 8 10 9 7 5 3 1

A CIP catalogue reference for this book is available
from the British Library

ISBN: 978 1 9069940 6 8

Typeset by Alma Books Ltd
Printed and bound in Great Britain by
CPI Mackays, Chatham

Birmingham City Council

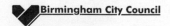

Supported by
**ARTS COUNCIL
ENGLAND**

To Jo

I

Frank went down the stairs, across the hallway, and into the back room. The windows beyond the bar were only just becoming grey and the room was nearly dark, but he didn't turn the lights on. He made his way carefully between the tables and through the far doorway into the snug.

He liked the dim fug, the whiff of booze on the air, the leftover warmth from the punters and the fire. There were still a couple of pink nuggets among the clinker in the grate. On the table in the corner a faint gleam from the rim of a pint glass, overlooked. He shook his head, picked it up and carried it over to the bar.

Then he walked back to the fire. He had a sense of something amiss. He bent down to look at it. Yes, one of the ribs in the grate that held the coal was all but burned through. Another thing to worry about – he had enough on his plate as it was. There was a sharp bitter smell from the exhausted coals.

He walked on into the public. It was cooler here, probably the draught from the front door just beyond. He went up to it and slid the bolt so Darren could let himself in, but didn't bother to open it. You could hear the rain coming down outside, no need to check. Instead he turned back and followed the bench that went the length of the public. When he got to the bar counter he tapped it sharply twice, as if he was ordering a pint himself, or testing the soundness of the wood. He stood there for a moment or two, getting the drinker's eye view. Then he made his way back through the pub and up to the flat to get breakfast.

Dawn could hear Frank clattering about in the kitchen before she even opened the door. She went past him over to the window and peered round the curtain. The rain sounded almost dry as it rattled against the pane. Nothing like rain for bringing the customers into a pub.

Then she wished she hadn't thought that thought. It brought to mind the regulars standing outside her dad's pub, getting soaked to the skin, more fool them, forty years ago this very day.

'Something Jerry said last night,' Frank told her, an egg in each fist, the smooth almost pointed tops poking through his big curled fingers.

'I don't want one,' she said. 'You always do me one.'

'Just in case.'

'I never want one.'

'It was the rain made me think of it.' He put each egg in turn on a slotted spoon and slid it into a pan of boiling water on the stove.

'That's the missionary position, that is,' she told him.

'What is?' he asked, looking guilty, as she knew he would.

Try it sometime, my friend. 'Being boiled alive in a cooking pot,' she told him out loud.

'Oh. Right-oh,' he said, moving quickly on. 'What Jerry said, if you have an ordinary sized face with stubble on it, then eat a lot so you end up with a great slab face, you'd have the same amount of bristles in total, but just spread out more – oh bugger.' There was a sharp short sound from the pan, like the report from a tiny rifle. 'Blumming egg cracked. They always do it on me.'

Funnily enough Frank had a large face himself, though not a slab. Round more than flat, in line with his head as a whole. But stubble, no. He had a way of shaving that made his stubble vanish altogether, chopped off below the level of the skin. When finished he looked like a shiny balloon.

'Water too hot,' Dawn said.

'It's got to boil. That's why they're called boiled eggs.' He shook some salt into the pan.

'It's our last morning for the books, that's what we've got to worry about, not what that know-all Jerry's been telling you.'

Frank's big shoulders slumped. One thing he didn't like to face up to was reality. Anything but. But today was the day they needed to find what was wrong with the books, get them to reconcile. Tim Green from the brewers had given them another week, said he would be passing through anyway and could pick them up then.

'Are you saying what I think you're saying?' she'd asked Tim.

'All I'm saying is, I'll give you another week.'

'We've got our fingers in the till, is that it?'

'No, of course not. I'm just giving you an extra week, to check through.'

He wasn't from the brewers in any case, or at least the brewers weren't brewers, not any more, they were a pub management concern. They'd discovered it was easier to move money and property around than brew beer.

'Been a landlord myself,' Tim said. 'I know how it's the last thing you want to do. But it's got to be got right.'

They'd been sitting in the back room, about half past three, between openings. It wasn't the pub's best time of day, particularly in winter, the morning sparkle gone from the bar. Sitting in wooden light at a table in the fag end of the afternoon, the dusk gathering through the windows beyond the bar, books spread in front of them, smell of used booze from lunchtime hanging in the air, Tim, in his sharp black suit and open-neck shirt, letting his coffee go cold: she could do without it.

Because Tim dressed young you got the idea he *was* young, from a distance anyway, but close up you could see fine lines all over his face.

'I've got a new set of wheels,' Tim said. 'Ford Focus.' He was changing the subject, for fear of upsetting her, or rather he wanted her to think that. In actual fact it was boasting, reminding her that as a bloke with new wheels, he didn't ought to be crossed. Still, it let her make a point.

'Frank and me don't run a car, as you know,' she said. 'We never seem to have the wherewithal.' Which maybe we would have, if our fingers were in the till.

'The miles I do a week, I need a decent car. This Focus buzzes along, I have to admit.' He paused, thinking about it. In his mind's eye it was probably a Porsche or a Lotus. Tiger Tim, she thought. 'But I'm getting to the point when I can't spend the rest of my life on the road. I tried to put the case to Mr Banks, I said it was time for him to think about a desk job for me. No joy at all. It's like getting blood out of a stone.'

Foxy was nearer the mark. Tim was making out he was willing to give his wheels up, those free wheels anyway, and come down to her level. He was telling them, telling her at least - Frank busying himself in the snug riddling the fire, keeping out of it as best he could – Tim was telling her that it was Mr Banks she had to worry about, not him.

'I'll be over this way next Thursday,' Tim had said in a whisper, friends together, maybe villains together even. The sheer cheek of it made her swell with rage. He touched the side of his nose. 'I'll pop in for the books then.' He made a popping noise twice by pressing his lips together then parting them suddenly, pleased with the sound.

Now it *was* next Thursday. Frank pulled out one egg with his slotted spoon, picked it up quickly by his fingertips and dropped it in his eggcup. For some reason he had an eggcup shaped like a chicken, with a hole in its back to put the egg in, wrong part of the anatomy altogether, as she'd pointed out. He'd had that eggcup all through his service life, so he said, and used to take it down with him to the mess room for breakfast. Probably something only a large man could have got away with. It had brown wings and body, red legs, and a yellow beak, with the tip broken off. This egg was the one that had cracked, and there were swirls of white on it, as if it had got interrupted halfway through putting shaving cream on its face.

Frank got the second egg out, laid it on the plate beside the chicken and sat down at the table. He had another plate with a pile of soldiers ready prepared. She shook her head at it all. There was his teaspoon and his knife, his salt and his pepper. It reminded her of how her brother Keith used to lay out his Meccano before building something.

He pointed to the spare egg and raised one eyebrow at her. She shook her head again. He shrugged his shoulders, then sort of snuggled down on his chair to make a start, secretly pleased, only not as secretly as he believed. She had a sudden temptation to change her mind and ask him for the spare egg, just to watch his face drop, but didn't. A cup of black coffee was all she could cope with in the morning.

As she sipped it and he put yellow-tipped soldiers into his mouth one by one she tried to get into his thick head what an emergency it was.

'Tim could be here this morning,' she told him.

Frank thought about it, then shook his head. 'No, not coming up from Dorchester and going to Taunton first. It'll be later on.' He shook his head again, as if he could shake Tim and the books right out of it. He was quite capable of convincing himself that Tim coming later on solved the whole problem.

'All the more reason for you to sit down with me this morning and try to get it sorted.'

He took the eggshell of the first egg out of his chicken, laid it on the side, picked up the second egg and offered it to her once more.

'No, Frank.'

Duty done he slid it into the chicken, gave the top a quick warm-up tap with his knife, then cut it off in one, using his thumb as a lever. He was practical as far as practical things went, presumably had had to be on a boat. But as soon as any problem appeared over the horizon he tried to duck. Perhaps he'd learned that on a boat as well.

After breakfast she got the books together, plus the big box-file of receipts, bank statements and the till record. She went downstairs because there was more room to spread out down there. Frank was down already, squatting in front of the fireplace in the snug. She put the papers down on the table in the back room where she had talked to Tim.

'All right, Frank,' she called.

'I'm just clearing out the fire,' he called back.

'Oh, for goodness sake, Darren can do that when he comes.'

'He's got enough to do with the floors and the bar furniture. Anyway, he hasn't been a lot of good since he got the heebie-jeebies.'

'It's what we pay him –'

'Plus we've got a bit of a problem here. One of the rib things on the grate has all but burned through.'

She got up wearily and went to look. It was the original fireplace, with metal boxes that must once have supported hobs on each side and curved iron ribs between them making up the grate front. One of them was tapered away, sure enough.

'You could hardly notice it yesterday,' Frank said. 'It must have given up the ghost all at once.'

'Don't try to wiggle it,' she told him, 'you'll make it worse.' His big paws fiddled with it like a child with a loose tooth. 'Let it alone.'

'It needs replacing, that's the point.'

'In the meantime we'll be careful with it.'

'How can you be careful with it, Dawn?' There were some things he *could* get aereated about, and one of them was his precious fireplace. He looked forward to winter just so he could get it going. With the central heating on as well, and a good crowd in, the snug could get like a Turkish bath by the end of an evening.

'You can poise the coals so they don't fall through, that's how.'

'Poise the coals? *Poise* them?' He stood up and dusted his knees. 'I don't think Health and Safety would make much of that.' He was wearing his working trousers, big fat jeans with a bib and brace on them. They always looked as if they could stand up by themselves, without his being present inside. 'Poise the coals,' he said again, shaking his head as if he'd been poising them inside his own brain, and seen them come tumbling down.

'We won't be worried about Health and Safety when we're in clink for fiddling the books.'

'It's bad enough us making the rolls for lunch instead of buying them in. If they found out we were doing that, we'd be for it,' he said. 'Let alone having a wonky fireplace.'

'Never mind,' she told him consolingly, 'if all our customers get burned to a frazzle nobody will ever know we'd given them food poisoning as well.'

'If we're in bother already, all the more reason to get this laid properly and not leave it to Darren,' he said. 'You make a start and I'll join you in a bit.'

She left him to it. She could at least check she'd done the actual sums correctly. When it came to ticking off the receipts against their outgoings, though, it would be better with two, if she could ever raise him from his grate.

It was a funny thing: however hard you had to concentrate, your brain still went off on its own somewhere while you were doing it. She started thinking about her brother Keith once more.

Playing tennis – Keith had been good at it, when they were kids back in Yorkshire. Even at their secondary modern school, where there'd be half a dozen of them on the court all at once, running every which way like flies on a cowpat, he shone. He was a skinny kid with a big racket that seemed to wobble when it hit the ball – his wrists were that thin – but still the ball would whizz across the sagging net like a bullet. One day he somehow or other ended up in the final of a tournament, playing a bloke burly enough to eat him for lunch. Keith won the first set and people were calling out to encourage him. The spectators named him Baby Garth. He was pale, like Dawn was, with fair hair that flopped to the side. He started well in the second set too, then suddenly went all to pieces.

Dawn talked about it once with Jason, one of the pub rugby team, who said that what it was, Keith had been in the zone and then come out of it. There was a kind of consolation in finding it had a name. She wished she'd been able to pass it on to Keith. You were in the zone, Keith, she would have said, and then you left the zone.

At the thought of long-ago Keith leaving his zone, a tear plopped out of Dawn's eye and landed on her ledger. It hit the 7 like a wet bomb and knocked it to pieces. Bugger it, she whispered to herself, just what I need when I'm trying to prove these books are pure as the driven snow.

Frank came in.

'Another thing Jerry brought up,' he said, 'say it's raining, for the sake of argument raining a very even steady kind of rain, a certain amount of drops each cubic metre.' Frank pointed at the air with his finger while he spoke, as if the problem was written on a blackboard. 'You've got to make a journey of a hundred yards, let's say, through the rain. Do you get not as wet if you run instead of walk? Or do you just get hit by the same number of drops, only quicker?'

Dawn wondered if he'd been reminded of this instalment of Jerry's claptrap by seeing her tear fall. He wouldn't say anything straight out, even if he had; he wasn't a man in touch with the emotional world. A career aboard ship probably squashed that out of you. All those sailors living cheek by jowl with each other, if they made the mistake of opening up, they'd be like so many oysters, showing their horrible wobbly insides to each other. Couldn't be done. You'd learn to keep your shell tight shut. Anyway, the rain was still gusting against the windows, that's what would have reminded him.

'Depends,' she said.

'On what?'

'On whether I'm carrying a load of shopping.'

He shook his head, wiped his hands on his dungarees, then smoothed his short, balding hair. 'I've set the fire, anyhow,' he said. 'Poised it, like you said.'

'Well, you better come and help me with the books then.'

'I'll just make us a cup of coffee first.'

'No, Frank, you can't time-waste for ever. We've got to get on.'

'It won't take a minute. We always have one. It'll help us get on better with the books.'

'We haven't got time –'

But it was no use. His big trousers had already walked out of the room, and she could hear them climbing the stairs up to their flat to put the kettle on.

She opened the box-file of invoices and receipts. The last thing she wanted to do was go through them. She felt like she did when their bank statement arrived and she knew they were overdrawn. While the bad news was safely inside the stuck down envelope it couldn't jump out and grab you round the neck. That's how Frank felt too. But you had to resist, you couldn't live in a fool's paradise.

She pulled open the spring clip, took the receipts out, and put them in a pile on the battered old table. Then she flipped the file shut and put it on the bench to one side of her.

As she straightened up again she realised there was somebody standing and looking at her, over by the bar.

While he was spooning coffee into the pot, Frank heard Dawn suddenly quack down below. That was how her voice always sounded in the distance: quack! quack!

Ducks in the Norfolk twilight, while Frank sat on a torn seat next to Pete in Pete's old open jeep, shotguns at the ready, the ducks flying in line over the smudgy marshes, so clear against the glowing sky you could see every detail of their outlines, necks strained straight forward, even see their beaks as they opened and closed to deliver each quack. Funny how seeing them whirr into the night-time like that lifted your heart but you still wanted to shoot the little buggers; no hard feelings.

In fact even from near-to, Dawn's voice would sound like a duck when it started up. It took a second to make out there was a word inside each quack.

One of the regulars, Alan, said to him once: 'That wife of yours, she's so Yorkshire, she's a Viking.'

'What's that, m'dear?' Frank asked him.

'They attacked that coast a thousand years ago. Look at her, how tall she is, she must be nearly six foot, with that blonde hair of hers. She looks like she only just got off the longboat. She ought to be wearing animal skins and a helmet. You know, one of those ones with horns on.'

Frank had looked at her, talking to a group at a table on the other side of the snug. She was tall all right, skinny and tough. Blonde out of a bottle, of course, but she must have been one properly years back, when young. When she took her clothes off, her skin showed white as bottled milk. Even her flat bosoms seemed hard, the nipples bolted on to big brown washers.

He wasn't sure whether Alan was admiring her or taking the piss. He had that way of talking, half sarcastic, half meaning it. Probably came from teaching at the university, keeping his students guessing.

'The way she talks,' Alan went on, 'that's Viking as well. Different rhythm than your bog-standard English. It's a harder intonation, more rasping.'

'We smoke a bit,' Frank had said.

'You had no defence, being west-country,' Alan told him. 'All those soft vowels. No point trying to reason with someone when she's coming at you swinging her axe.'

'She's not my wife,' Frank said. 'We're not married.'

'That's what I meant,' Alan had told him. 'Rape and pillage.'

'Keith!' Dawn called.

'You what?' whispered Darren.

'Oh!' she cried. She felt a lump in her throat like a bit of swallowed food she could choke on. Then she realised, and said 'oh' again, a little one this time. 'Oh. I was just thinking about somebody.'

Like I owe *you* an explanation, she thought, furious all of a sudden. Darren was standing there, just in the doorway, bang inside the only beam of light in the whole place. It was a grey light, given the rain outside and the dim room within, but just enough to turn Darren's dark hair fair. He had a parting too, which made his hair fall to the right hand corner of his forehead and, though he was taller than Keith had been, his body had a similar trembly thinness, like an alley cat's.

'Darren, I could well do with you not creeping about like that,' she told him.

Darren was looking at her wild-eyed. It was an easy look for him, because though he hadn't exactly got bags under his eyes he did have patches of dark skin, as if he never had enough sleep, or was taking some sort of drugs. Which might explain his addled brains. He looked as though his irises had run.

She'd noticed before how you could catch fright from somebody else.

'Come back down to earth, Darren.'

'You give me the key,' Darren said. 'You said to let myself in. You said you would have a lie-in sometimes, with the late hours.'

'Yes, well, I didn't mean coming through the keyhole like a genie out of a bottle.'

He shrugged, as if to say don't get you. He unzipped his anorak and hung it on the peg. 'I'll lay the fire first,' he said.

'It's done already, Darren. You walked right past it. Frank did it.'

'Oh.' He looked into the snug. 'I'd a done it,' he said. 'I don't know why he always does it.'

'Because he likes doing it. That fire's his baby.'

Darren looked back into the snug again, obviously trying to make out the baby in Frank's poised coals.

'I should start off with the fire because that's the mucky job,' he said obstinately, 'and then do the floors.' He sounded as if he was reciting a contract of employment, which he was, in point of fact.

'Look on the bright side, one thing less to worry about.'

'I worry about not having it to do. I worry about everything, me. Once I wasn't worried for a while and then afterwards I worried about not being worried. I thought there must be something bad I'd forgotten about.'

'Well, for the time being just worry about getting the mop and bucket up from the cellar and giving the place a good swab down.'

'Hello, Darren,' said Frank, coming in from the hall just as Darren was going out to it. 'I thought it was you.' Frank was carrying a little tray with three mugs of coffee on it and a plate of biscuits. 'I've brought you some coffee down, m'dear,' he told him. 'We thought we'd have some.'

'Frank, he's just this minute got here. Give us a break. Give *him* a break.'

Darren glanced at Dawn, as if looking for what to say.

'That's what I *am* giving him,' Frank said. 'A break.'

'I've just told him to start on the floors,' Dawn continued.

'I'm just going to start on the floors,' Darren repeated obediently.

'Won't do any harm,' Frank said. 'He's been rained on, coming over here.'

'We can't take the blame for the flipping weather, Frank. Save his elevenses till eleven, why not? It's only half past nine.'

'Have a swig or two, anyhow,' Frank told Darren. 'Get the chill out of your bones.' He handed him a mug.

'Oh well, if it's party-time I might as well go and have a cigarette.' Dawn got her packet from the bar, lit one, picked up her mug and walked through to the front door. She opened it and stood on the step, clutching her mug in both hands, the cigarette between her fingers.

Ever since the ban came in she'd avoided smoking in the pub even when it was closed. The last thing she wanted was smoke in the atmosphere if some council snooper came in when the doors opened.

There was a pile of dog ends on the pavement, from last night's regulars. There was a big ashtray outside nowadays, but half of them took no notice. She'd have to remind Darren to sweep up.

The rain was quite light for the moment, just a few drops brushing against her in the doorway, but the air had a greenish tinge and above the street the sky was purple, clouds piled on top of each other. The houses opposite looked peaceful enough, but she knew better. Because it was a Georgian terrace, same vintage as the pub, people going past thought they were all lived in by toffs, but in fact half of them were council and one was a bail hostel. Not just Darren: Jake, the tattooed man, lived across there too, even though most people would expect him to be squatting in some cave.

Frank read out the receipts in a big voice like a town crier, holding each one a long way from his face because his glasses weren't strong enough. She tried to shush him, not wanting others to know all their business, even though it was only Darren, and anything that wasn't a bogeyman went in one ear and out the other. Frank lowered his voice for a few moments then turned the volume back up again.

'It's not done any good,' she told him when they'd got to the end.

'Has it not?'

'Has it buggery. We had all the figures written down right in the first place.'

'That sounds OK to me.'

'No Frank, it's not OK.'

He looked at her with his big eyes, then took his spectacles off and looked at her with his normal-sized eyes a bit longer. 'Oh well,' he said, and shrugged.

'We wanted it to be wrong.'

'Did we?'

'Then we would have got to the bottom of it, wouldn't we?'

She got him to read out all the outgoings again, from the ledger this time, while she tapped them into her little calculator. The sum total was right too, or at least as close as dammit, just £10 and 48 pence out which was probably a couple of miskeys. She did the subtraction from the bank statement and there was still over nine hundred unaccounted for. In just three months.

She sat and looked at the little screen for a few moments, as if staring at it hard enough could make the figures start to behave. Frank stood in the middle of the room waiting for somebody to put new batteries into him, brawny arms hanging slightly out from his body like a pair of penguin wings. 'Bugger,' Dawn said finally.

'Oh yes?' Frank asked.

'Bugger and pisspots.'

'Not turned out well, then.'

'What are we going to do, Frank?'

'We've got nothing to hide, that's how I look at it. We can look anybody in the eye.'

'Mr Banks could sack us on the spot. If we're not criminals we must be a pair of dopes who can't keep track of their accounts. I suppose we *are* a pair of dopes who can't keep track of their accounts.'

'We'll have to try and appeal to his better nature,' Frank said.

She glanced up at him. He was nodding, as though in agreement with himself.

She'd been here before, she knew what it was like to convince yourself in the absence of the enemy that they would be reasonable and commonsensical, that you could twist them round your little finger. Then when you actually saw them again, or even before you saw them, when you were just about to see them again – like when you play a cassette and there's a sort of echo of the music before the music begins – you suddenly got a memory of what a nasty difficult unforgiving old sod Mr Banks really was, and all your hopefulness went out the window.

Because she understood exactly how Frank was managing to delude himself she became angrier with him than ever. 'Don't be such bloody fool,' she told him.

'I think I'll check the cellar,' Frank said.

2

Darren's vulnerable flat was on the top floor of its building, with just the roof above. It was only a bedsitter really, with a little kitchen and shower room off.

When he woke up early that morning, before morning in fact, he could hear the rain drumming above him on the tiles. He always felt relief when he heard that noise, as if not hearing it was a strain and a worry, even though most of the time you didn't even know you were being strained and worried. What it was, if the air was empty, the night air at any rate, there was room for God knows what to come into it, just like Stonehenge.

The first time he was taken to Stonehenge he understood what it was for, even though he was only a small lad. It was an enormous house that just had door frames and window frames, massive ones made of rock.

No doors, no windows. No roof or walls.

Just frames.

It was a building made entirely of openness. There was nothing else to it except the possibility of entering or leaving. Absolutely anything you could imagine, or even worse, could go in or out of it. Anything at all, anything that wanted to.

Except people, of course, it being shut to actual people. It was a place for other things than people to exit and enter. He had stood staring at Stonehenge in the twilight. When it was exactly twilight you could see things, even when you weren't at Stonehenge or anywhere else in particular, even when the only place you were was the twilight itself. There was a moment when things began to flicker in the air, things flying about in the sort of crack where daytime met the night. It was like lifting a stone or a plank and catching sight of all the creatures that secretly lived underneath. The join between day and night was very narrow but you could just get a glimpse of what was living inside, see them fluttering about, so long as you were watching at the exact right moment.

At twilight he saw those things flutter in and out of Stonehenge, flickering round the frames, a bit like bats though there weren't any bats.

The air above his flat was like Stonehenge, being full of openness. Darren would wake up sometimes and think of the night up there a few feet above his head. But not when it was raining. People complained about the rain, but not him. The rain was like nets or mesh, all over everywhere. He pictured it hanging silver in the darkness. It stopped the air being open, it closed the air.

Darren walked over to the pub. It was just across the road. It had rained so hard a few minutes ago that there were sheets of water running along the road itself, not just in the gutters. Because the water was transparent, and the road underneath it was grey, it looked like the greyness of the road itself had come loose and was sliding along.

It was still raining now but not so hard as just now. He had his anorak on, complete with hood. He felt like a snail in its shell. When he got to the front of the pub he took out his key. He kept it on his key ring with the keys to his flat.

He slid it in, turned it, and opened the door. He went in and shut it after him, then walked past the end of the public and across the snug.

Halfway across, he stopped, turned, and looked at the fire. Frank had cleaned it out and set it again.

Why did he do that? It was Darren's job. It was like stealing, it was as bad as stealing. It *was* stealing.

He bunched his hands in his anorak pockets in anger and disappointment. Then he walked over to the back room.

He stopped in the doorway. That was a frame too, like Stonehenge, no door in it. Never had had one, so far as he knew.

Dawn was sitting at a table, side on to him, busy working on some papers. She obviously hadn't heard him come in. He flipped his hood off his head.

Dawn began to raise her head and turn towards him. He knew, suddenly, exactly how she would look: scared; terrified.

Here he was, in the doorframe, like a ghost that had suddenly arrived out of nowhere.

Once he talked to Jerry about Stonehenge.

'There's a word for what you mean,' Jerry said.

'Is there?'

'Portal, that's the one.'

'Is it?'

'When anything goes from one world to another, it goes through a portal,' Jerry said.

'Beam me up, Scotty,' Alan said.

'That was a transporter,' Jerry said. 'Same difference. Remember when the crew are beamed? They go all shimmering for a moment. Like ghosts. If you travel from one world to another you're bound to be a sort of ghost. Stands to reason.'

So here Darren was, in a portal. Just for a second Dawn would see him shimmering there in the doorframe and think it was a ghost. And then she would realise it was only him and her panic would go away.

But knowing she was going to panic made him feel panicky too. A shock is much worse when you're expecting it.

Dawn's head turned. She looked at him. She saw him. Fright hit her face like a disease.

'Keith!' she called out and his heart nearly stopped.

She'd seen him, Darren saw her eyes clocking him, yet Keith was what she'd called. It was like looking in a mirror, and a different face looking back at you. Oh fuck, oh bugger, Darren thought, fuck fuck fuck: he was a ghost for definite. In his ghost form, he was called Keith. 'You what?' he whispered.

And then it was over. Dawn's face settled back to normal. Darren busily took off his anorak to cover up with its swishy noises the thump thump thump of his heart.

He made out he hadn't noticed the fire was laid. He wanted Dawn to see how it was a surprise. That wasn't a lie because he really had been surprised. It surprised him exactly the same way every single morning.

Laying the fire was Darren's job. Frank had said, when he started: when wintertime comes round the first thing you must do every day is clear the fire out and lay a fresh one. Darren had been pleased because it gave him the idea that he was here for the duration. It was all right working in the cancer shop but it paid you zilch.

'I think it's a nerve,' Dawn said, 'them shops paying people zilch.'

'It's a charity,' Darren pointed out.

'I'll give them charity. Charity my backside!'

'No, it is,' Darren insisted. 'It *is* a charity.'

'You know it is, Dawn,' Frank said. 'It's a charity shop, when all's said and done. That's what it is. What do you expect?'

'A young bloke like Darren here, he's got to have a few

25

pounds in his pocket, wouldn't you say so? And if this so-called charity won't give it him, the government has to. That's right, isn't it, Darren?'

'Is it?' Darren asked.

'Dole,' Dawn said, all lips and no volume, as if it was a rude word.

'Oh. Right. Dole.'

'What it boils down to, they employ you to do a job but let you be paid what you need to live on from the public purse. Then they have the cheek to call themselves a charity. It's taxpayers' money, is what it is, what you've been living on. They're nobbut a bunch of thieves. Or if not thieves, hypocrites.'

The thing about Dawn was she could get very bothered by stuff. She certainly got very upset with the people in the cancer shop. Darren thought they were OK. Usually Rebecca in charge, who was probably about fifty but very bubbly with it, all the customers said about her being a bubbly person, plus a girl called Gemma working at the counter with him, who was pretty good-looking. She had lovely tits, at least as far as he could make out. She usually had quite a low top on. Big ones, for definite. She was living with her mum and dad, who kept some chickens. He still went in for a couple of hours on Thursday afternoons. It made him feel guilty now, working at the shop for free. Gemma never said anything about a boyfriend. She talked about the chickens, mostly. Her thing was how they shat everywhere and pecked your legs.

The pub paid all right. Six quid an hour for twelve and a half hours a week. But part of that money was for laying the fire, which he never had to do.

Frank came down with some coffee. Dawn was in a bad mood and went off outside to have a fag. Darren took a few swigs of his coffee and then got on with his work.

First of all, sweep the whole ground floor. (Or as it should be, second of all.) Get rid of the squashed crisps and peanuts lying spread out under the tables where they'd got trod on like flattened hedgehogs. Once on Bean Street he'd seen one get run over and it let out a scream. He told Jerry about it because he'd never heard a hedgehog saying anything before. Jerry said it wasn't a scream, just sounded like one. It was just the sound of the air in the hedgehog being squashed out of it all at once through its tiny mouth, maybe its bum as well, like when you make a balloon fart by letting its air out after you've stretched the mouth-piece tight, and it vibrates. The poor little hedgehog's lips and maybe its bum vibrated as the wheel went over the middle of it.

He thought about Dawn while he swept, her seeing something else standing where he was standing, and calling it Keith. Like as if for the moment he, Darren, was dead, and somebody else was in the world in his place.

Darren came heavy-footed down the cellar steps as he always did, though he was a lean lad, could hardly weigh more than ten stone despite being the best part of six foot tall. It was a case of his horrors weighing him down. Certainly he seemed to suffer from double gravity and made Frank concerned about the future of the steps, which were old thin planks that gave at the best of times.

Darren made a racket because he wanted to let the spirit world have notice of his arrival, as Frank well knew. That was because, some weeks back, the poor lad had seen the ghost of a landlord of Victorian times who had fallen down the steps and broken his neck, apparently. Frank himself knew nothing of the story but Darren had got hold of it somehow.

Darren had come down the cellar and something beige flitted across his path. He reckoned it was a jacket or a smock that the old man had worn. Frank, not knowing what he was about, had jumped the wrong way at hearing all this. Instead of persuading him it was a trick of the light, given there was nothing more beige than cellar light, he'd gone off on one himself, telling Darren about a haunted alleyway in Portsmouth he went down once upon a time.

There had been a dog's hind leg at the midpoint of the alley with a lamp on the wall, and underneath a bloke taking a leak.

'Come to think, m'dear,' he'd told Darren, 'he was wearing something beige and all, or so it appeared. You get a beige light from those street lamps when they have them at low wattage. But it looked like a beige jacket, quite an olden times style of one. Long in the body. He was resting his forearm on the wall while he peed. That was the general impression, anyhow. I only saw him with half an eye. I was busy talking to my mates. There were three of us. I suppose we all of us saw him with only half an eye. Which would have made one and a half eyes in total, probably not enough to be sure. But as we approached the bend in the alley we all realised at the same time that he wasn't there any more. And when we got to the point when we could see the rest of the alley there was no sign of him. There was a good hundred yards of it ahead with tall walls either side, but it was clean as a whistle. One of my mates hared along to the end and looked up and down the street just to make sure he hadn't gone fast as a train and got there already, but the street was as quiet as the grave.'

'Bloody hell,' Darren said, and Frank realised at once that he'd taken the wrong tack. Darren's eyes practically revolved in his head. Frank tried to make light of it. 'What you got to ask yourself, m' dear, is why would someone come back to the earth and then waste his time having a pee?'

Same logic of course, if you'd broken your neck a hundred and fifty years ago, the last thing you'd want to do would be flit up and down the self-same steps all over again, even if you had no neck to break this time. But Darren had swallowed it all, hook, line and sinker.

'All right, Darren?' Frank asked him now.

Darren had a jerky way of walking, as if somebody was pulling his strings.

'I've brushed the floor,' Darren said. 'I've come down for the mop and bucket.'

'Good lad.'

Darren just stood there looking awkward. Frank thought he ought to say something. 'See that bulb up there, Darren?' he asked him. It was a bare bulb, dangling on its wire. Dawn was always going on about getting a shade for it, but Frank told her: it's a cellar, it's not our sitting-room. It's just a room to have barrels of beer in.

Darren sort of looked sideways at it, suspicious. 'Yep,' he said. 'I see it.'

'That's a hundred and fifty watt bulb, that is. If you had a hundred and fifty watt bulb in your bedroom, you'd know all about it. You'd need to have your sunglasses on.'

Darren just looked at Frank, then at the light, then at him again.

'It's a hundred and fifty watt bulb,' Frank said again, 'but this cellar's a big space.' He turned round to look at it himself. There were big humped barrels in a line, like a school of porpoises. They lay on cradles on a long wooden bench, like a butcher's bench almost. It could have been here since the pub was built. At right angles to the bench was an old Belfast sink with two taps poking out from the wall above it. The walls were whitewashed and a bit webby. There were boxes of wine, mixers, crisps, nuts, glasses, box upon box, stacked against the wall opposite the barrels. The beer lines hung down from the ceiling like tackle on a yacht.

He turned back to Darren. 'There's no window. It's underground. It's dark down here. There's a lot of darkness for one light bulb to shift. It's not surprising your eyes play tricks on you.'

'I didn't see a ghost this time, anyhow,' Darren said. 'I think it was Dawn saw one.'

'Dawn?' Frank asked. He tried to picture Dawn seeing one. She didn't have a mystical bone in her body as far as he could make out. He told her once about how he used to dream about dry land when he was at sea, not land as it actually was, but more like country scenes that you see in jigsaw puzzles, where everything is brighter and more colourful than in real life. He got through a load of jigsaw puzzles in his days in the navy.

He remembered one in particular, a thatched inn with big hollyhocks growing in front of it, and a bit of a lake behind in which there was a rowing boat partly sunk. The sign board dangled by one corner from its bracket. There was an old man sitting in a chair by the front door, with a beard and a clay pipe. He looked happy being old, as if he had been it from birth.

When Frank described it to Dawn she gave him short shrift. 'It's wishful thinking,' she said. 'You won't get me living in a tumbledown place like that in the middle of nowhere.' At the time they were looking for a pub to manage, and he liked the idea of a place in a village. 'And having a lake on tap is a recipe for midges,' she went on. 'I had enough of them back in Yorkshire.'

'Just for a moment or two,' Darren said.

'Oh yes? Where was this then?'

'Upstairs. In the back room. Where she was.'

'Did you see it too?'

'Oh no, I didn't see it.' He pulled and pushed at one corner of his lips as if he was trying to decide whether to be sad or happy. 'I *was* it.'

'I beg your pardon?'

'I was the ghost what she was seeing. Well, she was seeing a ghost spot-on where I was stood.'

'How do you know? Did she say?'

'No. She just got a horrible look on her face when she caught sight of me.'

'Well, everybody gets a horrible look on their face when they catch sight of you. You mustn't let it get you down, m'dear.'

'Then it went away.'

'That's the thing about ghosts. They go away. They've got no staying power.'

'That's not what you said about the ghost I saw down here the other day.'

'Was it not? What did I say then?'

'Long in the body, that's what you said.'

'Did I?'

'And it's true, when you think. That ghost we got down here has been in this cellar for a hundred and fifty years, long enough.'

I give up, Frank thought. Darren collected his mop and bucket. For some reason best known to himself he then went up the steps backwards. Maybe he found it easier to cope with the mop and bucket that way round. With a spindly form like his it was probably a bit of an ask to get sufficient lift. But going in reverse meant more of a levering motion than on the way down which at least saved the steps from being so clonked on. Of course he was in some danger of suffering the same fate as that landlord of times gone by, but that was his lookout.

'Careful where you put your feet, Darren,' Frank said.

'I'm doing OK,' Darren told him.

Frank unhooked the line from the guest beer barrel. Then he thought: if me and Dawn were living in that thatched pub we could lie on a big fluffy bed in the morning, with sunlight streaming through the windows, and shag like a pair of bunny rabbits.

Darren came bum-first through the door from the hall, carrying the mop and bucket. That same second there was a banging on the front door like the knell of doom. Followed by a horrible crash as Darren's bucket hit the floor.

'Bloody hell, Darren,' Dawn told him.

'Sorry,' he said, picking it up again.

'You *know* who it is,' she said. We hope, she thought.

'Yeah.'

31

'Well then.'

Darren tried to rub his forehead with his knuckle even though he was holding the bucket, which clanked in front of his face. The row from the front door continued. What Darren had thought was, the ghost. That's all he ever seemed to think. There was room in his pea brain for one idea, and unhappily that was it. No wonder he wanted to rub it out of his head.

But she was as bad. In fact she was getting annoyed with Darren because really she was irritated with herself. As the thumps continued she couldn't shake off the fear it was Tim already, with horrible dry bookkeeper's eyes, Mr Ford Focus come to call her to account.

Of course she was sure it wasn't. Frank had said he wouldn't be able to make it till after lunch. But it was like she needed to tease herself with the possibility of Tim just for good luck, to stop it being him in actuality.

Every morning the bread van man knocked at the door like a man possessed, always at about this time, coming up for ten o'clock. That's who it was, solid gold assumption.

She went to the front door, opened it wide, not a care in the world.

Yep, van man, caught mid-knock.

He was pear-shaped, one of those legless wobbly men that always sprang to the upright when you were a child. Thin hair no colour at all, though catching a bit of dark from the wet, as the rain had just started coming down once more.

He looked up at her. She had the advantage of the step, but he was small anyhow, harried-looking. His problem was a fear of parking on double yellows. There was his van, engine still going, anyone could see he was just making a delivery, but he wouldn't be convinced. He dreaded the unreasonableness of traffic wardens, having had a bad experience with one once, in London.

The van man worked for a firm called Half a Loaf, which was written on the side of the van, yellow letters on a green background. You're supposed to say better than no bread, he'd told her. Whatever rings your bell, she'd replied.

'I thought there was nobody in,' he said now. He sounded put out. One thing she'd learned in life, nervousness leads to bad temper.

'Well, there was,' she replied quite sharply.

'Three dozen rolls?' he asked, business-like straightaway.

'Correct.'

'Righty-ho.' He stepped over to his van and slid a tray of rolls off its rack. Dawn stepped back to let him into the pub.

He put the tray on the bar. Darren was filling his bucket at the sink, angling it awkwardly to get it under the tap.

'One thing I like,' the van man said, 'is the smell of yesterday's beer in pubs. Loved it since I was no more than a nipper. My dad had a rented room in a pub once upon a time and I would inhale the smell as I walked across the bar when I was on visits to him.' Dawn pictured a little pear-shaped boy waddling across, inhaling.

'I can't say it ever did much for me,' she replied. She used to be ashamed of that pubby smell when she was a girl. She went to school wondering if there was a sniff of it on her clothes, or even her skin. A girl in her class lived in a fish and chip shop, her mother known to all and sundry as Greasy Gert, and she certainly used to have her own private cloud of battered cod hovering over her, especially in warm weather. Here's a little fishy on a little dishy, the kids would nastily sing in her direction. But nobody ever teased Dawn and Keith about the pong of beer. The other children seemed more envious than otherwise.

'It's not a bad life,' the van man said. 'First thing, I'm loading up at the bakery and there's the smell of fresh baked bread.' He seemed to have put his double yellow anxiety on hold for the moment. Darren came out from behind the bar, lugging his bucket of water. 'Next thing, here I am,' the van man continued, 'smelling stale beer.'

'You can have one if you want,' came Frank's voice from under the floor.

'Bloody hell,' the van man said. 'What's that about?'

There was a creaking and groaning from the cellar, then the trapdoor in the middle of the bar floor rose up and Frank's great ball of a head appeared underneath it. The van man stared at it, boggled.

Darren trotted over with his mop, slid the shaft back like a snooker cue, and made as if to take a good pot at Frank's head.

'My good lady will pour you a pint if you require one,' Frank's head said.

'Fuck me,' the van man replied, then turned to Dawn: 'Beg pardon.'

'And now, goodbye.' The trundling noise came again, and Frank's head slowly sank from sight, the trap door lowering into place as it did so.

Darren gave out a high-pitched squiggle of laughter and trotted off to where he'd left his bucket of water.

'His party trick, that,' Dawn said, going over to the trapdoor and pressing it fully home with her foot. Suddenly she imagined it was Frank's head and she was pushing it down into his shoulders: if she took her foot away his head would ping back up again. She kept her foot pressed on the trapdoor. 'He likes to take a ride on the barrel lift.'

'I never seen anything like that before.'

'We get his head popping up all times of the night and day. Some say this place is haunted. Don't they, Darren?' she called to where Darren had started mopping the back room floor.

'Yep,' Darren replied in a small voice, as if he was too busy with his cleaning to care.

'It's like those pumpkins at Hallowe'en,' Dawn said. She stepped away from the trapdoor. It stayed put, of course. She went over to the hand-pumps. 'What can I get you, anyhow?'

34

'Oh no, best not,' the van man replied. 'I'm driving all morning. Save it till some other time.'

'Offer won't last till another time. You'll be an ordinary punter then.'

'Not to worry. I just appreciate the smell of it.'

'You're easy to please.'

He smiled, easily pleased, then his eyes clouded over, recalling the double yellows. 'Best be off, anyhow,' he said.

Darren made sure he got the mop just right. When he first came he'd made it very wet and Dawn had told him off about it. She said there would still be lying water at lunch and the punters would leave footprints in it. Plus when you slosh a lot on, the dirt just rides on the water and then sinks back to the floor again. But when you don't have that much you can shift the dirt on to the mop and then rinse the mop in the bucket. Dawn had thought the subject of cleanness through from A to Z.

For a moment when the head came up through the floor it looked like a head rising from the grave to tell him something. So Darren cued it with the mop handle to remind it it just belonged to Frank.

Maybe the head really wanted to say Keith, which was the word Darren hadn't mentioned to Frank when he told him about Dawn seeing the ghost.

He hadn't told Frank that Dawn had called out Keith. He had needed Frank to tell him it wasn't a ghost Dawn had seen in that split second. Like it *officially* wasn't. Especially since Frank was his total boss, even though Dawn was bossier.

But not saying something was as much a lie as telling one. Darren had told Frank a lie when he hadn't said about Keith. Maybe that's what Frank's head wanted to say when it popped up from the cellar. It wanted to tell him Keith was true. If not saying about him was a lie, then he must be true.

So Dawn had really seen a ghost called Keith, after all.

3

Dawn and Frank had their usual row about fetching nosegays. Worse than usual, because the rain had come back.

'Listen to the noise of it,' Frank said, and listened, putting his hand behind his ear to point it at the rain beating on the big grey window behind the bar. Darren listened too. It made a noise like an untuned radio.

Dawn didn't listen, not wanting to be contradicted by weather. She didn't like being contradicted by anything, full stop. 'If you're too mard to go out,' she told Frank, 'I'll blinking well go.'

'I'll go if you like,' Darren said. 'I don't mind. I like rain.'

'You know what they say,' Frank told him, 'not enough sense to come in out of the rain.'

'We live in England. It rains. It won't melt you,' Dawn said.

'Right-oh,' said Darren.

'No, no,' Dawn said, 'you've got your own job to be getting on with. There's the whole bar area to clean yet. You know how it's got to be?'

'I know how it's got to be.'

'Like a big brown jewel, that's how it's got to be.' She ran her eyes over the bar's counter and windows and shelving as if to clean them with a look. 'A big brown *diamond*,' she explained. Darren knew given half a chance she'd take the cleaning away from him just like Frank had taken the fire.

'How can *you* go?' Frank asked her. 'With all them rolls to do?'

'They won't take but two minutes. Anyway, you could do them.'

'Me?' Frank pointed at himself as if Dawn didn't know who me was. 'Fat chance.'

'It's filling rolls, it's not rocket science.'

'Look,' Frank said, holding his two hands out as if they were a pair of fans, the backs towards Dawn. His fingers rippled like seaweed. 'Look at them.'

Dawn looked, also Darren. Each of Frank's fingernails had a little black roof. 'Oh per-*lease*,' Dawn said.

'Blowed if I'll get rid of it in a hurry,' Frank said. 'I can dig at it with a nail file but it'll hardly lessen. Just go greyer.'

'And you wonder why I won't have an egg for breakfast.'

'It's only soot from doing the fire. But my nails aren't amenable to cleaning. What it is, they're quite raised up from the finger ends, which means they shovel up any dirt that's going.'

'If they're that raised up, they ought to be easy enough to clean. If it can go in, it can come out again.'

Frank lowered his eyes and wiped his hands on the bib front of his dungarees as if they'd got wet. 'It doesn't work like that,' he said. 'Tight nails work best, for some reason.'

'Honestly, Frank.'

'It's true. You can spring dirt out of tight nails like a cork out of a bottle.'

'How would you know, being as yours are so loosely fitting, according to you? Oh, I get it.' She nodded her head. 'I get it,' she repeated. 'You've been cleaning someone else's nails for them.'

'I've never cleaned somebody else's nails for them my whole life.'

'How do you know, then?'

'I *don't* know. I just picture it. Perhaps I dreamt it.' He paused. Darren guessed he was running his mind back over his dreams. 'Maybe I *have* cleaned somebody else's nails for them, I don't know,' he said finally. 'I can't remember doing it.'

'I think you would remember something like that. It would have been like those monkeys grooming each other and eating the bugs.'

'Thank you very much. What it is, I think my own nails were tighter when I was young. They've just gone proud of the finger ends with the passage of time. Anyway, the point is that with my nails being like they are *now*, it's not a good idea for me to fill those rolls.'

'It's clean dirt,' Darren said, 'soot is.'

'Shut up, Darren,' Dawn told him.

'Yes, shut your cakehole, Darren,' Frank said, being sharp just in order to get himself on Dawn's side of things again.

'You don't need to pick on me,' Darren told him. He began mopping a bit of floor he'd already mopped once. In fact he'd already mopped the whole of the floor, taken the stools down from the table tops and put them in place, wiped the table tops and put beer mats out, as well as gone outside, emptied the outside ashtray, and swept the wet fag ends up off the pavement.

'Anyway,' Frank told Dawn, 'you know what I think about us making our own rolls.'

'We're not making them,' Dawn said. 'That's the whole point. No cooking is taking place on the premises. Read my lips. All we're doing is filling them.'

'I'll fetch the blumming nosegays,' Frank said.

'Anyway, it's me that makes them rolls, not *us*.'

They had made a pig's ear of their accounting somehow or other, but the mathematics of the rolls was simple enough.

Thirty-six filled rolls delivered daily by Half a Loaf cost £36 and sold for £72, profit £36. Thirty-six unfilled delivered daily cost £12, fillings bought from Morrison's twice weekly amounted to about £8 for each daily batch of rolls, total £20, sold for £72, profit in the region of £52. Fifty-two pounds per diem, as her dad used to call it when doing the reckoning at their place long ago.

Even Frank ought to be able to follow the ins and outs of that calculation. Plus the money didn't belong to the brewers, just to them. They kept it in a separate tin.

Up in the apartment Dawn gave her hands a thorough scrub and tied a scarf over her head, Queen of England style. Remembering Frank's anxieties she glanced at her own nails, which were clean as a whistle.

Then she spread her oilcloth on the kitchen table, and put out a chopping board, cheese, sliced ham, sliced chicken, onions, chutney, margarine, mustard, a pack of salad, mayonnaise. Frank had carted the rolls up before he went out, and she took a dozen from the tray to make a start. She cut them not quite through with her bread knife, so as to retain a little hinge, then flipped each one open to await buttering.

Frank was right about one thing. It was a job that took more than a couple of minutes.

Halfway through she remembered the radio, went over to the windowsill to turn it on, and got 'For You Are Beautiful' by Roger Whittaker, perfect buttering music. She sang along for a moment or two, deliberately badly as she knew she couldn't do it well, then fizzled out and let the voice fill her ears. The melancholy of it made her think of Keith again, and suddenly she wept, for the second time that morning.

She was just at that moment slicing up a piece of cheddar and as she pressed the knife down, it slipped sideways off the firm surface of the cheese, and cut her. She saw a thin red line on her finger, like a sketch of the blood to come.

She knew why it had happened. It was subconscious, to give her a reason for weeping that wasn't Keith. Didn't work. She thought of him more than ever as she watched the skin around go white and beads of blood come to the surface of the cut. One slid right out and splotched on to the roll below.

Quick as a flash she picked up the roll and took a big bite, no idea why, hiding the evidence maybe. Then walked over to the sink to run her finger under the tap. More drops ran as she went, she heard one plip on the lino, but at least the rest of the rolls were safe. With her uncut hand she stretched over to the radio and turned it off, right in the middle of *beaut*. When she washed the cut the cold water triggered a deep bone ache, as she knew it would.

She got a big plaster and put it on. Should have been blue but that would be like a confession that she was doing catering after all. Didn't have blue ones anyhow.

By the time she got back to the rolls the finger was just throbbing. It seemed to have done it good, having the plaster on tight. She picked up the roll with one bite out of it and stuffed it in her mouth, pushing at it till her mouth was so full she could feel her cheeks bulging out and there was no room to move her jaws and begin chewing. Some of the roll was pressing against the gag button at the back of her throat and she had to keep telling herself to be calm so she wouldn't retch. The important thing was, it was all in. For some reason that seemed to ease her mind. She pushed at the roll with her tongue. Jerry said one time that snails eat with their tongues. They have teeth on them. Or maybe Alan said it. Pair of know-alls, the both of them.

After a few moments the roll got workable and she could begin to chew on it. By the time she'd got the whole thing down her, she felt as tired as if she'd done gymnastics. She held the edge of the table and gave out a couple of shaky sighs.

*

Frank went down Bean Street, crossed the junction and turned into Butler Way, rain pattering on his brolly. He thought of that conundrum about falling rain that Jerry had described, and speeded up to put it to the test. No joy, you just walked all the faster into your own soaking trousers. He needed to change them when he got back, three pairs in one morning.

A Green Thought was the next shop after the Spar but he walked straight past it to the one beyond and stood looking in the window.

It sold doll's house miniatures, really minute ones, including little trays and plates of food. He always liked to look at them if he was in the vicinity. A cottage loaf with a slice cut off, butter on a dish, a pot of jam. Right by it, a plate on which stood a colander full of sprouts, with several sprout leaves scattered round the base. Next a joint of beef, cooked medium rare, a carving fork stuck in it and the matching knife balanced wonkily on a pile of carved slices, each with a sliver of white fat on its rim.

The dinkiness of it all was what appealed. Everything was clear and hard and sharp in that world. Being big had a diluting effect, somehow, the same way a fat face had thinner stubble. He could vouch for it.

He turned and went back to A Green Thought, lowering his umbrella and giving it a shake at the pavement before going in.

There was nothing more comfortless than a flower shop in wet weather, the smell of green, of cold surfaces, of water. Talking of which, Father Thomas was standing at the counter, a comfortless sort of character himself, though nice as pie in a doleful way when similarly stood at the bar of the Old Spring. He had his old grey mac on, a bit short, dark grey suit trousers beneath and grey hair above, also short so it looked composed of metal filaments, the type of head you could scrub limescale with.

'Hello, Father,' Frank said. 'Buying a bunch of flowers for your girlfriend?'

Father Thomas turned slowly, sure enough carrying a bunch of flowers. They reminded Frank of an advert where everything was in monochrome except the thing being advertised, whatever that was. Father Thomas's face was pale above his dog collar, with grey stubble, and he had pale grey eyes; but the flowers were yellow and rust and mauve. 'Ha,' Father Thomas said, seeing it was Frank. He didn't offer an explanation. 'Smell them,' he said instead, pushing his bouquet in Frank's face. 'You don't get much in the way of perfume this time of the year.'

'You could kill me doing that,' Frank told him, his face suddenly covered in soft impacts.

'I beg your pardon?'

'I might have been allergic.'

'Not a chance, given you have a bunch of flowers on every table of the Old Spring.'

'Nosegays,' Frank said.

'You what?'

Wendy, the florist, came through plastic strips from the back of the shop, bringing a waft of more of the same with her: dampness, coolness, the thin churchy perfume of late season plants. 'Nosegays,' Wendy agreed. 'Here's your change, Reverend.'

'Thank you.'

'We do three sizes. Big are bouquets.' Wendy had a squarish face, also pale, green-framed spectacles, curly old-fashioned hair. She always reminded Frank of the serial killer Rosemary West, only with a flowery backdrop. 'Medium are bunches. Yours is medium,' she told Father Thomas.

'Ah, indeed, thank you,' Father Thomas replied. He shook his flowers a little, as if he'd just won a race.

'The littlest of all are nosegays.'

'Nosegays used to be carried in the hand,' Father Thomas said, 'so that they could be raised to your nose in case of a bad smell.'

'Charming,' Wendy said.

'That's what we have on our tables,' Frank said. 'Nosegays.'

'All done,' Wendy told him. 'They're in a bag in the back.'

'I thought for a moment you were going to say bad smells,' Father Thomas told Frank.

'Dawn has never liked the smell of beer, that's true.'

'You don't say?'

'Or the taste of it, come to that.'

'Perhaps she was an imbiber in a previous life.'

'*I* must have been a cow,' Wendy said.

'A cow?' repeated Father Thomas, wagging his bunch of flowers at her like a big jolly finger.

'If you keep shaking that little lot, you'll bend the stems, and then they'll droop. I spent my former life eating plants, so now I've got to spend this one putting them in water and arranging them.'

'Maybe you killed somebody,' Frank suggested.

Wendy raised an eyebrow at him above the frame of her spectacles.

'Never,' Father Thomas said. 'I can't see you ever giving anyone the chop.'

'You know how to flatter a girl,' Wendy told him, 'even being a man of the cloth.'

'You can't be blamed for something you did when you were still somebody else,' Frank told her, feeling suddenly he'd gone too far. 'Even if you *are* being punished for it.'

'That's one of the great spiritual mysteries,' Father Thomas told him. 'Or at least, near enough.'

'Is it?'

'Original sin is the name.' He thought for a moment. 'Causing folk despair, the game.'

'There's not much original about killing someone,' Wendy said. 'People seem to be at it all the time.'

'I just meant,' Frank said, 'if you killed someone in a past life, that might be why you're spending this one doing flowers.'

Wendy and the Father looked at him.

'You know,' Frank went on. He felt like you do when a joke falls flat. 'You have flowers at a funeral.'

'Good point,' Wendy agreed. 'I wonder if I stabbed him or shot him.'

'You don't know if it *was* a him.'

'Oh, it was a him all right.'

'Any rate,' Frank said, turning back to Father Thomas, 'she does like a gin and tonic. Dawn.'

'So she does. The Old Spring hardly qualifies as purgatory in her case.'

'We have our good days and our bad days,' Frank said cautiously. 'It's just a pub, when all's said and done.'

'I'll get the flowers for you,' Wendy told him.

While she was at the back, Frank asked Father Thomas, 'Will you be in at lunch, m'dear?' He felt vaguely that he'd been off-hand with him in some way.

But Father Thomas was cheerful enough, by his standards anyhow. 'Is the Pope a Catholic?' he asked.

The floor under the beer pumps was always sticky. Darren hated the way his trainers half stuck on it as he cleaned up the bar. It reminded him of a social worker he used to have, Rubber Lips by name, whose lips had a thick tread to them so when she opened her mouth to speak they clung together for a moment and then slowly separated like velcro does. But if he did the bar floor first before cleaning the counter and shelves and pumps, he'd just be treading in the wet and dirtying it again, so he had to listen to his trainers tearing free of the floor while he wiped and rubbed the woodwork, squirted it with furniture polish and rubbed it again, then windowlened the bar-glass. He worked so hard he felt a sort of anger in his rubbing arm.

When he'd finished he stepped through the counter and round to the back room to inspect what he'd done, going on tiptoe so his trainers wouldn't deposit stickiness on the floors he'd washed earlier. The windows beyond the bar had darkened while he'd been at work. The bar didn't shine like a brown diamond, not in this rainy light, but it did gleam softly, like some old galleon sunk beneath the waves.

When he turned round, he realised how dark the rest of the place had got. They didn't switch lights on until opening time, because it would only encourage people to bang at the door, thinking they were open already. The glow of the little copper vases on each table, waiting for their nosegays, made the air around them seem dimmer still. There were patches of darkness all over the room, the shadows of the bar counter, of the tables and stools, patches of dark in the corners and under the benches, the sort of shadows that didn't need bright light to be opposite to.

Darren realised it was all a single darkness, seeping up from the cellar through the gaps in the floorboards, lying around in separate bits but waiting for one false move on his part for it to shrug itself together. Once, when he was little, he'd watched a TV programme where a scarecrow came to life and walked about the countryside with arms outstretched. He dreamed about it for years, still did sometimes. Darren pictured an even worse kind of a scarecrow patched together from the blacknesses here, coming stiff-legged towards him across the room.

He started back the way he'd come, tiptoeing extra carefully this time, trying to walk the exact same route like returning across a minefield, back through the doorframe, across the snug, then turning left at the far door into the public. Just as he turned he slipped somehow, maybe on a damp patch, and flung his arm out, catching the shelf where they kept old books and stuff to make the pub seem homey, plus tins of snuff for punters who wanted their tobacco fix without lighting up. Books and snuff tins flew through the air. He heard them thump and clang as they hit the floor. He staggered a couple of steps like a scarecrow himself, then got his balance back.

45

Then Frank's voice: 'Hello, m'dear, what's going on here then?'

Darren's whole body ached with the strain of not falling. He could have told Frank: I slipped. But he didn't. He didn't want to be a person who slipped. No chance of getting the fire back if Frank got evidence of lack of coordination. Any rate, it wouldn't be true. It would leave out what had really happened, the scarecrow. So what he said was: 'Poltergeist.'

'Poltergeist?'

'Fucking poltergeist.' Suddenly he could see it, not so much a scarecrow now, more like a monk, in a black robe, black hood, flinging the books and tins down along the public.

'No need to swear,' Frank said. 'And stop pulling my leg, m'dear.'

'It seemed to go dark, like an eclipse.'

'It can't have been an eclipse. There wasn't any sun. You can't have an eclipse of the rain. What you can do, you can get soaked to the skin, take my word for it. Sometimes I think to myself: stuff the bloody nosegays. More trouble than they're worth.'

'Then the things just got flung. They were whizzing right by me. I fell over, near enough.' Darren could see the fury and spite involved, the long rage, a hundred and fifty years of it.

4

'Hello, Brother,' said Brother Julian. He stood there in an old green woolly, his stomach curving forward as if he was offering it as a present. Maybe it was the dull day, but his plump face looked grey, almost deliquescent.

'You need the light on,' Brother Paul told him, and switched it on. No good, Julian looked just as poorly, worse really, as a sheen of sweat became visible on his upper lip.

'You've been buying your flowers,' Julian said.

'I have been buying my flowers. Our flowers. All for one, and one for all.' Paul got the big green vase from the sideboard, went into the kitchen, filled it, brought it back and put it in the middle of the table at the dining end of the room. Then he stuffed the flowers in it. 'Bugger flower arranging,' he said.

'It's easy to have contempt for what you don't know,' Julian informed him in his uncompromising fashion. You could mistake it for pomposity, if he'd been capable of pomposity. He had seated himself in an armchair by the French window. Beyond its panes, greenery shook and swayed in the rainy gusts.

'My ignorance must be wide-ranging, in that case.'

'Sign of a good education, to admit it.'

'One of the drawbacks of a confessional culture, in my opinion,' Paul said, 'is the way it encourages us to think our vices are our virtues.'

Julian pursed his lips, as much as to say, hark at him. He believed in keeping faith simple. Or rather, he had his own particular way of complicating it. 'You need to give yourself a good drying,' he added, being nice to make up.

'I think I'll have a quick bath. Even my socks are soggy. After being out in the weather you feel like getting properly wet, to clinch it.'

'Then afterwards come down for a spot of lunch. I thought I'd do some Welsh rarebit. We have that cheese left over from making the macaroni cheese. Serve it piping hot.' Julian's fat cheeks slightly pinked at the prospect. 'I could bury some sliced tomato and onion in it.'

'Nice try. But I have a pub to go to.'

'You should give yourself a day off in weather like this.'

'It's my own little ministry.'

'Oh Paul.'

'Quite true. They think I'm a priest in the Old Spring. They call me Father Thomas.'

'My lord!' The sacrilege sent Julian round-eyed as a fish. 'How did that come about? Brother Paul, what on earth are you up to?'

Good question. Imposterhood had been achieved in two easy steps. Perhaps true of all falsity: you take a step out of virtue and then, while you're exposed on *terrain vague*, something comes along and pulls you into the mire. Lower your guard, Old Nick takes advantage.

A person in the pub had asked him his name. Alan it was, that ass of an English lecturer up at the university. 'I'm Alan, by the way,' he'd said after some grumpy mutterings about this and that. And Paul had replied, 'I'm Thomas.'

There was nothing more authentically Catholic than taking on a new name in order to cope with a new aspect of one's

48

life. Children did it when they were baptised, women when they were wed. Paul had gone from Joseph O'Connor to Paul when he became a brother in the De La Tour order. But that wasn't fraud or false pretences. Even God lived a double life when he became Jesus. A triple life in fact, since at any given time he was the Father, Son, or Holy Ghost.

In point of fact Paul was still Joe in certain recesses of his imagination, always had been, when he thought about his childhood and his parents for example. That's why it wasn't fraud – each name covered a different aspect of himself.

By the same token, that was why he felt a need to give himself a new name in the pub. He'd just retired from teaching, he had no intention of spending all day every day pottering round the De La Tour house. 'Why don't you take an interest in the garden?' Brother Julian had suggested, wanting to keep the kitchen all to himself.

I'm going to be a local, Paul decided during that first session in the Old Spring. He'd had his entrée to the big wide world with the children at school; now he needed another. Another door to put his foot in.

But of course his name was a lie. It may not have been a fraud but it *was* a fib. Or at least, underhand. When Paul had taken his vows everybody knew he'd been Joseph up till then. But he'd let Alan believe he was Thomas all through, like Blackpool in a stick of rock.

From the moment Paul spoke to Alan, everyone at the Old Spring had called him Father Thomas. He'd freed up his identity and that left them free in turn to make of it what they wanted. He tried to explain that he was a Brother, a member of a lay teaching order and not a Father, but Frank and Dawn and the regulars took absolutely no notice, regarding it as a technical distinction.

So he gave up. Anyone could act as a priest, *in extremis*. He himself had been one once before, when the Cuban crisis erupted while he was a first year student. One night he and his friends convinced themselves that the world was at the very point of extinction and he conducted mass in his room, enjoying the terror of the moment, eating Mother's Pride and drinking Spanish sauterne and feeling them turn into the authentic body and blood of the saviour. In fact, no mass since had given him such a sense of spiritual drama, of sacramental engagement. It must be like, in the world of human love, first love.

'They seem to see me as pub chaplain. It's the dog collar. They don't understand it's monastic, not clerical. Thomas is as good a name for me as any. You know what people say: any Tom, Dick or Harry.'

'It's not the Thomas I'm worried about,' said Julian. 'It's the Father.'

'Most of the men in the world are fathers.'

'But we're not. That's the whole point.'

'Look on it as a term of endearment.'

Julian looked out of the window for a moment, obviously deciding to let his anxiety skitter harmlessly into the vegetation. Then he turned back. 'I spent my morning tossing up whether I dare rhyme *regina* with *vagina*.'

He gave Paul a crafty sidelong look, conspirators together. He was being nice again. Being a brother. That was what life in the house was all about.

'What did you decide?'

'Thumbs down. People these days wouldn't know what *regina* means.' When he wasn't cooking hot dinners Julian spent his retirement writing hymns to the Virgin. Mary was one of us who had become one of them, unlike Jesus whose journey had been in the other direction. That's what the Assumption meant, as far as Julian was concerned. She had been taken directly into heaven, which meant that she was the one earthling there, the rest having to wait for the day of judgement when they would be transmogrified into heavenly material. Therefore she should be celebrated robustly. She was the mother of us all, our representative in the divine. For Julian this meant that she validated the human condition, and made innocence possible, particularly sexual innocence. It got him round the long and endless implications of the Fall.

But for the sake of solidarity Julian was prepared to pretend that his insistence on innocence was tinged with guilt. It only made him more innocent still. 'Anyhow those compound rhymes are clunky,' he said. 'It would be like pitting *fiesta* against *siesta*. It could only work in a limerick.'

'That would never do.'

'Oh, I don't know about that. I have written limericks about the Virgin in my time,' Julian said stoutly. He said most things stoutly.

'Funnily enough, I came out with a couplet myself,' Paul told him. 'In the flower shop. It was on the subject of original sin.'

'It must be catching,' Julian said.

'Where do you think you're going?' Frank asked.

'Off,' said Darren.

'Off, he says. Off!'

'Off,' Darren agreed, in a smaller voice this time.

'But you haven't finished yet.'

Darren looked worriedly round the rooms, then at the bar itself.

'Final chore,' Frank said. He pulled a box of matches from under the bar counter as if he was pulling a rabbit out of a hat. 'Here you go.'

Darren opened them and looked inside, as if expecting to find something unexpected in there.

'It's for the fire, bonehead.'

Darren's face lit up like a kid who'd been given a toffee. Like a kid who'd been given a box of matches, to be more accurate.

'You be careful,' Frank warned. 'It's all ready to go. I don't want that fire roughed up. Them coals have been poised, by Dawn's strict instructions. One of the bars burned through.'

Darren knelt before the fire, holding the box of matches at arm's length as if he was going to light a firework. He delicately lit an edge of paper at one side of the fire, then another at the other side. The flames shot up promptly and licked around the kindling and the coals of solid fuel. Darren rose to his feet and watched it catching for a moment or two. He looked at ease for the first time since he'd sent the snuff and books flying.

'Good lad,' Frank told him.

Darren came over and put the matches on the counter. 'Bye then,' he said.

'See you, Darren,' Frank replied. He looked at the bar clock. Spang on eleven-thirty. 'Leave the door on the latch as you go. It's time.'

Darren did up his anorak to the top, and jerked his hood toggles tight. Funny thing about blokes who weren't bright, they always put their clothes on to the nth degree. Frank had noticed the same thing among the dopier sailors in the navy. Every button buttoned, as many layers as possible on top of each other. Satisfaction of a job well done, presumably.

As soon as he'd gone out the front door, down came Dawn. She gave the bar a looking at.

'He worked his little butt off,' Frank told her.

Dawn licked her forefinger and rubbed at some stain on the counter.

'Give the lad some credit,' he said.

She shook her head, at Darren or maybe herself.

'You got a plaster,' Frank told her.

She shrugged. 'Did he do the fag ends?' she asked. 'On the pavement?'

'He did.'

'Them baps are up top.' She pointed to the ceiling.

'All right, I'll fetch them. The outside door's open so you better watch the bar.'

He went up to get the rolls. They were in their wicker basket, all ready. Each was wrapped in cling-film, just like they would have been if they'd been bought filled from Half a Loaf. For some reason it made them look like a pile of shrunken heads, to Frank's eyes. To complete the disguise they all had a label on, computer printed. *Chicken and Mayo. Cheese and Ham. Cheese and Chupney.*

He'd shown her one of the ones with the mistake when she first started doing them. 'Read it,' he told her. 'Cheese and chupney,' she'd replied without batting an eyelid. He realised she really thought that was how chutney was spelt, so said no more. She just gave him a puzzled look, as if wondering how come he'd forgotten how to read all of a sudden.

He picked up the basket, carried it down, and put it in its place behind the bar.

'I been rushed off my feet while you were upstairs,' Dawn told him. She looked around the empty rooms.

'Give it half an hour. The Father said he'd be in, so that's one. I saw him down at A Green Thought.'

'Father comes rain or shine. Got nothing better to do with his time, I suppose, except religion. What was he doing in the flower shop, anyhow?'

'Well, he wasn't buying himself a drink.' Frank flipped the hatch and went behind the bar. Dawn took her chance and went out into the snug. She loved her bar but didn't much go for being behind it, if she had the choice. She liked to go from table to table, taking away the empties and crisp packets, having a word and a joke with the punters. That was being mine host, according to her definition.

'There's no need to be sarky,' she said. 'It just seems strange for the Father to be buying flowers.'

'Well, *I* was doing it.'

'Maybe he's got a lady friend somewhere. Just because he's religious doesn't stop him having fire in his belly.'

'Well,' Frank said, 'That must be why he comes here to drink beer. To put his fire out.'

'Why don't you save being a clever Dick for when Tim comes this afternoon and we have to explain away that nine hundred pounds?'

About twelve a CAMRA bloke came in. Dawn was upstairs, having another look at the books.

He was a big man in a zip-up hunting jacket, a bit like the one Pete wore when they went duck-shooting in Norfolk, green canvas-type material cut quite long so it came down to mid-thigh, lots of pockets, only Pete's was worn with use and this one was in new condition. Just used for hunting down real ale, in all probability. There were little beads of rain on the surface where the waterproofing had stopped them from sinking in.

He had a little smile on his face, a look that said: You may think I've come in here for a drink, but in actual fact I'm a man on a mission. 'I'll have half of the Buckman's,' he said.

'Come far?' Frank asked him, carefully pulling the hand-pump to show he cared.

The man flinched slightly. The smile on his face stayed exactly as it was, but now it looked regretful. What did he expect? He could hardly be taken for a regular. Frank didn't know him from Adam.

'Brighton. Came on the train.'

'Did you then? You must have started out bright and early.' He passed over the half pint. The man raised it to his face as if he was going to take a sip, then just sniffed it instead.

'It was early,' he said, lowering his glass again, 'but it wasn't bright, not by a long chalk.'

'Nor here, neither.' Frank turned and looked toward the window. It was silvered by rain, like the bloke's coat, but in sharp little lines, each coming to a point like so many needles. He had the notion of collecting different kinds of raindrop just like the CAMRA bloke collected makes of beer. 'As you can see for yourself.' He turned back to the customer and shook his head sadly, by way of saying, rain, rain.

The man raised his little glass again, put his lips to the rim, then lowered it once more. 'Remember that bloke Reggie Maudling?' he asked. 'That politician, years ago.'

'Oh yes,' Frank said. 'That takes you back.' He'd nearly said, bit of a dodgy character I recall, but stopped himself in time. You learned as a landlord not to have opinions about politics.

'When he was Foreign Secretary,' the man said, staring at his drink, 'he arrived in some British embassy somewhere or other at nine in the morning, and said to the officials, I know this seems a funny thing to ask, but could you let me have a gin and tonic. You've got to remember there's a three-hour time difference from back home, he told them by way of explanation. So they get him one, and only afterwards did they remember the three-hour time difference was in the opposite direction. He was pouring G&Ts down himself at six in the morning.'

'What an operator,' Frank said, still cautious. He shook his head as if he couldn't help admiring Reggie Maudling's cheek. 'Ha,' he added. He tried to put it together, like working out a crossword clue.

'I'm on Brighton time, me,' the bloke said. He looked up from his glass to see if Frank got it. 'I've been on the go so long it feels late to me, that's all I mean. Could be mid-afternoon, from where I'm standing.' He was excusing himself for having a drink this early in the day, not that he'd had one yet. He stared down into his half pint like he was a high-diver about to dive into a pool far below. He lowered his top lip over the bottom one, then did likewise with the bottom lip over the top one. Then he took a swallow.

'Hmm,' he said, neither for nor against, and went off to a table in the back room.

Frank fiddled with the basket of rolls, stacking them neatly. Poising them. The basket rested at an angle behind the bar, so that people could see what was on offer. At that moment Jake, the tattooed man, came in, and sat down in his usual place in the public, up by the bar counter. The public was just like a corridor really, coming to a dead end at the bar itself, with only room for a single bench running along one side of it.

Dawn didn't approve of Jake sitting there. She complained that other customers had to pass the end of the public on their way to the snug or the back room, and couldn't help getting an eyeful of all his blueness. It covered his face, neck and ears, and probably all the bits of him you couldn't see, in the form of snakes and dragons and roses and God knew what, much of it already blurry with age. Dawn didn't approve of Jake full stop. She wanted him banned.

'Good name for him: Jake,' she said once, when they were having a row about it.

'How do you make that out?'

'Don't you know what Jake means? Well, jakes.' She leaned towards Frank. 'Toilet,' she whispered.

Frank had put his foot down. You couldn't bar someone for being tattooed. It was against the law.

'It's against the law to bar someone because they're black,' Dawn said. 'There's no law I've heard of against barring someone because they're blue.'

'Only if he causes trouble,' Frank said. 'Which he hasn't.'

'Not yet, you mean,' Dawn had said darkly.

'You stacking them rolls?' Jake said now.

'What you got to watch with rolls, they might roll off,' Frank replied.

Jake gave a small serious nod.

'Doing this reminds me of a lady who had a greengrocer's in Tiverton when I was a boy,' Frank told him. 'Just her hands, mauling about with the piles of caulis and onions and all the rest of them. Red raw, they were. I suppose she suffered from chilblains or allergies or something. I don't remember the rest of her at all.'

Again Jake gave a nod, as if he was cottoning on exactly, as if he too could remember the hands of that long ago vegetable woman in Tiverton, a small blue chap watching her red fingers among the spuds.

At twelve-thirty on the dot in came Darren. As always, he was dressed totally differently from how he had been earlier. He wore a little imitation-leather bomber jacket type of thing instead of his anorak and had brushed his hair with some sort of gel so it stood completely upright, like a crew cut somebody had forgotten to cut. It made him look like he was getting the fright of his life, non-stop. He had carried an umbrella over in lieu of his hood, to stop his hairstyle being beaten down by the rain like a small field of wheat.

He took his jacket off and hung it on the peg. His shirt was long-sleeved and loose-fitting, hanging outside his trousers, a bit like those worn by acrobats and fire-eaters in a circus. It had palm trees and parasols and bits of bright blue sea patterned all over it. One of the regulars had complimented him on it the other day, and even though she was a mature woman, he'd blushed in reverse, went white as a sheet with pleasure. 'He's had some knocks in his time, that lad,' was Dawn's theory.

Darren stood by the fire a moment, rubbing his hands. Then he picked up the tongs and carefully repositioned a coal that had worked loose. He didn't need permission now, being a punter. Then he came over to the bar.

'What can I get you, sir?' Frank asked him.

Darren thought a moment, like he always did, as though not having faced this array of beer pumps before. Then said, 'A pint of Buckman's,' like he always said.

'Good choice,' said Frank and pumped it.

The CAMRA man was on his second half pint, Mendip Best this time. He'd ordered a roll with it, chicken and mayo, and was munching away in the back room. In the public Jake was drinking his pint and staring at the wall opposite. Once Frank had suggested to him he might want a paper from the rack, and Jake said, 'No, ta,' in such a definite way it made Frank wonder if he knew how to read. There was writing on his fingers but that didn't prove anything, it would have been dictated in any case. And now here was Darren at the bar in the snug. It was lucky each room gave on to the bar, just partition walls separating them like spokes on a wheel.

'Here you go, m'dear,' he said, and passed Darren his drink over.

'Hello, Jake,' Darren said, peering round the partition into the public.

'Ho, Darren,' Jake answered. Jake's leg was vibrating as he sat, as if he was impatient to be up and off. He was wearing his horrible blue shellsuit with white stripes down the sleeves and trouser-legs. He could remain like that for hours.

'Going back today?' Frank asked the CAMRA man in the back room, taking Darren's money as he did so.

The man assumed he was talking to Darren for a moment and then started as he realised Frank's eye was on him.

'Oh, later on. This evening. I'm off to the White Hart next.'

'Nice pub, that.'

'Yes, well. Is it then?'

'Nice pub, isn't it?' Frank asked Darren, giving him his change.

'Is what?'

'The White Hart.'

'Nice pub,' Darren said.

As it blustered its way down Bean Street the wind seemed to craze the falling rain, turning it from transparent to white with each buffet. Father Thomas had learned from his drenching on the errand to A Green Thought, and had pulled a floppy clerical umbrella from the stand in the hall, but you had to angle it dead to windward like mariners of old their prow or it would be inside out in a flash. All this for the sake of a pint, he thought with some satisfaction.

Finally he made out the pub signboard beyond the edge of the umbrella. It pictured a small fountain spouting in a rocky grotto, the whole thing glazed and dripping with the rain, a double whammy of wetness rather as his bath had been earlier on, the board swinging in the gusts. Dim electric light showed through the frosted windows of the bar, like a car's headlamps through fog.

Inside, a fire glowed pinkly on the snug's hearth. Yes, worth being wet, just for the sight of that.

Maybe that's what one could say on arriving in heaven after life on earth, or at least something similar, though Thomas found it hard to envisage making such a cosy, comforting remark in the absence of a mouth.

'Father,' said Frank.

As if on cue a customer in a big green Barbour jacket walked through from the back room and left the pub, giving Frank a curt nod as he did so. Father Thomas pointed at himself and raised an eyebrow.

'Don't take it personal,' Frank told him, 'I think he was one of them devil-worshippers.'

Darren started at the mention of devil, and Father Thomas clapped him reassuringly on his back, rather as one might burp an infant, not that he'd burped many in his time. Darren looked adrift in a shirt several sizes too big for him.

'*And* he couldn't be bothered to bring his glass back to the bar,' Frank continued.

'That's the trouble with devil-worshippers,' Father Thomas said. 'That's why we're so against them in the church.'

Frank pumped him a pint of Buckman's.

'I think I'll take a roll with that,' Father Thomas said. 'You know what I'm passing up today? Welsh rarebit, to keep out the rain. With tomato and onion added.'

'At the monastery?' Frank asked.

'That's called buck rabbit,' Darren said.

'Yes,' Father Thomas said to Frank. 'No,' to Darren. 'Buck rarebit's with an egg on top.'

'Oh.'

'You get to know your rarebits when you lead the monastic life.'

Frank brought the basket over and Father Thomas surveyed it. 'I'll have the cheese and chupney,' he said. 'In homage to the rarebit I'm not eating.'

'You got to be here to tend your flock, Father,' Frank said, handing it over. 'That's the point.'

'I'll have a cheese and chupney as well,' Darren said. While Frank was taking the basket back, Darren turned to Father Thomas and asked, 'You know about devil-worshippers?'

'Ye-es,' Father Thomas agreed cautiously. He took a bite of his roll. He'd forgotten one thing about this particular creation of Dawn's. You compress the roll between your jaws and the chutney inside bolts for the nearest exit. He used his paper napkin to shepherd some from his cheek into his mouth.

'I saw a poltergeist this morning,' Darren said. He looked nervously in Frank's direction, but Frank was leaning over towards the public, having a word with Jake.

'I wish I had sharper teeth,' Father Thomas said.

'Do you?' Darren asked, eyes wide, hair on end.

'Then I could do a clean bite and the chutney wouldn't get all over the shop. What did it look like?'

'It was just a smear.'

'The poltergeist.'

'Oh, I didn't see it.'

'Ah.'

'You don't see them. As such. Just what they do.'

'Like the wind?'

'You what?'

'Like not being able to see the wind. Just what it does.'

'Yes, that's right, just like the wind.'

'Darren, it's very windy out there now. Wet and windy.'

Darren took a swig of his beer. 'It wasn't the wind, Father. It was just invisible *like* the wind.'

'Do you mean to say you can tell one sort of invisible from another? No, don't answer that question. Of course you can. *I* can. I wouldn't be what I am, if I couldn't tell one invisibility from the next.' He took another bite of his roll. Again, the chutney squidged. This time he used his knuckle to collect it, then sucked his finger. Nothing but discriminating between invisibilities, in his calling. Nothing but invisibilities where he lived, spiritually speaking. Nothing but inaudibilities too.

That was what spiritually speaking actually meant, when all was said and done.

'I told you,' Darren said triumphantly. He was looking over towards Frank. 'I told you it was a poltergeist.'

Frank gave a grin across distance, even though he was only a yard or two away. He was in the orbit of the public, not the snug, for the moment. He waved in their general direction, and turned back to Jake.

'Yesss!' Darren said, clenching his fist in triumph. 'Father says it was.'

Thomas almost said something then thought better of it. Let it go. Let the boy feel vindicated, if that's what he needed.

5

When Keith left school he got a job in a rubber composition factory. He worked on a mill like a gigantic mangle, which squeezed the artificial rubber into flat sheets. There was a fog of chemicals in the air, and the bloke who owned the place used to come round to check up on the men with a big cigar stuck in his gob, like a bad boss in a cartoon.

Keith had gone there from school and was just doing it for a couple of years until he was old enough to work in their dad's pub. It was a rotten job and the hours were terrible, six till six weekdays, six to twelve on Saturday, but the money was all right, especially for a young lad, twenty-one quid a week. But Dawn didn't like the way Keith came home tired out, white as a sheet. Their dad thought it would be the making of him. 'You'll work longer hours than that in the hostelry,' he said in his boomy voice, 'you mark my words.' He always thought horrible things were the making of you.

Saturday lunchtimes Keith went with his workmates to the pub, not their own pub but another one, near the factory, one that would serve them underage. He wheeled his bike there and chained it to a fence in the car park. Then after they'd had a pint and a pork pie, they would all walk off together to watch Bradford playing rugby league, if it were a home game, anyhow.

It was raining cats and dogs, just like today. Luckily there was a roof over the stands that kept the worst off them.

After she'd finished clearing up from dinnertime opening, teenager Dawn hung around in her bedroom for a while, playing records. But she had itchy feet so she decided to go out to the shops. The problem with living over the business, she still felt it to this day, you were never free of it while you were in the building. She put on a miniskirt and a tank top, did her hair up just as if she was off on a date, slid on some heels even, and clopped into their kitchen.

'You're never going out,' her mum said. She was sitting at the table reading a magazine. Dad would be in the other room, watching sport on TV.

'Am that,' Dawn said.

'It's bucketing down.'

'Oh well. Won't do no harm.'

'You can't go in that clobber, any road. It's small enough as it is. If it shrinks any more, people'll see the lot.'

'What's *the lot* supposed to mean? What's a lot, when it's at home?' She wished she'd kept her mouth shut. It was her mum who had a lot.

'You're tall enough, when all's said and done.'

'Being tall has got nowt to do with it.'

'It has when you're wearing them high heels.'

'Oh for goodness sake. Being tall's not a crime. It's not because I eat too much, you know.' Serve her right, after all.

'You'll get drenched, all the same,' her mother muttered, giving her big bosom a shake as if to settle it back into place.

'There is such a thing as coats in this world, mother.'

Dawn always remembered what she did that afternoon, which was nothing much. She went and looked at records. She had some coffee, hoping one of her friends would come into the coffee bar, but no one did that she knew. She wandered round clothes shops. A car swished through a puddle and wet her shoe.

'Bloody Bradford,' a little boss-eyed man with a large flat cap said, seeing it. He had a dog with him on a lead, a poodle of all things, not a bloke's dog at all, especially in Bradford.

'It weren't Bradford, it were that car,' she told him.

'Bloody potholes are Bradford's. And the bloody puddles.'

'Oh well.' Him being indignant on her behalf cheered her up. 'Never mind,' she said, 'shake a leg.' She shook her wet leg and her shoe came off. 'Whoops.' Being high heeled it lay on its side as if it had been shot, or she had. She hopped over to where it was, flipped it upright with her toe, and slid it on again.

The man watched her sourly. His dog watched her sourly too. 'You mark my words,' he said, shaking his head and his big cap. 'Bloody potholes.'

When she got home, the pub was still closed. There was a group of men standing outside, looking indignant.

'We're stuck out here in the weather, duck,' one said.

'It's the right weather for ducks, and all,' another one said, and they both laughed.

'Never mind,' Dawn told them. 'You wait here a minute and I'll get it sorted out.'

It was awkward sliding her own key in the lock and letting herself in without them following too. But her dad was the landlord, not her. She slid sideways through the door as if it was only opening unofficially, just a crack that she had no right to be going through either.

There were no lights on in the pub. What she thought was, her dad must have dozed off in his chair, and perhaps her mum was asleep in the kitchen too. She went up the stairs. Her mother was standing at the top. She was wiping her hands on her skirt as if she'd just that minute finished the washing up. She was looking at Dawn with her forehead wrinkled, as though puzzled to see her.

'Where's Dad?' Dawn asked. 'Them blokes outside are getting restive. It's still pouring down.'

'He's not here, Dawn. He went off. He went off with a policeman.'

Dawn in that second knew everything, knew what she was going to know for forty years, for ever. She felt herself go weak, imagined lurching backwards down the staircase. 'Keith,' she whispered.

Then her mother said something stupid. 'He fell off of his bike,' she said.

Just for one second Dawn's old life came back as if it had never gone. She felt herself go weak a second time in succession, this time with relief. He fell off of his bike. That's all he did. He was in hospital with a big bandage round his head. Maybe with his leg up on one of those little crane things. Big bunch of grapes on the table. Just fell off of his bike.

When you totted up the anniversaries, Keith dead for ten years, for twenty years, for forty years, you'd have to say, to be accurate about it, Keith's been dead for ten years all but a second, for twenty all but a second, for forty all but. Because for that one second Dawn was given again a world in which Keith wasn't dead, and therefore had the pain of losing him twice. She could keep her books accurately for Keith, even if she couldn't for the Old Spring.

Mother said: 'He's dead.' She suddenly sounded confidential, woman to woman, asking for advice or an opinion. 'Dawn, the policeman said he's dead. He told us he's dead.' She said the word as if it hadn't ever been said by anyone before. She looked at Dawn expectantly, wanting her to say what the word actually meant.

'I'll make a cup of tea,' Dawn said.

'What about the blokes outside?'

'Sod the blokes outside.'

It was November 17th, 1968, forty years (minus one second) ago today. It was always minus one second no matter what the time of day, what the anniversary, it was always whatever time had passed since Keith died minus one second. If she could buy a ticket, Dawn would travel to that second and live her life out there, a different life, visiting the hospital with a box of chocolates for the invalid, working with him at the pub when he got better, not running off with Arthur to get away from home. Maybe taking over the licence with Keith when their parents retired. Maybe he would have had a limp.

She thought of that second as a little door. If she could only find it again and go through she could have the life she should have had.

It was raining today just as it had then, as if it was the same day coming round again, as if there were only so many days invented, and they were shuffled when they'd been used up and dealt out again.

Her dad had come back about half an hour later. He was just *her* dad now, not *their* dad anymore. Fine catch that was. 'He's gone,' he said. 'He has gone.'

'It might still be a mistake,' Mother said. 'It might have been somebody else.'

'I told you, didn't I? Listen to what I say, woman. He's gone. It was him. I saw him.'

'Was he . . . ?'

'No, he was just like normal, only dead.' He put his arms round Mother but they were a bit short or rather his belly was too fat and her bosoms were too fat too, so his arms didn't reach all the way. Dawn felt like a stick insect compared to them and was glad to be one. Keith had been thin too. She could see his thin arm, holding that tennis racket. After a while dad said, 'I'll go and open up.'

'What you mean, open up?' Dawn asked him.

'There's blokes down there, waiting in the rain. I told them I'd be down shortly.'

'More fool them, if they're waiting. There's other pubs to go to.'

'They're our regulars, those chaps are. They come here day in, day out. They're our bread and butter.'

Song of the publican. She got to know that tune well enough, over the course of her life. 'It's a pity they haven't got a home to go to, then. Who cares about our fucking bread and butter?' Dawn realised she was hissing at her dad like a snake. 'Keith won't be eating any bread and butter where he's gone, will he? He won't be eating anything, ever again.' She suddenly pictured him eating his lunchtime pork pie in that pub, his last meal on earth, and heard herself making a choking sound, as though Keith's pie had stuck in *her* throat.

'Yes he will,' Mother said unexpectedly. 'He'll eat manna.'

'Great,' Dawn said. 'And what's that when it's at home?'

'I don't know. I think it's made of locusts. But apparently it's very nice. It might be some sort of honey. I hope he likes it.'

Dawn gave her a long squashing look. Mother seemed to have become a halfwit. She looked down to avoid Dawn's gaze and suddenly her face folded into sobs. 'He was always a fussy eater,' she said.

Dawn's thought was: maybe your cooking had something to do with that. She turned back to Dad. 'You can't open up as if nothing happened. Your son died today.'

'I know he died today, our Dawn. I went and looked at him, didn't I? It wasn't an easy thing to do, you know. The bloody copper started blarting his eyes out, for a start. He knew Keith at the tennis club, a year or two back, apparently.'

Perhaps you might have cried too, then, Dawn thought, the two of you could have cried together. It might have stopped you looking so big and fat now, and barking in that voice of yours.

'Why do you think I'm going to open up?' he asked, pushing at her shoulder, almost hitting her. She could feel what was inside that shove: I get left with the girl out of the two of them, just my luck. The boy was bad enough, couldn't even ride his bike properly. 'Because I don't want to sit up here thinking about it all night, that's why.'

Dawn recollected her dad's belief about horrible experiences: they will be the making of you. That's what he'd told Keith about working in the rubber composition factory. Well, Dad, Dawn thought, if that's true, you should be pretty well made by now. You should be just about the most made bloke in the whole of Bradford.

No other vehicle was involved, apparently. Nobody actually saw what happened. He was found lying half on the road, half on the pavement. His bike was in the road. He must have hit his head on the kerb. Nothing was said about whether he'd hit a pothole, but that's what Dawn concluded. She inspected the spot and sure enough there was one nearby, not deep, but disguised by a puddle and enough to make a person lose his balance if he was unlucky.

Often she thought of the squinting man with his poodle on a lead and a flat hat too big for him, saying, Bloody potholes. Saying, You mark my words. It was like as if he had been a messenger, come to warn her. Come to tell her to beware.

She looked out for him on the streets but didn't see him again. Maybe that proved the point. Or maybe she was being daft: there was no shortage of men with flat caps in Bradford, it would be like trying to pick out a particular ant from an ants' nest. A large percentage of them didn't have eyes that pointed in the same direction. The poodle didn't prove anything at all.

The other day, maybe having in the back of her mind the anniversary coming up, she asked Alan about messengers from God, from the gods.

'Hermes was the messenger of the gods,' Jerry said, butting in. 'He was also called Mercury.'

'He had little wings on his heels,' Alan said, 'to help him get speed up.'

She couldn't quite picture that little long-ago man in Bradford with wings on his heels, couldn't picture anybody

68

in Bradford with wings of any kind, come to that, but still. When the man had told her about the potholes, Keith would have been still alive. So what? What could she have done? Rung the police? Rushed to the pub car park and tried to catch him before he mounted his bike?

Yes, yes, yes, that's exactly what she should have done, if she'd listened properly. What would it have mattered if she'd made a fool of herself?

It was about a quarter past one when Dawn came back down into the pub. She had taken her watch off when she washed her hands before making the rolls and forgot to put it on again. Frank being so fearful about the council checking up on their foodstuffs must have given her the willies too and she'd scrubbed up like a surgeon in *Casualty* (being that was the only bit of an operation the actors knew how to do). But you didn't need a watch down here, you could tell the time in pints.

Father Thomas was about one third down his. It would be his second, and he'd make it last out till he left at about a quarter to. Darren likewise his second, three quarters down, off any minute. It being a Thursday he'd have the charity shop to go to, more fool him.

It made her seethe, the thought of her and Frank paying Darren good money for a couple of hours work during the morning, and those cheapskates giving the poor lad zilch for the whole afternoon. He was furtive about going there too, even though it was them in the shop that should be ashamed. They no doubt banged the same drum as her old man, said it would be the making of him.

Darren was out of his depth standing by the Father, and moved his head from side to side above his beer in a slow fashion as if it had gone heavy on him despite not being over-full of brains. The movement reminded her of a polar bear she once saw in a zoo, looking and looking with its big head, wondering where all the ice and snow had gone, most likely.

Behind the two of them, Colin had raised the shove-ha'penny board and was lining up the snub of his palm to give one of the little discs a bash.

'What you up to, Colin?' she asked him. As luck would have it he made his move the same second and, distracted by her voice, knocked his ha'penny so hard it shot to the end of the board and pinged part way back again.

'Thank you, Dawn,' he said in his muttering voice. 'Much appreciated.'

He was small and thin, hardly more than eye level with the board to start with. He was known as Colin the Coach. The pub hired him and his charabanc for outings from time to time. It was funny watching him climb aboard like a monkey and then get into the driver's seat. The bus looked too big for him the way someone's clothes might be too big. He was very neat in that department, in point of fact, always in a dark blue blazer. Bang on for the captain of a ship, or in Colin's case, bus. And flannels, with a white shirt and a tie. The tie let the side down when you looked close, since it had girls on it, the girlie type of girls, pink on a blue background, wearing bikinis and holding up glasses of champagne.

'You can't play that game on your tod, Colin,' she reminded him.

'Practising.' He stretched up to the mantelshelf, got down the arrowroot pot, gave it a good shaking over the table and rubbed it evenly in as if he was talcing a baby's bottom. Then he banged his hands together to get the arrowroot off.

Practising shove-ha'penny made as much sense as practising ludo, as far as she could see. It called to mind Keith and the other lads playing fag cards or marbles in the primary school playground as though their lives depended on it, while the girls just stood around in sensible little groups being nasty to each other. Keith would lick the edge of his fag card then eye along it as if he was sighting a rifle before flicking it away.

'You going anywhere interesting this afternoon?' she asked.

'My goodness,' Colin said. He put the arrowroot pot back and picked up his pint glass from the table nearby. In his hand it looked like a large amber vase. 'I wouldn't be drinking this, would I?'

'Oh. I suppose not.'

'Be out on my ear, caught drinking before a job. Got a couple of days off.'

'Have you, then? It's a shame about the rain, in that case.'

'Doesn't worry me. Going to Hamburg tomorrow, crack of dawn.'

'Are you really? Hamburg.' She tried to dredge up some thought about Hamburg but her mind stayed a blank. 'How long for?'

'Just overnight. Back on Saturday.'

'You won't have time to get off the bus.'

'Oh no. Flying.' He glared at her stupidity. 'Went down the travel agents. Got quite a good deal. Good hotel overnight.' He sniffed sharply. He always sounded to Dawn as if he had narrow nostrils. Her dad had had a stubby metal thing, a bit like a thimble only with short spikes all over it and a sort of butterfly nut on the top. He used to twist it back and forth in the bowl of his pipe to uncoke it. Suddenly she imagined shoving it up Colin's nose, enlarging his nostrils for him. 'Three stars,' Colin added. 'Breakfast included. Continental.'

Dawn had assumed he was getting a free ride in a colleague's bus. 'Good for you,' she said.

'Been wanting to see the place for years.'

'Have you then?'

Colin was silent a moment, looking back at her. He dusted his hands again, then looked at her a bit more.

'Hamburg's where the Beatles got up and running,' Frank said. He was picking up empties.

'That's it,' Colin agreed, happy to have a straw to clutch at. 'Where the Beatles.'

'The oldest fan in town, in't you, m'dear,' Frank said, clapping Colin on the back. He turned and winked at Dawn. 'You OK, Dawn?'

'Why shouldn't I be?'

'I thought you might be worrying. About you-know-what.'

'Oh well.' She shrugged her shoulders. Depends what you-know-what you mean, she thought. But Frank's reminder of the approach of Tiger Tim suddenly made her stomach sink so sharply it seemed to press on her bladder and made her want to wee. It was as if the prospect of him coming had been gaining in horribleness all the while she'd not been thinking about it.

Father Thomas turned from the bar. 'I hope nothing's the matter, Dawn,' he asked.

He was a good man but somehow his concern seemed exaggerated. As if it was what he was obliged to show, with that dog collar round his neck. Silly for her to think that: she knew he liked her well enough. Being a woman you had a sort of man-gauge, which even worked with priests. In any case, what *was* liking someone, or loving them, but a sort of exaggeration? What she felt about her Keith, *that* was exaggerated, for starters. For starters and finishers. 'I just need to check the Ladies,' she said.

'I did *do* the Ladies,' Darren said, all aggrieved.

'Want another, Darren?' Father asked him, to take the wind out of his sails.

'No thanks, Father. I got to go.' He took his jacket from the peg and put it bad-temperedly on.

Dawn realised he was glad of an excuse to stalk out in a huff. It put him back on the high moral ground even though he felt guilty about going to the cancer shop. 'Any rate, they might have been used since then,' she said to him.

'There's not been a lady in,' Darren told her.

'I'm in,' chirped up a woman's voice from the back room. She was sitting there with her husband, an oldish couple with bags of shopping on the bench beside them.

'Oh yes,' Frank said, 'but are you a lady?'

'Cheek.' She laughed and shook her head.

'Don't take any nonsense from him,' Dawn told her. 'I don't.'

'I haven't needed it, anyhow.'

'I'm not sure I need it, neither,' Dawn said, looking at Frank as he wiped a table.

'The Ladies, I mean.'

'I'm off,' Darren announced, picking up his brolly.

'Bye, Darren,' Dawn said. Bye, bye, the others echoed. 'See you,' she heard Shrek grunt from the public.

'Nice bird?' Frank asked Colin, just at the moment when Colin was taking another swing at his ha'penny. Frank was full of beans at having teased the woman in the back room. He loved by-play with the female customers. It seemed to be all he needed in order to stay topped up in that line, sad to say.

Once again Colin's ha'penny zoomed to the end of the board.

'Bloody hell,' Colin said, disgusted.

'Sorry, m'dear. Bad timing.'

'What bird? When it's at home?'

'The bird in the travel agent, who gave you that sweet deal to Hamburg.'

'Oh, her.' Colin tugged down his blazer sleeves, remembering. 'Yes, very nice.' He wriggled his neck in his collar, making sure all his clothing was hanging just right in case the nice girl in the travel agent popped into view.

Frank brought the glasses up to the bar and gave them a clatter. 'Saw *him* coming, anyways,' he said in a low voice to Dawn and the Father, 'sending him off to Hamburg. Poor old goat.'

'I'll be down shortly,' Dawn said, and went up to the Ladies.

*

Harry came in. He inhabited a farmer's barn in the village of Wadley, half a dozen miles to the north of town. He had everything sorted out nice, though it was still a barn, not a conversion, the sort of place where the next-door neighbours were a rabble of chickens. The farmer let him use it for free. He had a camping gas stove and an old wardrobe to keep his clothes in. For years he'd sold crayon drawings of household objects, a chair, a table, a cup of tea, even a house, to passers-by outside the Priory, but had now retired. All a bit much, since he didn't have a house of his own.

Frank and Pete went to visit him once, when Pete was over from Norfolk to stay, but they'd been disappointed, at least Pete had been. Pete was into the rural life. Once upon a time he'd been taught how to cook a hedgehog by a couple of Travellers he met, but Harry wasn't interested in country ways, or any other ways but his own. He was just a bloke that lived in a barn. In any case, he never said a lot.

He didn't say a lot now, only, 'A pint of Buckman's.' He didn't even say please. He'd timed his arrival just right, while Dawn's back was turned. She didn't approve of him any more than she approved of Jake, and likely as not wouldn't have let him be served if she'd been on duty, though Frank had told her it was none of their business where people chose to kip. But once he was installed she'd no doubt leave him be, for the sake of peace.

Harry took his pint to a table in the back room, the next one to the couple where the lady hadn't used the Ladies. He put his beer on the table, hoisted one leg on top of the knee of the other, and unlaced his boot.

'Oh no,' Frank said.

'Oh no, what?' asked the Father.

'Harry's taking his boot off,' Frank told him

Sure enough Harry pulled it off and put his hand into it. He had a curly pepper and salt beard and tufty eyebrows on a high tanned forehead that was wrinkled with the effort of feeling about in the depths of his boot. The couple at the next table looked interestedly over at him.

'He looks like Moses trying to decipher the Ten Commandments,' Father said.

Harry placed the boot under the table, and picked up his pint.

'Diddle diddle dumpling,' Father added.

'What?'

'Went to bed with his trousers on.'

It was so strange to hear Father spout nonsense with that serious look on his pale face that for a moment Frank had thought he was saying Latin, maybe a prayer.

'One shoe off and one shoe on,' the Father continued. 'Diddle diddle dumpling, my son John.'

'Dawn will go ballistic,' Frank said.

'Well, you could tell him there's a dress code in this pub.'

'I like to live and let live, if I get half a chance.'

'Maybe she won't notice. He's got his feet tucked out of sight now. Mind you, if she glances under the table she'll think he's got three legs.'

'No law against that,' Frank said. As if conjured up by the word 'law' a hand suddenly felt his collar. 'What?' he asked, turning round.

'Hello, Frank love,' Shirley said. 'Where's your lovely missus got to, then?' She put her other arm round his neck too and clasped her hands to bring his head forward and down, then pushed the red O of her mouth towards his face. She stopped when their lips were an inch apart, looking straight into his eyes. 'When the cat's away, the mice can play, choochy face.' Then she looked across the bar at the snug. 'Sorry, Father. Can I get you another?'

'Don't mind me,' Father said. 'No, thanks all the same.' He took the last swig from his glass. 'I've got to go now, anyway.'

6

One thing that drove Dawn bonkers was seeing an unauthorised person behind the bar. Being landlady of her own pub had given Shirley the idea she could make free with theirs. And with Frank, for that matter. She was giving him a good old mauling. It didn't help that she was got up like the Queen of Sheba, with bright red lipstick on, her hair piled up on her head and a lime green coat cut like a cape.

'Hello, darling,' Dawn said. Frank started; his round head went like a traffic light on stop. Not to fret: she'd welcome a bit of hanky-panky as a sign of life on his part, and he wouldn't get far with Shirl in any case, she being all show and no follow-through. But it took another woman to sniff that out – even the Father was abandoning ship as fast as his legs would carry him.

'Oh botheration, Dawn,' Shirl said, 'if only you'd given us another minute.'

'Oh, it wouldn't have took that long, mark my words. See you tomorrow, Father.'

Father stopped in the doorway, spun round and did a little bow. Then he was off, out into the outside. 'Oh sod!' Colin muttered, obviously having miscued another ha'penny.

'Colin, I don't tolerate language in my pub,' Dawn said sternly, mainly to show Shirl who was boss. Frank winced.

'Beg pardon, Dawn,' Colin said.

'It was only sod,' Shirl said. 'And just whispered, poor muffin.'

Colin opened his mouth to say something indignant, but couldn't think what, so closed it again. It was being called muffin that stung. 'Sod might be all right for the Grapes,' Dawn told Shirl. 'But we have standards here.'

'Watering hole to the clergy,' Frank said.

Dawn turned to Colin. 'Save your swearing for Hamburg,' she said, letting him off the hook, 'they'll appreciate it over there.' It was her business to dole out justice and injustice, that was the point. 'Let's sit here,' she told Shirl, pointing to a table in the snug, beyond the shove-ha'penny board. 'We can keep an eye on this rascal while we're at it.'

Shirl exited the bar in the public. 'Ooh, let me squeeze,' she said, obviously easing past Jake who guarded that bar-flap like a rottweiler even though it was Jake himself who should be guarded against. She came over to the table. 'I nearly ended up in that fellow's lap,' she said. She shook herself like a wet dog. 'That would have been interesting.' She leaned over the table. 'Do you think he's had *it* done, as well?'

'For two pins I'd have him out.'

'You'd have everybody out, if you had your way. There'd only be you and Frank here. It would have to be a snake, stands to reason. Or a dragon.'

She undid her coat, slipped it off and hung it on a peg. She was wearing a white blouse with a tied neck in a bow, a medium black stripe running down the left side with a narrow orange stripe just beside it, making a thin white one in between the two, a black skirt down to her knees, shiny stockings and high heels. There were gold necklaces round her neck and a muddle of cuffs and bangles at each wrist. Her nails were varnished to buggery in red.

She sat down opposite Dawn. 'A dragon would work best, when you think about it.' She raised her eyebrows and pursed her lips, pretending to be shocked at herself. Her mouth poked forward like a strawberry that had been stuck on underneath her nose. 'How horrible to see it rearing up.' She wrinkled her nose so it looked like a strawberry too, an unripe one.

'What can I get you?' Frank asked, over her shoulder.

'You do creep,' Shirl told him. She put her hand on her left bosom as though to say, Be still, my beating heart. 'I'll have a G&T,' she said, suddenly business-like.

'Two G&Ts please, Frank.'

Frank touched where his forelock would have been and went off.

'Nice fire,' Shirl said. 'I told Bob, that's what we need in our place. To give it a heart and soul.'

Dawn saw Harry approach the bar from the back room. He seemed to bob as if he was walking along the slope of a hill. 'Where did *he* spring from?' Dawn asked.

Shirl followed her gaze. 'Another one you want to chuck out?'

'I never said.'

'Any rate, why I'm here, I could do with a word of advice.' She caught sight of Colin glaring at the board and gibbering to himself. 'How can a grown man get in a lather all by himself at a shove-ha'penny board?'

'That's the difference between us and them.' Dawn shut her eyes against the picture of Keith and his fag cards, but it was there inside her head in any case, all the clearer. Colin had been sighting along the board, one eye shut, in the exact same way Keith used to sight along the edge of his fag card and into the air beyond.

'Drinks, ladies,' Frank said, arriving with a tray. He put their glasses on the table and retreated to the bar.

Shirl leaned forward. 'What it is, Bob's at me every morning, regular as the milkman. He won't leave off. Not for a day.'

'I didn't know you were shagging the milkman,' Dawn said.

'It's like getting hit with a blunt instrument,' Shirl told her, not interested in Dawn's quips.

A bloke came into the public, quite a big fellow, wearing a mac and a winter-weight baseball cap. He had a grey pigtail poking out of the hole at the back. Perhaps it acted like a mooring rope when gusts hit the beak of his cap. Frank hadn't seen the man before but he seemed to take Jake in his stride, giving him a nod. Jake gave a two millimetre nod back.

'Yes, m'dear?' Frank asked.

'Dog all right?'

For a stupid second Frank thought he was asking if dog was on for lunch.

'Oh yes,' he said, as it dawned. He peered over the bar. There was a small wet dog there, maybe a terrier, looking back up at him and panting a little, with its tongue hanging from one side of his mouth. The pong of dog wafted up, released by the rain, but Jake was in no position to be fussy. 'There's a bowl of water under the bench.'

'Oh, thank you,' the man said, bending down to look for it.

'He probably drank his fill from a puddle already.'

The man pulled the bowl out and put it in front of his dog. 'He's always ready for a drink,' he said.

'Come to the right place then,' Frank told him. Jake was looking at the dog intently, as if he hadn't seen one before.

'I think his kidneys are a bit duff,' the man said.

'That so?' Frank found himself peering down at the dog as if he had X-ray vision and could check the dog's kidneys from the outside. Being a landlord you had to make out being concerned about everything, even the insides of a dog you'd not set eyes on before. The dog looked up, saw three men eyeballing him, one of them blue, yapped once, and turned back to the water.

'Name's Ted,' the man said.

'How do, Ted.'

'No, the dog. I'm Simon.'

'Ah ha. Frank,' said Frank.

Simon looked at Jake, but Jake just carried on looking at the dog, oblivious. Or maybe shy. That thought had never occurred to Frank before: maybe shy. Some people thought he was threatening, which was why Dawn wanted him banned, but all he ever did was sit there.

Shyness was a form of fear. Young Jake lying on a tattooist's table, hoping the little cold pinpricks were bit by bit taking away his scaredness. Possible anyway. A way to make social hobnobbing easier for the rest of his days, to make it more or less non-existent, in point of fact.

Alternatively: a big stupid bastard who thought wall-to-wall tattooing would make him look good.

'That's the pub mascot,' Frank said. 'Name of Jake.'

'How do, Jake,' Simon said.

Jake moved his head another tiny amount, this time from left to right, as if he was saying no to how-do.

The man of the couple in the back room came up to the bar and asked about the fillings of the rolls. Frank passed him over the whole basket, to show his wife. He went back to their table with it and held it out for her to inspect. She ferreted around, destabilising the pile, obviously in hopes that some sort of gourmet roll would be lurking at the bottom.

'Just the bog standard,' Frank told her.

She blushed, as if caught out. 'They look nice,' she said.

'Bog standard *is* nice, if you ask me. Any rate, I don't know any better.'

She picked one out then raised her shoulders, ducked her head and flashed a little apologetic smile at Frank. Then she looked up at her bloke, who nodded at the rolls in general, both hands gripping the basket. She picked out one for him too, holding one up in each hand for Frank to see, like a pair of cymbals she was about to clash.

Just at that moment there was a fracas in the public, two-tone barking, and a bloke came through into the snug, looking harassed. He was a short man, wearing a large flat cap and a trench coat. A poodle followed him on a lead, also looking harassed, one of those bigger poodles that don't have their coat carved into shape. It lay down on the floor, resting its head on its front paws, obviously brooding about being barked at by the dog next door. Colin was still egging himself on at the shove-ha'penny table and in the corner Dawn and Shirl were deep in their conversation. Every now and then a faint rasping noise came from Colin's direction. Sometimes it was the ha'penny, travelling over the board on a layer of arrowroot; sometimes it was Colin sniffing; oddly they sounded exactly the same.

Dawn glanced up and saw the bloke and his dog. She stared for a moment with her hand gripping her neck, as if she wanted to strangle herself lightly, then rose to her feet.

'Oh no,' said Shirl, 'not dogs and all.' Oddly she'd put her hand to her throat as well. She looked at Dawn's back, then towards Frank, caught his eye, raised her own eyebrows and did a sort of pout with her lips.

'You OK?' Dawn asked the bloke.

'Yes, fine.'

'I'm the landlady.'

'Oh. Right. Nice pub.'

'I thought for a minute I knew you.'

'I don't think so.'

'No, well, it were a time ago, anyhow. You'd be dead by now, any road.'

'Ah. Thanks a lot.'

'It was just he had a similar dog.'

'*I* haven't got a dog.'

Dawn looked slowly down at the poodle. The man looked down at it too. 'My mum's,' he explained. 'Just taking him for a walk.'

'Any excuse,' Frank told him. 'What'll you have?'

Dawn went back to her seat. Frank poured the bloke a pint. 'You want to warm up by the fire,' he told him as he passed it over.

'I will, thanks,' the bloke said. Dawn glanced up at him again, but Shirl's loud confidential voice got louder still and brought her attention back again.

'My wife's got a cheese and chupney one,' the man from the back room said to Frank's back.

'Sorry, m'dear,' Frank replied, turning to face him. 'I got distracted.'

'And I've got –'

'They're all the same price. Two quid a pop.'

'Ah.'

The man fetched out his money. Behind him, Harry got out an old leather purse and began counting pennies. He'd obviously earwigged the amount per roll and was seeing if he had enough for one himself. I worry about a shortfall of nine hundred quid, Frank thought, and that poor sod can't take for granted the price of a barm cake.

He was tempted to slip Harry a roll, but if he tried, Dawn would clock it. She might be busy talking to Shirl, or listening at least, but a sixth sense would detect he was doling out something for nothing. In any area of life important to you, you could pick up vibrations others didn't detect. You learned that fact by living cheek by jowl with people. You could notice the way a person's antennae would suddenly wag.

It wasn't that Dawn was mean exactly – yes, it was, she *was* mean, though kind in her own fashion. She wouldn't give you her toenail clippings but was fond enough of the human race, some of it anyhow. The thing was, she protected their business, or tried to, and it had a £900 hole in it already. Times were hard, that's how she saw the issue. The smoking ban had cut down their trade something terrible. Pubs were going to the wall left, right and centre. The £900 was the last straw. He could hear her saying the very words. He already hated the number. He'd even prefer if it was a thousand, just for a change. What would it matter? They were liable to lose their jobs either way.

Anyway the couple might be well peeved if they saw another punter get his roll for nothing. That was why a landlord never said on the house without good reason.

Frank gave the man his change plus a couple of paper napkins. As he went off Harry limped up to the bar.

'I'll have one,' he said, nodding at the basket.

'Which?'

'Any.'

Frank held out the basket and Harry plunged his arm in, not looking. It reminded Frank of bran tubs when he was a kid, feeling in the sawdust for the shape of a toy, just a shape, the shape was the exciting part, the toy itself would end up being just a toy in the light of day, like any other toy.

Harry's paw reappeared, clutching its roll.

'Good choice,' Frank said, wrinkling up his eyes to read the label, 'ham and cheese.'

'That it?'

'That's it.' Blimey, Harry wasn't any better at reading than Jake. Frank remembered those crayon pictures Harry used to draw to flog to tourists outside the Priory: TV sets, flower beds with bright flowers in, plates of grub. He would write EGG AND BACON underneath in a wobbly hand. Perhaps he'd just learned particular words for the sake of art. It didn't prove he could read, any more than Jake having LOVE and HATE tattooed on his fingers did.

'Is it what the Father had?'

Perhaps he wanted to be sure he was getting the best value for money, on the basis that the worst person to short-change, short of a doctor, must be a man of God.

Frank learned that lesson yesterday, going to visit Romesh, one of their regulars, in hospital. Dawn had gone the day before and couldn't bring herself to go again so soon. 'I hate to see him that poorly, I hate it,' she told Frank. The nurse wouldn't let him on the ward: only family. Too poorly for other visitors. She seemed as wide as the corridor. How had Dawn managed it? He pictured her sweeping through in her horned helmet like Alan had described.

'He's one of my flock,' Frank had said.

He was going to explain about Romesh being a regular at the Old Spring, but the nurse cut across him.

'Oh. Oh, I see. I didn't think, being as he's an Asian gentleman. Come in Reverend, that will be fine.'

It was odd to see someone so fat give in so quickly. He would have expected that size of person to need more of a push. And in he went, to find poor Romesh gasping on his hospital bed like a stranded fish.

Father had had the chutney; so had most of the customers today. Frank ran his eye over the basket. None of those left, to all appearances. Still, no point upsetting a punter.

'The very same,' he said.

Harry passed over his small change, content.

'Hi thang yow,' Frank said, jollying his side of the transaction so as to take the sting out of Harry's two pounds.

As Harry hopped back to his seat, Frank put the rest of the rolls in order, lining them up alternately in their basket as if building a soft wall.

'What you want with that bloke with the poodle?' Shirl asked in the middle of her own pause for breath.

'I don't want anything,' Dawn whispered. 'He gives me the willies.'

'Some willies I wouldn't mind being given,' Shirl whispered back, 'but his isn't one of them.'

The rain had stopped for the moment, though clouds rushed around the sky, their edges tufted as a cardinal's eyebrows.

A few sodden people scuttled through the temporary let-off. Water reflected here and there. The sharp gusts of earlier on had dwindled to a quixotic breeze that lifted Father Thomas's hair from behind and then pressed his cheeks from in front. It felt moist as a grape.

The front garden of the De La Tour house, like the back, was stuffed with Victorian vegetation, dank rhododendrons and hydrangeas. They swayed stiffly, topped up by the downpour the way Frank topped up a pint, staring fixedly at the convex surface as his hand edged the pump handle to the exact angle. Each to his own. Brother Julian would probably call them tumescent, to rhyme with heaven-sent.

The thought of Julian gave Brother Paul a pang. Julian was right: somebody did need to take the garden in hand. It needed – well, it needed bringing up to date. Brisker, more modern plants should be planted. *With it* was the phrase that came to mind, the garden should be made with it, *it* being the everything that was now, *with* the rush to connect, the phrase as a whole catching the click of contact. Even garden plants should be made to click. Though Paul had a vague monastic qualm that *with it* wasn't with it any more.

Paul let himself into the hall, put the umbrella in its stand and hung up his coat. The hall needed to be fixed too, he suddenly saw that. It had small black and white tiles on the floor, many cracked and some missing, leaving lozenges of grey cement behind like bad teeth. The varnished panelling on the walls was dark and crazed. The Old Spring was old and battered enough but it had a cared-for look. Darren did the business, under the eagle eye of Dawn.

Perhaps that was what was missing here, a woman's eagle eye. A pub had to be a home from home, and the De La Tour house should be that too, given the ultimate home was above and beyond, for the present at least. That was the trouble with Christianity: it was posited on the notion of a journey. The Holy Family was hardly a model for cosy domestic life, camping in that stable. Mary might have been the Mother of God but no one ever made any claim for her housewifely skills. How would you tell, with straw and animals everywhere?

A faint smell of Welsh rarebit hung in the cool atmosphere. Paul went into their big room. Rain was spitting against the French windows again. Julian was at the other end, hunched over the dining table. Paul turned and took some steps towards him, then realised he was dead.

7

Julian was sitting at the table, his head slumped forward on his own Welsh rarebit as if he were munching it directly from his plate, like an animal. In the middle of the table the vase of lilies stared upwards, like a bunch of nuns in white habits.

Paul stood where he was when he'd realised, halfway across the room, needing a moment to arrive at how to react.

When something like this happened you had to learn how to be you all over again, work out what thoughts you thought, what feelings you felt. It was all very well to have views on death but they evaporated at once when you actually saw it.

Paul was aware of willing his cheeks to go pale, his eyes to become shiny, his ears to turn pink. He was etching shock on his own face the way engravers might etch it on stone or iron. When you entered a social occasion you plastered a silly grin on your face; when you entered a death event, you used whatever sharp tools and acids that lay to hand in order to appear suitably horrified.

It was worse than that. Hypocrisy nestled inside hypocrisy, like Russian dolls.

Paul was pretending to mourn his friend, his brother, when in fact he felt nothing: that was the first hypocrisy.

He was pretending to feel anxious about pretence, when really he was frightened and repelled: that was the next. He simply didn't want to go near Julian now Julian had become a thing.

He took a step, then another, working wobbly legs as if he was both puppet master and puppet. As he drew near, he finally made himself look at his old friend.

There was Julian, and his lunch. He had sat here all alone, eating the Welsh rarebit he'd cooked for himself. Paul had known Julian always ate lunch alone, while all the younger members of the De La Tour household were at the order's school, watching over the boys as they devoured their burgers and chips, and he, Paul, was in the Old Spring talking poltergeists with Darren, hearing Colin the Coach agonising over shove-ha'penny, observing Shirley make her moves on poor old Frank. But you can know and not know, both together. If you didn't understand that eating was a communal act you could hardly call yourself a Catholic, even a Christian. What other religion had sitting down to supper with companions as a central image? He had deliberately avoided picturing Julian munching his midday meal day after day all alone.

That was better, he felt his eyes smart.

As he came up to the table, Paul caught a bitter whiff in the air, death, no not death exactly. Next best thing. Vomit.

It wasn't Welsh rarebit that Julian was lying upon. Or only in a reconstructed form, a soft and surreal jigsaw puzzle of itself. Julian had finished his lunch and cleared it away, then he'd sat back down to work on his poems before being overtaken by sickness unto death.

Paul stood beside the table and imagined him here in the quiet room staring out across the intervening space, those chairs and sofas not being sat in, the TV not being looked at, across to the French windows and the garden beyond them, where the plants sucked water up their roots and waved stiffly

in the rainy wind; testing words in his head, *regina, vagina.*
Trying to pluck some lyricism from their opposition, to get
counterpoint from their counterpoint, to complete the quest
of his whole life, of everyone's life one way or another, by
reconciling body and spirit.

Julian was a minister too, in his own way, devoted to
transubstantiation, the task of transforming Welsh rarebit
into melody. And then, like stormwaters in a drain, the vomit
roared up his throat and drowned him.

Call the police. No, that would be over the top. There was
no question of a crime having been committed. Julian had had
a dicky ticker for years. And recently he hadn't looked well.
He'd gone on holiday with his sister and her family in the late
summer, perhaps to recuperate, perhaps to say goodbye. He
was the most alert of men but lately there'd been a look of
abstraction on his face and a film of perspiration on his upper
lip. Just the doctor, that would do for now.

Not now, not exactly now. There was something Paul
needed to do first, before anyone came.

Paul stood and breathed deeply, despite the stomach acid in
the air. It was a relief to have a duty to do. He needed to perform
some difficult, unpleasant service. Christ had washed the feet
of the disciples, and that can't have been pleasant, however
holy the atmosphere in which the task was undertaken, easing
toe-jam from between manky toes, scrubbing embedded grime
from hard-worn soles, a personal service in the rather leery
sense of the word personal, and of the word service. This
too. He needed its nastiness to cut through the cop-outs and
blankings and bad faith of the last few minutes.

Under the vomit, acting like its plate, was Julian's notebook. He couldn't leave it where it was. It might be read by
a coroner, or by Julian's sister, by someone who wouldn't
understand and who could be wrong-footed by such work
in progress, who might think that it was spoiled trash and
should be discarded.

Whatever words were there, they were Julian's last words, and deserved some respect and understanding. They might be words in a language that only Paul could read.

Gav came in, nodded at Jake, sat down beside him. Jake was still looking at Ted, the dog, who was curled in a ball half under the bench. Simon was sitting on the bench just beyond him, reading a *Daily Mail* from the rack, his pint at his feet. He still had his baseball cap on, but his pigtail curved round and rested on his near shoulder, like a second pet.

Gav followed Jake's gaze and looked at the dog too, glaring at it almost, as if to discover what was the deal. Then he turned to Jake, and said nothing. Jake raised his eyes from the dog, looked at Gav, and said nothing back.

'Do you want a roll?' Frank asked Katie. She was sitting on a stool, at the snug part of the bar. It was nice just to look at her, and to smell her for that matter. After all the old lags, she was fresh as a daisy.

'I thought Gray was going to be here,' Katie said. 'He said he was. I took a late lunch especially.' She raised her fizzy water and looked at it with her eyes screwed up, as if to check on its clarity.

'You won't get fat on that,' Frank said.

'I don't want to get fat. Hey, I've chosen the dress.'

A roll unsold, Frank thought, looking at her slimness. She was wearing an orange type of woollen jumper with a raised collar and a little slit on the front of the neck, with a rim on it of embroidery, like a tunic on a toy soldier. She had black hair like brackets each side of her face, curving into her jaw. Lips in between, curving slightly down but happy-looking. He had a sudden sense of exactly what they'd feel like, kissed, and had to stand quite still while his heart thumped sharply. He could feel the cool firmness they'd have, then the sudden give in them.

In the far corner of the room Dawn and Shirley were still on the go, lips opening and closing. What's it all about, he wanted to ask, lips opening and closing all the time. The most flexible part of the whole body, lips – that tells you something.

'Dress,' he said, trying to get the thread.

'Dress, Frank. For my wedding?'

'You could have a pickled egg in a bag of crisps.'

'You what?'

'Open the bag, drop the egg in.'

'Jesus, I thought you meant to wear at my wedding.'

'Scrunch the crisps round the egg, kneading the bag with your hand. It's like a do-it-yourself scotch egg. They stick to the vinegar, the little crisp bits.' Katie's small face, skin white and slightly moist, made him think of a hardboiled egg when it plumps from its shell into the palm of your hand. 'The egg looks like a little hedgehog when you take it out the bag, with little shards of crisp stuck all over it.'

He remembered Pete's story about cooking a hedgehog one time. Pete must have been in his element, out on the fens, squatting on his haunches with two gypsies from the village, night behind them, fire in front, swigging scotch from his hip flask. The animal was coated in mud, half buried in a fire, and slowly baked. Tandoori principle, Pete said. When it was done they dug the hedgehog out and cracked the hardened crust. It came off in one, he'd said, bristles, the lot.

That's how Katie's face was, moist and soft and white, newly peeled.

'Oh, thank you very much,' she said.

'All right then.'

'No, Frank, thank you: no.' She shuddered. 'My dress? Wedding dress?'

She opened her handbag and got out a piece of paper that she spread out on the bar. It had obviously been cut out of a catalogue. She turned it for him to see. There was a woman in a white bridal dress.

'Very nice,' he said. £600 was printed in a small box to the left of the photo. Two thirds of the amount he and Dawn were stuck for. Think of it that way, getting all in a lather for the cost of a dress and a half.

'What do you really think?'

'I told you, very nice.'

'Men.'

'True enough.' Truer than Katie knew. Graham popped in an hour ago, told Frank to make his excuses, and popped off again. He couldn't cope with any more dresses for the time being, with any more wedding arrangements, for that matter. 'It's doing my head in, Frank,' he'd said. He was a long-legged big-chested bloke with long hair. Frank liked to lie as little as possible, so he didn't say outright Graham had stood her up, just said nothing and let Katie think the two of them had got their wires crossed. Half a lie.

'The whole thing'll go tits up, if we're not careful,' Katie said sadly, and took another sip of her drink.

'I think you're jumping the gun a bit.'

'We jumped the gun already. I'm due in April, remember.'

'I mean, the wedding. You're just getting your knickers in a twist.'

'If Gray can't be arsed to meet me in a pub, fat chance him turning up at the church.'

Across the snug Dawn got up and placed some more coals on the fire with the tongs, poising them with care. 'Lovely girl like you,' Frank told Katie, 'course he'll show. He just needs noddling on a bit.'

'You think?'

Dawn went back to her table and sat down opposite Shirl once more. 'Fellas get nerves as well as girls, you know,' Frank said.

'He plays rugby, Frank.'

'Thanks a lot,' Simon said.

'Sorry, m'dear,' Frank replied, turning towards the public. 'Similar?'

'No fear. If Ted sucks up any more of that water, he'll keel over.' He plonked his glass on the bar. 'See you.'

92

'See you,' Frank said.

'See you,' Gav said.

Frank watched for the blue head. It did a sudden sideways shake, as if a fly had settled on its nose. Simon bent down, hitching on the lead no doubt, then went.

'Funny about water,' Katie remarked. 'It does make you tiddly, after a while.'

'Ted's a dog,' Frank explained.

'You what?'

'A dog.'

'A dog dog?'

'Yep.'

'I suppose what it does, it dilutes the brain.'

'Perhaps you should have something stronger. It might have a weaker effect.'

'I'm back to work in a min.'

'Playing rugby doesn't prove anything.'

'Does it not?'

'Different sort of fear.'

'But he doesn't fear, that's what I mean. He plays prop forward.'

'It's a different sort of being brave, too, that's what I'm getting at. Same as me. I was in the Falklands, you know. Shells whizzing over. I was OK there, but getting fixed up with Dawn, different ask altogether.'

Another half lie. Yes, he was in the Falklands. But the shells didn't exactly whizz over, at least over him. He did see a ship being hit in the distance one time, smoke rising. You could make out a little tiny gleam of red, like the tip of someone's cigarette being dragged on far away, and black smoke in a straight line at an angle, as though the ship was being swung round on a black rope pinned to the middle of the sky somewhere. The sea was royal blue and very flat, the sky pale blue, not a cloud. You could imagine the South Atlantic was a hot part of the Mediterranean, only with the heating turned off.

'Were you scared, getting married to Dawn?' Katie whispered. She glanced quickly over her shoulder at Dawn in the corner.

'Terrified. We didn't get married, matter of fact.'

'What do you mean? Did you do a bunk?'

'No, nothing like that. Just decided it wasn't necessary, that's all.'

'How could you be terrified getting wed if you never got wed?'

'I meant the commitment.'

Katie leaned over the bar. 'Do you live in sin?' she asked.

Frank ran a cloth over the bar counter. 'That's right,' he told her. 'That's where we live.'

Shirl pushed her head at Dawn over the table. It was like the way somebody jumps forward at you when you put your glasses on. Too much detail, Dawn thought. She could make out the powder on Shirl's cheeks, especially because the cheeks themselves had gone red and veiny. The whites of her mascaraed eyes were a bit yellow too, and seemed slightly dented.

'It's like being shagged with a stick,' Shirl whispered loudly. It was a good job Colin the Coach had gone. He would have whacked his ha'penny into outer space. And the bloke in the flat hat had gone too, along with his poodle. The snug was just the two of them now, except for Katie sitting at the bar and turning old Frank to jelly.

What Shirl had done was circle back to where she'd started. Too much detail in more ways than one.

'For goodness sake, Shirl.' For two pins she would get up and walk off. She didn't have to listen to this sort of thing. Plus she felt got at. She had the feeling Shirl had guessed Frank went off her several years ago. One morning he just looked at her with new eyes, didn't want to know any more.

Of course even if she and Frank had been at it like rabbits she wouldn't've let on to Shirl. But she had a horrible feeling that Shirl could sniff out the difference between not telling a lot of dirty secrets and not having a lot of dirty secrets to tell.

'I can't help it,' Shirl said.

'You could always chuck a bucket of cold water over him,' Dawn suggested.

'I like sex as much as the next person. You know that, Dawn.'

'I don't recall us going out on the pull together.'

'You know what I mean. I'm not dead yet, that's what I mean.'

I've got ears like radar scanners, Dawn suddenly realised. Even while Shirl was confiding in her like she was, she was picking up the odd little word from the conversation Katie and Frank were having at the bar. Tits, she heard, in Katie's silvery voice. Knickers, in Frank's. Arse, Katie's again.

'Fire's burning low,' Dawn said. 'I'll just put some more coal on.' 'Lovely girl like you,' she heard Frank say, while she was doing so.

'The thing is,' Shirl said, when Dawn got back, 'I like to be respected.'

'Don't we all.'

'Bob might just as well be barbecuing a chicken.'

Shirl gave a long wobbly sigh. Dawn had the urge to confide back, to tell her about the missing nine hundred quid. She opened her mouth to speak. But if she did it would just be a spot of bother. It would just be an inconvenience, and she would feel called on to belittle it herself. I don't know what we've gone and done with it. Must have added up wrong. We'll have to find it somewhere I suppose.

Even as Dawn opened her mouth it occurred to her that Shirl's sigh was one of contentment. She liked being a barbecued chicken. She was just exactly the sort of woman who would. She even looked a bit like one, when you thought about it.

She was probably making it up in any case. Bob was a lean bloke, wiry, with thick grey hair and legs that wouldn't stop a pig in an alley.

A little puff of Katie's words, floating down like stars from a rocket: 'Weren't you scared, getting married to Dawn?'

At the bar, Frank's big head nodding.

Across the table, Shirl looking long and hard, waiting for Dawn's reply, expecting her to try going one better, all set to squash her riposte.

Katie's voice again: 'Sin?'

A sob slid out. Big fat sob, glistening between the two of them on the table top.

'What is it, Dawn? Whatever's the matter?'

Dawn opened her mouth to speak but another sob came out instead. Her heart banged in panic. Whatever would Shirl think? And Frank?

She peered over at the bar. No worry on that score, Frank too busy making goggle eyes.

Dawn swallowed, took a breath. 'My brother died today,' she said.

Shirl froze. After a long second she blinked. Dawn watched each set of blackened eyelashes meet its opposite number. Sorry, sorry, Keith, Dawn said in her heart. Sorry to use you to stop being embarrassed in front of Shirl. You had that dying to do when just a boy and this is the use I put it to.

'Dawn,' Shirl said. 'Oh Dawn.'

Even in the middle of guilt Dawn felt a little glow of triumph, trumping Shirl's ace.

Shirl's hand came over and grasped Dawn's wrist.

'Dawn, Dawn, whyn't you tell me, Dawn? Letting me go on like that.'

Dawn tried to answer but only another little sob came out. The strain of trying made it more like a squeak.

'Was it this morning, Dawn? It must have been this morning. Oh my God? Was it sudden? Was it an accident?' Suddenly tears were coming from her battered eyeballs, catching on the thickened sticky lashes and hanging there like little silver fruit.

'No, no, Shirley. It's forty years gone.'

'What? What do you mean? I don't get you, Dawn.'

'My Keith died forty years ago today. It's like his birthday, only death. His deathday.'

'Oh. I see.' Shirl gave Dawn a look through her teary eyes, much as to say, I've been led up the garden path here. 'I'm sorry, Dawn. It must be hard for you. Did he have cancer?'

'No. He just fell off his bike. He fell off it in Bradford, where we used to live in them days. Not the Bradford down here. The real one, up north. That Bradford had very potholey roads at the time.'

'He went down one, did he?'

'I don't know what he did. He died, that's what he did. I wish he *had* died this morning. Then he would have had forty more years of life than he did have.'

'Round numbers are always the worst. I've had enough of them in my time, believe you me. I dread them rolling up on me. I've got another in a year and a bit.'

Shirl's way of reminding Dawn that she was eight or nine years younger than her, as well as being ten times more desirable. Keith had only had the one round number, Dawn realised, when he was ten. Unless nought counted.

Katie got down from her stool at the bar and gave each half of her bum a smack in turn, as if to knock the dust from it. Cheek, given cleanliness was the pub's top priority. Two cheeks. Dawn felt a laugh shake her chest and looked as glum as she could so Shirl would think it was another sob being stifled. Katie just liked the sound her tight jeans gave out when struck, or rather she knew poor Frank would like it.

'I'm sorry to mither you about it,' Dawn said.

'That's what friends are for. I've been bending your ear with *my* woes.'

'It was because of what you said.'

'Was it?'

Now it was Dawn's turn to whisper. 'It made me think, Keith probably never went to bed with anyone his whole life.'

Shirl reflected on this. Shirl's confidences about Bob hadn't made Dawn think about Keith being a virgin, in point of fact. Nothing could make her think about that, because she thought about it always. All the details of Keith were in her head at any given moment. She just said it so as Shirl could make sense of the turn their conversation had taken.

'You never know,' Shirl said, 'you don't know what he got up to when your back was turned. How old was he?'

'Seventeen.'

'There you are then, seventeen.'

'Seventeen's not very old. Especially in them days. I hate to think about all the life he never lived. I hate to think of it.'

'Bye, Dawn,' Katie said. 'Bye,' she added, in the general direction of Shirl.

'Bye, duck,' Dawn said. 'Take care now.'

Gav said: 'Rufus said he wants to see you. This afternoon. Half three.'

'Here?' Jake asked.

'Not here you prat. They're closed, in't they? Three? At half three?'

'I got painting to do. Shop front on Pomeroy Road.'

'What you doing here, being you're painting? Supposed to be.'

'Dinner time. I got to go back after.'

'If you're so busy painting, where's your overalls? You making out you been painting in your track suit? There's not a spot of paint on them. Maybe a bit of pizza stuck on the trousers, but not a spot of paint on them.' Gav pointed his thin head right at Jake's groin. 'One of those Hawaiian ones, bit of pineapple chunk on it.'

'Fuck off.' Jake pushed Gav's head away, bent down, pulled a plastic bag from under the bench, and shook it at Gav. 'I took them off in the bog.'

'You sucking up to Dawn, that's what you're doing. You should have took your tattoos off at the same time. That would have done the business for her.'

'Black bastard.'

'What you mean? She's blonde, in't she? Or was once upon a time.'

'Fucking Roof.'

There was a pause. 'You don't want to call him that.'

'Why not? He is a bastard. Have you seen his poncy hat?'

Gav lowered his voice. 'Not bastard, you stupid bastard. Black. You didn't ought to call him black.'

'Why not? He is black.'

'Yeah, but you don't want to say it like it's an insult. It's bloody racist.'

'It's bad enough not being able to have a fag.'

'Anyhow, look at the colour of you, if you want to talk about what colour someone is.'

Julian had his lunch all alone at this table, where he was still seated.

You are conscious of the little sounds you make when you eat alone, the crunchings and lip smackings, the soft gobbles, the whole poignancy of being a body. People can't do it with dignity, like a cow does, tearing grass all day, surrendering simply to the long process of mastication, digestion, excretion. People need to tart up the proceedings, to eat together, as if chewing were a form of language. Maybe that's where language began, in fact, in those movements of the mouth: little subtle grunts of appreciation or disapproval, modified belches of satiety, an agreeable murmur to signify *après vous*, a moan or whimper for pass the mammoth steak. Once upon a time talking with your mouth full was all the talking there was. Thus food became community; and community, Christianity. In the beginning was the meal.

At the heart of Christianity there is a table, with men sitting round it, each one with nicely washed feet, eating together, talking, taking communion. But Brother Julian ate his last supper alone.

When Julian had finished his carefully made Welsh rarebit (with buried onion and tomato), he cleared the dish away, and then returned to his seat and got out his notebook. He looked across at the rainy window and chewed his biro.

The earlier pages, that had been flipped over and therefore not vomited upon, were full of scribbling on the vagina regina topic. The Queen (earthly) of Heaven (heavenly). Christ came from heaven to earth through her vagina. Saved, we go from earth to heaven, through his sacrifice, her mediation. His direction through the vagina: being born. We go the other way. He exits, we enter.

Julian didn't actually write that we screw the Virgin to get to heaven but that's what he implied. He wrote around it. He scrabbled for something to rhyme it with, to say it at a safe distance.

Suddenly it all seemed pathologically repetitive and obsessive to Paul, like some kid giggling over dirty words at the back of the classroom. A grown man spending his time trying to convince himself that his celibate existence had a sexual meaning after all. If sex meant so much to him why hadn't he gone off and had himself a shag? That was the great advantage of a confessional culture: room to manoeuvre.

Paul got to his feet and walked out of the cloud of sickness and death to the other side of the room. It seemed stupid to note that Julian meanwhile stayed exactly where he was, but he did, and Paul noted it. The rain was beating so densely against the window that the glass looked as if it was melting and sliding, and so did the greenery beyond. There was a cool layer of air here, out of reach of the living room's predatory central heating. Paul breathed it in and wrapped it round himself, in preparation for his return.

Back at the table he seated himself by prone Julian once again and opened the notebook at the spattered page. There were just two phrases on it: *Song title, Dung beetle.*

8

The smell of the cancer shop was even stronger in wet weather. It was like the stew witches make, with eye of newt and toe of frog. Alan had told Darren about the recipe in the Old Spring once upon a time. Only here it was armpits and crotches and baby sick and body dirt and sweat from summer days and old perfume, all brought back to life by damp getting into the clothes, like you pour water on powdered soup and – hey presto – soup.

The dresses on the rack looked like a line of long-dead women, each one flat as that hedgehog on Bean Street. People always saw clothes when they saw ghosts. Shrouds, that was the main one. Naturally enough, being they were the last clothes most people ever wore. Most ghosts just looked like walking sheets. Then armour, which clanked. Lady ghosts in big dresses. Or bloke ones in beige jackets, like the one Frank saw in Portsmouth that time peeing against a fence, and the dead landlord of the Old Spring who haunted the cellar steps. If you wanted to know about fashions of times gone by, you only had to check out a few ghosts, same result as visiting the cancer shop. It was basically the clothing that lived on, looking for the bodies that used to wear it.

Whisper: 'Why don't you try one on?'

Darren jumped in shock, hitting the rack with his elbow so the dead women swung out to one side like a line of dancers all in formation. 'What?'

'When no one's about,' Gemma whispered again. 'Excepting me.'

'What do you think you're doing, Darren? Look. *Look* at it.'

Rebecca, red faced, was pointing at one of the dresses that had fallen off its hanger and pooled on the floor. It looked like the Wicked Witch of the West after her beautiful wickedness was gone.

'You know something, Darren?' Rebecca asked. 'All those dresses are washed. And then ironed. Each last one of them.' She almost had a smile on her face but Darren had seen that sort of smile before. Her eyes looked hot. 'And when one drops on the floor it has to be done all over again.'

'It was my fault, Rebecca,' Gemma said. 'I made him jump.'

'Ah well,' Rebecca said, 'not to worry.' She became suddenly lively again, flirty almost. She could switch her hot eyes off like you switch a light. She picked the dress up and held it against her. 'What you think, Gem? Suit me?' She twirled. Her tits and hips swelled the dress out so it looked as if someone invisible was inside it.

Gemma clicked her tongue, winked, and did thumbs up at her. Rebecca put the dress back on its hanger, replaced it on the rack, turned away, wiggled her hips and went off to the back of the shop.

'She's very feisty,' Darren said.

'She's a cow.'

'No, but.' He clenched his fists and punched his arms in and out as if he was jiving.

'Plus all that bollocks about washing and ironing it again. She just put it straight back. Hey, Darren, guess what, Princess Leia's done a bunk.'

'Has she? Who has?'

'Princess Leia. One of the hens. Chickens? Chick-*ens*?'

'Oh. Right.' Darren suddenly realised how short Gemma was. He was usually so busy looking at her tits he hadn't picked up how close they were to the ground. Seeing her stick up for him to Rebecca made him realise. Gemma was like a bird herself, not a chicken though, a very small bird, robin maybe, pushing its chest out at the world.

'We've been looking for her high and low. I'm dead scared a fox might have got her.'

'I thought you were pissed off with them crapping on your foot and not being intelligent.'

'I never wanted them *dead*, Darren. I never wanted a *fox* to eat them. Anyway, Princess Leia is my favourite one. She's cleverer than the others. She comes to my hand and eats her grain.'

'If she's so clever, how come she buggered off?'

'That's proof, for God's sake. She sort of made a hole in the bottom of the chicken wire. I think she must have kept putting her neck under it and pushing upwards until it made a gap. It's just like in those war movies when they get away from the Germans.'

'Perhaps she'll get safely home to chicken-land and join her wife and family.'

'How can she have a wife and family, dope, when she's a she?'

'Hey,' Darren said. He glanced round the shop. There was one little old lady going along a rack of tops, feeling each one carefully. Maybe she was blind and that was like a Braille way of choosing clothes. No sign of Rebecca: she must be sorting in the back room. 'Hey, Gemma, what you say about me wearing a dress for? What was that about?'

'I thought you might like it.' She said I *thought you might* ordinary and then more or less sang *like it*, giving the quickest look at him with her eyes and then looking off, away, over his shoulder.

'Like wearing a *dress*?'

'You were inspecting them hard enough. Some men do like it, you know. That doesn't mean you're queer. Eddie Izzard for one. And then there's that guy who does art, he always wears a little frock. But he might be an actual gay, I can't remember.'

'For fuck's sake,' Darren whispered. He felt suddenly like he was in a foreign country where he didn't speak the language. That could be any foreign country, being as he didn't speak any languages. Didn't know any of the roads, and didn't have a map.

Gemma leaned forward and whispered back. 'Maybe I'd like to see a guy in a dress. Maybe it would turn me on.'

Darren puffed his cheeks out. Then suddenly he slipped off his jacket. He held his arms out and up as if he was a weight-lifter holding a loaded barbell above his head. 'Shirt,' he said.

'That's a start,' Gemma said.

'No, Gem. I'm a bloke. I wear a shirt.'

'Very nice shirt,' said the little old lady from behind him. 'Did you buy it here?'

'You hungry?' Dawn asked Frank.

'I had a couple of rolls and a cup of tea while I was serving.'

'You looked like you was taking bites out of young Katie from where I was sat. Anyway, it's not good for you to have them rolls every day. You ought to have an apple or a banana for lunch sometimes.' She remembered stuffing a whole roll in her gob this morning and shuddered. She pictured it still intact inside her stomach. If she took her trousers off it would poke out like a hernia or being pregnant.

'You sure you're all right?' Frank asked her.

'Bit hot in here, that's all. I'll get a breath of air.'

'It's still chucking it down.'

'I'll stand in the door.'

Frank frowned. He was always leery about opening the door again after afternoon closing, for fear some passerby would think they were open all day and try to come in. She couldn't see the problem, she'd just tell whoever, I'm shut. His attitude was it might cause bad feeling. He had a fear of offending anybody. She wondered if that was at the bottom of his being off her these days, as if having sex required a certain amount of nastiness. Which, if you believed half of what Shirl told you, it did in her and Bob's case, nastier the better.

Dawn unbolted the front door. Yes, still coming down, a finer, furry rain now, the sort that could truly drench you. It softly brushed her face when she poked it an inch forward of the shelter of the lintel. The green light of this morning had gone and the air was blackish, even though it wasn't yet three o'clock, the rain a lighter grey on top of it. On the pavement were some fag ends from lunch punters that had missed the ash-tray, grey with wet.

Nobody on the pavements now, just an occasional car swishing past.

Keith walked out of the stadium with two pals. Score, Bradford 6, Wigan 9. The brown and blue crowd shuffling along through the rain, a bit quiet with the defeat, so many wearing caps it made their heads look flat enough to walk on, like stepping stones. Not Keith and his mates: too young, though one of them had one of those dinky Dutch style ones in brown cord. He wore it to the funeral the following week. Keith in a short fawn mac.

The mates peeled off. Keith proceeded by himself to the pub where he'd left his bike. People always proceed when coppers have anything to do with telling the story, as if they were ocean liners going from port to port.

Got his plastic cycle cape out of his saddlebag, put it on so he looked like a black triangle. Got on his bike and set off, his tyres hissing on the wet tarmac.

Not much to tell. Suddenly the handlebars lurched down, the saddle shot up, and he was flying through the air, unable to put his hands out because they were inside the cape. A black triangle flying over the front of its bike, heading head-first at the kerb. Bang.

He died so quickly maybe he never even realised he was dead. Maybe not even to this day. Just wondered who switched the lights off.

Dawn dragged on her ciggy. Coming round the corner of Warren Lane she saw someone, Tim Green, out of the corner of her eye. He must have found a space to park his Ford Focus just up there. She didn't turn to look full on at him, just let him come gradually into her field of vision. It seemed to lessen the pain to have him approach like this, got her used to seeing him.

'Hello, there,' he said.

She pretended to jump with shock. 'Frightened me to death,' she said. He was wearing a sharp-looking black raincoat.

'Seen my shoes?' he asked.

She looked down at them.

'They've got like an external tongue, coming over the laces,' Tim said. 'Neat, eh? It means water doesn't get in. Plus they have a sheer look. They're Italian jobbies. Don't ask me how much I paid for them. They cost me an arm and a leg.'

'If they cost you an arm and a leg, you'd only have had to buy one of them,' Dawn said.

'Ha ha. Very droll. You know how they always try to make you buy their liquid polish? Didn't touch it with a barge pole, never do. I have a tin of old-fashioned polish. I just apply it with a bit of elbow grease. That makes them fully waterproof even on a day like this. It gives a proper seal. Also it's a dull shine. I don't like those mirror shines.'

'Good for seeing up girls' dresses.'

'Is that so?'

'That's what the lads used to do in Bradford. You'd see them coming down the streets, their shoes so shiny you'd be dazzled. Of course, us girls couldn't afford to buy ourselves knickers, in them days.'

Tim looked put out, as if the edge had been taken off his polish. 'Oh well, I like a more subdued effect. My polish gets them the same black as my coat. A moody look, that's what I go for.'

'That's the exact look you've got,' Dawn said. 'Dead moody.'

Dawn brought Tim into the snug. 'Suh,' Frank said, clicking his heels. 'What can I get you, suh?'

'Hello, Frank,' Tim said. 'Coffee would be good.'

'I'll make it in the flat. Got the proper stuff up there. I'll fetch down the books first.'

Dawn had said not to invite Tim up. 'We'll do it in the snug,' she'd said. 'I don't want him worming his way in.'

Making the coffee upstairs was a good let-off. There was no point him and Dawn doing a Morecambe and Wise on the books. Dawn was much better at numbers than he was, in any case. She was probably better at coping with that little creep as well.

Tim Green was one of those blokes it was hard to get a handle on. When you saw him at a distance in all his gear he looked mid-thirties or so. When you got close to, there were fine wrinkles all over his face, like an old plate, and you saw he was well into his forties. He often sounded a complete prat, but there was something shrewd about him at the same time. He was the sort of fellow who kept his attention on getting what he wanted. Frank had known blokes like that in the navy. If you made sure nothing ever got past you it was almost as good as having a brain. At least that's how it looked from the outside, where Frank was stood, not being that bright himself and not bothered enough to make sure of always being number one.

Basically, if they had to shell out nine hundred quid, they'd have to. Borrow it and hope for the best, if the bank still had anything left to lend. No point in letting it get them down. One strategy he had for when things were getting you down was to think about sex instead. It took your mind off other considerations. That was probably the big advantage of being one of those sex maniacs you read about in the papers, no time to worry about your mortgage, you had to give sex so much attention. It would be like having a very demanding job.

While he waited for the coffee to infuse in the cafetière, he thought about Katie and what Dawn had said about him taking mouthfuls out of her. It cheered him up, that he could still make her sarcastic on the subject. It was like being given permission to think dirty thoughts, despite being the age he was.

One thing Frank knew, even while he was thinking his thoughts: Katie wouldn't be thinking thoughts back.

Tim looked up from the books as Frank brought the coffee down to the snug.

'You OK, mate?' Tim asked.

'Yes. Why wouldn't I be?'

'Dunno. You look a bit red in the face, that's all. You need to get out and take some exercise, in this line of work. When I was running a pub I always made sure I went out for a jog every morning.'

'Is that why you got your new shoes?' Dawn asked. 'Have you seen Tim's shoes, Frank?'

Tim slid his shoes out from under the table for Frank to look at.

'Look fast, don't they?' Dawn said.

'Good God, I wouldn't run in shoes like these,' Tim told her. 'I had a proper pair of trainers in them days. Cost almost as much as these, though, allowing for inflation. You know, those ones with gas-filled chambers for good bounce, reflectors on the heels, the whole works. Nike, they were. I went on one of those gait machines, to work out the exact sole I needed. But these ones are very practical from a walking point of view, as well as being designer shoes.'

'Sleek enough, anyhow,' Frank told Tim.

'Sheer, is the word. That's what the girl in the shop said. Sheer is the look of the moment,' Tim said. 'Flavour of the month. Sheer. With the external tongue over the laces. Italian jobbies. Hand made.'

'New car one week, new shoes the next,' Dawn said. Frank could see her drift. We're the ones being accused of having our hands in the till, while it's Tim who's out on the spend.

'That's a point,' Frank agreed.

'Heating the pub up like a furnace doesn't help,' Dawn said.

'Help what?' Frank asked.

'Getting red-faced.'

'I thought you must be talking about global warming.'

'Just your mush warming is enough to be going on with.'

'It's nice to see a bit of a fire, though,' Tim put in.

'Talking of which,' Frank said to Dawn, 'I thought I'd go down Silver Street and ask around to see if I can get anyone to come over and take a look at the grate.'

'You what? We've got these books to go through, for goodness sake.'

'Your missus is the one with the business head on her shoulders,' Tim said. 'It's fine by me. And the exercise will do you good.'

Dawn gave Frank one of her Viking looks. There'd be hell to pay later, rape and pillage not in it. Though come to think, she might by then be too busy thinking about what they had to do to sort out the £900 business to remember to be upset about being left in the lurch. And the fact of the matter was she had more chance of getting on the right side of Tim Green if she was left to her own devices.

In the meantime Frank was off out down Silver Street, on shore leave.

Mixed oddments was a set of shelves on the left-hand side of the shop as you went in. It had glasses, little vases, odd plates and cups and saucers, candlesticks, things to burn incense in, a present from Corsica which Darren didn't know exactly what it was, serviette rings, a red plastic cruet set with black bottoms, a thing that you put a peeled hardboiled egg in and then lowered a sort of frame with stiff wires that sliced the whole egg in one go, a salad spinner, a picture of cows in a field. Every time a customer looked at the mixed oddments they moved them about so instead of being rows they kept turning into a jumble, and one of Darren's jobs was to go over from time to time and sort them out.

He was putting the glasses in order of descending size, first off some pint beer glasses, then dimpled water glasses by name Jacobean, then smaller water glasses, then wine glasses, then smaller wine glasses, then whisky glasses, then sherry glasses, then tiny glasses that you could hardly drink anything out of. Gemma came over.

'What you up to, Darren?'

'Just getting the glasses straightened out.'

'They look like a load of ducklings following big mum and dad ducks, the way you've done them.'

'I thought you'd say chickens, being in the chicken game.'

'Hey, guess what? I got a text from my dad.'

'Oh yeah?'

'Princess Leia's showed.'

'Wow, Gemma.' Darren turned to face her properly, caught his shoulder on one of the pint glasses, and knocked it off the shelf. It landed on the floor and made a bang like a bomb going off so a lady over by the dresses shouted with fright. Darren bent to gather the glass.

'Careful, Darren,' Gemma said, 'you need a dustpan and brush.'

'Great news about your chicken, Gem,' he told her, following his thread.

'What on earth do you think you're up to?'

Rebecca, suddenly in his ear, like she'd been beamed over from the other side of the shop. Darren straightened up to escape the nearness of her voice, hit his head on the bottom oddments shelf, sent a brass vase flying. Rebecca was still bent down to talk into where his ear had been, and it hit her on the top of the head with a loud dull bong, then clattered down on the floor and rolled off, crunching on the broken glass. Rebecca sort of uncurled from her crouch, holding her head in her hands.

'Oh no, you all right?' Gemma asked.

'Fuck, Rebecca,' Darren said. 'I'm really really sorry.'

Rebecca looked directly into his face with her hands still clasping the top of her head. 'If you were really sorry, you little bastard, you wouldn't compound it by using obscenities in my shop, in front of my customers.' She spoke while hardly moving her mouth, like a ventriloquist.

'It was just an accident,' Gemma said.

'I'm really sorry,' Darren said again.

'There's violence in you, Darren. I can always tell. I used to run the battered wives shop. You learn.'

'He didn't mean it, I'm positive,' Gemma said. 'He was pleased about my chicken.'

'I'm not saying on purpose,' Rebecca said. 'But subconscious. It's there. And don't forget, I saw your CV. I'm the one who decided to give you a chance. But you hum with violence.' She took her hands down, then raised one again and felt where she'd been struck. 'I can feel the swelling already. It's like an egg.'

'It was a heavy vase,' Darren said.

Rebecca stepped forward. 'You said it, boy. The heaviest thing in the whole display.' She sniffed. 'And you've been drinking, my God.'

'No, I haven't. Just a pint in the Old Spring. Two pints. I work there.'

'Well, I can tell you one thing, young man. You don't work *here*, that's for sure. Not any more.'

The doctor went, the priest stayed. 'Which is how it should be,' Father Benson said in his sonorous voice. 'The body has died but there is still a living soul to work on.'

'Amen,' said Brother John, hotfoot from school. He was kneeling against the back of a dining chair that he'd positioned close to Julian's body, which was now lying on the floor.

The doctor had asked Paul to help him lower it there. 'We don't want it setting hard in a seated position,' he said. 'It'd be a pig of a problem for the funeral people.'

Paul had pictured a coffin like one of the old sedan chairs that once upon a time wobbled along the streets; the funeral people compelled to take Julian to his grave upright as if he were a powdered dowager or some Aztec emperor to be buried in his pomp.

'No, we don't want that,' he said, his voice dying to a whisper as he suddenly anticipated his forthcoming wrestle with inertness.

The doctor had slipped his hands under Julian's shoulders; Paul bent down to pick up the feet. Julian's head nodded in floppy agreement. Paul held his breath not so much to avoid any smells released by the removal as in hopes of suspending his own bodily processes for the time needed, to achieve a kind of mini-death, an editorial cut in his life's narrative from before he did it till after it was done.

Now the doctor was gone. Natural causes. A massive heart attack.

Massive seemed a tautology to Paul, or an exaggeration. Julian had had a heart attack. He had died. The heart attack had been exactly big enough. Death itself defined its scale.

Julian had been under medical supervision; this outcome was always on the cards. No need for a coroner. The doctor almost chirpy at getting to his dotted line so fast.

Now Paul wanted to ask the priest a question. It rose in his throat just as the death retch had risen in Julian's.

He wanted to ask, if a soul is defined by the life to which it was harnessed, why pray for its well-being after death? Surely by then it is what it is? Could you, for the sake of argument, pray for it to be worse? If not, then how can one make it better?

Prayer for the soul's redemption, after the body had died, seemed to Paul to cast a shadow over God's justice, suggesting that left to His own devices He might not clearly see and appropriately reward the soul for what it was, and wasn't.

Paul knew Father Benson would have an answer. He had an old priest's wiliness: there was always an answer. The Church was composed of all its souls, living here and in the hereafter: in praying for Julian, it was praying for itself. The minister in leading the prayers was a representative of the divinity; in identifying the mercy to be awarded, he was simply a visible component of the process of grace.

Paul's Adam's apple felt engorged. It was like a loaded gun. Bobbing in his throat was a way of formulating his question that would cut through the rigmarole. He didn't know what it was but it was there, ready to be asked. The words were assembled: sharp, tough, undodgeable. The tone was in place, harsh, no-nonsense, impatient. He only had to open his mouth.

He opened his mouth.

'I need to leave for a little while,' he said in a hushed, holy, responsible voice. 'I have to visit a sick friend in hospital.'

'I got to leave in ten minutes,' Darren reminded Gemma. 'Before ten minutes is up.'

That's what Rebecca had said. I want you out of here before ten minutes are up. I'm off out back. You be out of here when I return. And don't expect a reference from me, either.

If I need one I could get it from Frank and Dawn, he'd told her, to set her mind at rest.

'And who are they, when they're at home?' she'd asked him.

'Well, more like when they're in their pub. It's just downstairs.'

'I suppose they could write how much beer you drink, that would be a nice reference.' And off she went, out back.

'It won't take a minute,' Gemma said. 'Just come in the changing cubicle with me. There's nobody about.'

True, the lady by the dresses who'd shouted had gone off pretty fast when all hell broke loose. See what you do to customers, Rebecca said. People don't want to get hit on the head with vases, in case you haven't noticed.

'It's a funny thing, Gem,' Darren said now. 'I think I'm like an attractor of poltergeists. It's like I suck them towards me. I must be a type of portal that they can enter through.'

'Come with me,' Gemma said, curling her finger.

'Cool,' Darren said. His heart thumped as they went towards the cubicle. Partly in fear, in case she wanted him to put on a dress. Bad enough to get the sack, he didn't need to go pervy at the same time. But also hope. Jerry in the pub had told about the mile-high club, when people do it in the toilets of planes. This would be like the cancer shop club, doing it in the changing room. Not that they'd have time to do it as such, but even a goodbye snog would be good, a cheerer-upper.

Gemma zinged the curtain open. 'I got something I want to show you,' she whispered to him over her shoulder as she stepped in, and his heart beat so painfully he felt his eyes throb in time with it.

He followed her in. You want a portal, he thought, *this* is a portal. Plus, if you want a changing room, this one will do the works. He felt like Clark Kent going in somewhere, and coming out Superman. He turned and pulled the curtain shut behind them.

He turned back. Gemma was squashed close now, her head just by his chest. He wished he'd taken his jacket off first. He could do with his shirt being on show now. It always made him feel toned and up for stuff in his shirt.

The cubicle was so small with the two of them in, the last thing either of them could do was take any clothes off. All he could do from where he was presently stood was kiss the top of Gemma's head like he was her dad.

Before he did, she pulled her mobile out of her pocket and said, 'It's on here, what I want to show you.'

His heart sank, then lifted up again. He had a sudden idea: she was going to show him a picture of herself in the nude. Nice one. Next best thing to real life, and there wasn't room for real life in here.

She thumbed the scroller. 'Here, get this,' she said, and passed the mobile over. 'I've never showed it anyone before.'

He took a look. In the dim light of the cubicle the picture was bright and clear. There was Gemma, all her clothes on, standing in a garden with a chicken perched on her head.

'It's Princess Leia,' she said.

9

It was a rambling garden-furniture and wrought-iron shop, old and new and reclaimed bird tables, gazebos, flowerpots, even a staircase for sale. Nobody about. Like A Green Thought this morning, it seemed the wrong type of place for a rainy November, cave-like and cool, all stone and pottery and iron, with unlit log baskets and fireplaces propped up against the wall.

'Hello,' Frank said. He didn't like talking to no one, but a statue of a woman was the best he could do. He rested his dripping brolly against her plinth, very aware of the chilly smoothness of her hips and breasts. Statues always seemed to be going about their business without a stitch on, which was more than he'd usually come across in real life. Hello trees, hello flowers, oh, by the way, I forgot to get dressed this morning. 'Hello!' he said more loudly. He had a feeling his voice echoed slightly, or rather that it seemed to get transmitted on its way by all the objects lying around the place, taking on their flavours of marble and wood and hammered metal.

'Anybody there?' More loudly still.

A man appeared from behind a pile of Britannia tables. 'Hoo,' he said, 'aren't you loud?' He was small and slight, in his thirties maybe, but wearing boring old-fashioned clothes, a wool tie, V-necked jumper, sports jacket, cords, except he had dyed blond hair in a big eighties type of perm, which gave him a look of having popped out of an Easter egg.

'Sorry, m'dear,' Frank said, 'but I wasn't sure if anyone was home.'

'Tell you what, if I was dead you'd have raised me.'

'Fair point.'

'Where did you learn to project like that, then?'

'Project?'

'You know. Project.' He swung his perm with a touch of impatience. 'Shout,' he explained, as if Frank was being a dope on purpose. 'To shout like that.'

'Oh. I was in the navy, once upon a time.'

'Well, that didn't take long to come out into the light of day.'

'It's a loud place, a ship.'

'So I've been told. Did you have to shout Land Ahoy?'

'No, I never had to do that. That would have been more in the olden-days navy.'

'What a shame.'

They looked at each other a moment, until Frank dropped his eyes. He took a few steps around the floor, as if to size the place up. He nearly gave the statue a pat on its bottom to show which side his bread was buttered on, but stopped in time, realising that might send out the wrong signal after all. Everything he said seemed to egg the bloke on. It was all meaningless, just words, he reminded himself, but he could feel the smallest beginnings of panic stirring inside himself, like the first moment of tide-turn. They still had tides in the modern navy.

'What it is –' he said. He was just about to say, m'dear, which was what he always said, but stopped himself at the last moment. Wouldn't be a good idea, in this set-up. The trouble was, not saying it seemed to leave a hole in what he did say the exact size and shape of *m'dear* anyhow, which made it more blatant than if he'd actually said the words out loud. 'A mate of mine said you might –'

'A shipmate?'

'No, no. I been out of that game for years.'

'Oh. Right.'

'A mate in my pub. I run a pub.'

'Do you just? How neat.'

'The Old Spring, on Bean Street.'

'Oh yes. I know it. Never been inside though.'

'Nice old pub, m' – anyhow, my mate, one of the regulars, he said someone here he knew could do a bit of spot welding on the grate of the fire we've got in our snug. It's been burned through. It's been burned through with the heat over the years.'

'Nothing like a fire for getting hot.'

'No.'

'That's me.'

'What is?'

'The someone who can do a spot of spot welding.'

'Oh, is it?'

'I recondition all the old fire baskets and the like we get in.'

'What do you know.'

'You didn't bring it with you?'

Stupidly, Frank patted his pockets as if he might have slipped the grate inside one of them. 'No,' he said.

The man must have thought the pats were sarcastic. 'I thought you might have put it down somewhere,' he explained.

'I wouldn't know, in this place.'

'It's still got a fire in at the moment.'

'Ah. Best just to drop it off some time or other and I'll see what I can do.'

'I was hoping, m'dear, you could do it quickly.' Fuck, just what he didn't want to say. Not saying it that time in such a way you could *hear* it not being said, made saying it now all the more of a come on. No chance of pointing out everybody said *m'dear* in the Tiverton of his youth, at least as he remembered the place.

'It doesn't sound like a long job.'

'Like today?'

'Today?'

'I could take the hot coals out and riddle it through. The grate would cool soon enough. It's a bit of a hazard to the public as it is at present, but I don't want to be without it, not this time of the year. We're in the *Good Pub Guide* as having a welcoming fire. Welcoming fire on a winter's day is what it says. We get people from all over who come because they read about us in there. We had a fellow from Brighton just this morning. I wouldn't like to be accused of false pretences.'

'What time are we talking about, then?'

'What time do you close?'

'Half five. It's a bit after four now.'

'Oh.'

'You could come along this evening,' the man said quietly. He had stepped over to fiddle with some galvanized buckets, so his back was to Frank. His curly head bobbed as he clanked the pile about. It was like being spoken to by a bright gold clockwork octopus.

'Oh yes?'

'I've got some work to do in the workshop anyway. Say half six.' He turned and looked up towards him. 'Knock three times and ask for Frankie.'

'Frankie?'

'That'll do it.'

'*My* name's Frank too.'

'Is that so? How do, Frank. We must have more in common than meets the eye.'

It was disturbing, seeing a brown man turn grey.

Romesh was detailed, intricate, courtly. Thomas had watched him give advice on carpeting to a regular at the

Old Spring like a diplomat counselling a prince. From time to time he'd caught sight of Romesh through the window of the shop where he worked, the curtains and floor coverings outlet of a local furnishings company called Dogget and Son, standing solemnly in the centre of his domain, chin resting on chest as he listened to a customer's requirements, his tape dangling down from each side of his neck like a stethoscope; once, drawing attention to various samples with tiny arm movements like some orchestral conductor who'd opted for a non-flamboyant style.

One Tuesday lunchtime Romesh had stood at the bar of the snug in the Old Spring looking strangely animated and bright-eyed. He worked weekends so always had a day off in the week.

'I have had a very narrow escape indeed,' Romesh had told him.

Dawn came up. 'We nearly lost him, Father. I all but lost my Romesh.' She put her arm round Romesh's shoulders. He cocked his head a little towards hers in acknowledgement and even that intimate gesture had a quality of restraint, of good manners. 'What would I have done without him?'

'I saw my whole life flashing before my eyes,' Romesh said.

That was part of Romesh's secret: his ability to use clichés as if they were new-minted and true. You must gain an automatic originality merely from straddling two cultures, an ability to detect the electric charge deep inside the platitudes of each, to feel the feelings and experience the experiences that generated those formulae in the first place. Sipping his pint, Thomas had felt his eyes pain over with a vision of compacting carpeting, a flattening snug, of all the many-handed complications of Romesh's existence, whatever they might be, being crushed to diamond in the pressure of a single moment.

'I was driving north out of town,' Romesh said, 'very late last night, in fact at about two a.m.'

What on earth Romesh, fifty-year-old carpet salesman, might have been up to at two in the morning, Thomas couldn't imagine. Dawn had told him there had once been a wife, someone in a glittering sari presumably, with long glossy black hair, made-up eyes, a red spot on her forehead – that's how Thomas, with the admitted sentimentality of celibacy, pictured her anyhow, moving shyly like a deer as she negotiated the invisible impedimenta of another culture's take on gender; consigned to an early grave.

Romesh: man of inscrutable roots, unopenable baggage, mysterious journeyings.

'That sounds ominous,' Thomas said.

'I thought all was quiet. I had no sense of danger. I was travelling at about fifty miles an hour, the speed limit at that spot. Then out of nowhere, bang!' He said it loudly, so his beer rippled.

'He got whacked into by a Porsche,' Dawn said. 'If I could lay my hands on whatever prat was driving, I would –'

'I think he suffered enough, to be quite frank,' Romesh said.

'They drive them type of cars,' Dawn said, 'in hopes it will give them a bigger willy.'

'Did *you*?' Thomas asked. 'Suffer? Whether you did or not, I think I'd better buy you another pint.'

'Nobody buys my Romesh a pint today except me,' Dawn said. She went behind the bar and poured them one each.

Frank leaned over while she was doing so. 'That's Dawn for you,' he said. 'The only time she does any work behind the bar is when she refuses to be paid for it.' He paused. 'And that's not often, let me say.'

'Here, let me,' Thomas said, putting his hand to his inside pocket.

'No fear. More than my life's worth. Any case, you're welcome, m'dears.'

'It was a tremendous wallop,' Romesh said. 'I span round twice. I could see the headlights of the other car flashing across my windscreen as I span. Dazzle one second, darkness the next. I ended up crashing into the crash barrier in the middle of the road.'

'Oh well,' said Frank, 'I guess that's what it's there for.'

'But Lady Luck was on my side, twice over. First off, I didn't hit another car after the initial impact, for which I can thank time of night. Second, I slid into the barrier sideways, not head-first. As a result I stepped out completely unscathed. Also, my car was no more than dented. The poor Porsche was a complete write-off, and the driver was trembling from head to foot. He had to be taken to hospital.'

'Probably on drugs,' Dawn said darkly. 'That would give him the shakes. Or the DTs.'

'What do you know about it?' Frank asked. 'It was likely shock.'

'I know my fair share. We've got one of them comes in here. That Jake you're so fond of shakes so hard sometimes inside those tattoos of his, looking at him's like being at the pictures.'

'Give it a rest, Dawn. He's a customer. He's one of our own.'

'Not one of mine, he isn't. He's on something, if you ask me.'

Thomas had never seen Jake shaking, if indeed it happened at all and wasn't just a projection of some shakiness in Dawn's own outlook. From where Thomas stood in the snug, Jake in his place on the bench in the public seemed possessed of stillness; not serenity, because there was no discernible wisdom in it, more the quiet patience spiders have, or plants, even.

'A car is just a tin box,' Frank said.

'A slightly bashed box, in my case,' Romesh replied. 'But I was lucky, sure enough.'

His luck hadn't held. From that day on, the colour leached out of his skin. He had been a stocky man but he seemed to shrink, or rather to give out an impression of smallness, of dwindled potential, as if a diminutive man inside him was knocking to get out. His speech, which had been rounded, almost plummy, became frailer, sketchy. Then one day he was taken to hospital. An ambulance came to the shop, apparently.

Dawn was beside herself. 'I should have seen it coming,' she kept saying. 'I knew there was a change in him. I kept telling myself it was just the shock.'

'We all thought it was the shock,' Frank said. 'The hospital knew no better.'

'It *was* shock,' Thomas said, 'whatever they decide to call it. You could see it in his eyes.' He nearly added: I think he saw something as his car span round, but realised it would sound too much like Darren. But that remark about dazzle and darkness was in his mind. As Romesh's lifetime compressed itself into the span of a second, everything resolved into its basics: day and night, starlight and space; a black screen with an arbitrary flash of light crossing it, like the last cough of a defunct TV.

Thomas hadn't visited Romesh in hospital. He didn't know him as well as some, and Dawn went regularly in any case, always bringing back bad news. But now Julian had died, Thomas felt an almost panicky need to go and see Romesh. The two illnesses had progressed in parallel, Julian becoming bulky, uneasy in his body, hot-looking; Romesh going pallid as darkness descended, shrinking in a chill wind no one else could feel. Thomas felt he'd neglected the one; it was natural to feel an urgent need now to pay attention to the other.

Or maybe he just wanted a reason for escaping the atmosphere of mournful piety that was enveloping De La Tour House.

At the entrance to the ward a large nurse blocked the way.

'Yes?' she asked. Her largeness was uncompromising, as if it related more to being a wall than a body, as if, almost, she had been chosen because she had it to offer. Also, she was neither young nor old but some predetermined hospital age. It reminded Thomas of the medieval belief that everyone in heaven would be thirty-two because that was what Christ had reached when crucified.

I can talk, Thomas thought: I'm an institutional being myself. But religious orders seemed to emphasise age, not eradicate it, maybe because it was so poignant to see the younger members with all that chastity ahead of them, and the old ones with it all behind.

'I've come to see Romesh Mehta.'

'I'm sorry but he's very poorly.'

'I know. That's why I'm here.'

'No, but it's relatives only, I'm sorry.'

Romesh might have become pale, but not that pale. 'Oh.'

The nurse's eyes wandered to Thomas's dog-collar.

'Ah yes,' Thomas said. He collected himself for a moment. It would be his first downright lie on this topic. But all in a good cause.

He wondered if he would confess it later. No fear. Father Benson would be apoplectic. It would challenge the whole priestly edifice; more importantly, it would challenge Father Benson. It was all very well to see the confessional as giving Catholics room to breathe, but not if it choked the recipient. In any case, Thomas had to believe the lesser of two evils wasn't, logically, evil at all; therefore there would be nothing to confess. But still, as he felt his own collar, he had a memory of Julian, now suddenly in death become portable and on tap, Julian the acme and essence of liberalism, Julian who brooded over the Virgin's vagina (odd how those words folded into each other), of how even open-minded Julian had been stunned to hear of his impersonation.

'I'm his priest,' Thomas said. 'Romesh's priest.'

'It looks like this number has been interfered with,' Tim said.

'You what?' Dawn asked.

Tim shut one eye and peered at it with the other. 'It looks to be the number seven,' he said.

Dawn shut one eye as well, and peered, angling her head to look exactly along his line of sight, doing her best to show willing – to show that whatever it was that wasn't right was as interesting to her staring eyeball as it was to Tim's, like she was his intelligent assistant.

'Oh yes,' she said. Looking at it so hard gave her an optical illusion. The account book page was a flat white sea. Someone flying over it had dropped a tiny, hard, black number seven, like the littlest horse-shoe, and it had fallen down down down until it hit the surface of the sea; and at that exact moment, just as the water was springing up around it, everything had suddenly stopped dead, so there it was for good, caught in mid-splash.

'Seven,' she said. 'It does say seven. Does that column add up?'

Tim's mouth buzzed through the numbers in the column. 'Yep, it adds.'

'Something's gone and splashed it, is all.'

'I suppose so. The thing is, it mustn't just *be* legit, it's got to *look* legit as well. The tax people hate it if it looks like a number has been fiddled with. Bold crossing out is one thing, so long as you can still see the number underneath, but rubbing out and smudging gets their backs up no end. Believe me, I been there.'

'As long as it adds up.'

Keith, little-boy thin, maybe ten or eleven, diving into the water at Bradford baths, big green gloomy building echoing with kids' screams, his legs all a-wag with water bursting up around them; then afterwards him and Dawn, blue-lipped and goosy, eating Wagon Wheels and drinking Vimto in the pool café.

Keith caught in his fall, the exact moment he hit the kerb, head down, legs up with the cape swirling round them like a black splash.

'Something doesn't add up *some*where,' Tim said. 'That's the trouble.'

'If needs be, me and Frank'll just have to fork out the amount.'

'Doesn't solve the prob, though, does it?'

'Doesn't it?'

'Well, it would look like an admission of guilt. You know what Mr Banks is like. The whole licensed trade is based on trust, that's his watchword. And he proves it by not trusting anybody further than what he can throw them.'

'What we going to do, then? We can't find what's wrong with the books. And we can't pay the nine hundred back. We're stuck.'

'Yep, you're stuck, Dawn, that's the bugger of it.'

Dawn looked over at the bar, gleaming softly brown, at the different coloured bottles, ruby red, brown, fawn, yellow, green, at the faint glitter of glasses and optics, at the grey windows beyond. There was the gentle sound of thudding as if rain was knocking on the windows with watery fists. Like one of them ghosts as seen by young Darren, come to evict them from the premises. She sighed. Stuck was the word.

There was a pat on her hand. Then Tim's hand lay lightly on top of hers as if having done the pat he'd forgotten it. She looked down at it.

She was just going to pull her hand away from underneath when Tim spoke. 'But what's stuck can be unstuck,' he said.

'Can it?' she asked. She felt suddenly wobbly. What did he think he was up to, Tiger Tim, with his Ford Focus and snappy clothes? She was a good ten years older than him, had never been a beauty to start with. Kept herself slim but that was mainly so as not to turn into her mum and dad, with big bosoms like a great pillow between you and the outside world, muffling everything, or a fat voice that thought it was always right when it was always wrong.

Of course Tim was creepy, that was evident from the beginning, but it hadn't occurred to her he had any intention of creeping in her direction.

Got to think, she thought. Maybe he fancied older women? Maybe he liked to come over all little-boysey with them? Maybe he needed to feel like he was doing you a favour? One thing you learned after years of being a woman, after the same number of years being in the licensed trade: rumpy-pumpy comes in all shapes, sizes and flavours.

She wanted to pull her hand away more than ever, but it was harder to do now she understood Tim's wasn't where it was by an oversight. Stupid: why had she had to wait for the penny to drop? Hands were never where they were by an oversight, that was another thing you learned in the licensed trade, as well as just by being a woman.

'I told you this month's word already,' Tim said. 'Sheer, it is. That's the word.'

'Is it?'

'You know what it means? Sheer?'

'Terror, as I remember. That's what people say, isn't it?'

'No, no, it doesn't mean that. That's just like an add-on.'

There was a pause. Got to get my hand free, Dawn thought. It was almost as though it was in a prison and you had to find a clever way of getting it out again, like smuggling a file in inside a cake. Of course she could just give it a yank, but that didn't seem wise, not before she knew what Tim had in mind.

'Stockings,' she said.

'Getting warmer,' Tim said. He wasn't quite looking at her, but just to one side, as if eye-contact might distract him from his rigmarole. He was thin-faced with a tiny deliberate stubble showing, and lots of fine lines on the surface of his skin, as if he had put many different expressions on his face in the course of his lifetime and each one of them had left behind a little track, thin as the lines you get on the inside of a teacup when it's never been properly washed.

'I give up,' Dawn said.

'You can fall off it, like a cliff. It means a smooth, steep surface.' He patted her hand with *smooth*, again with *steep*, a final time with *surface*. Each time, Dawn nearly moved hers away. She could have done it without contact, like playing Paper, Scissors, Stone, but didn't quite have the nerve, needing to see exactly what was in Tim's mind. Then his hand settled back on hers again. 'Tell you what, Dawn,' he continued, still not looking at her square on, his eyes sliding from just below hers to just to one side of them and back again, 'I'm staying over in town tonight.'

'Are you just?'

'Friend of mine manages the Fielding Hotel. He lets me have a discount room from time to time. When I can't be bothered to drive all the way back home.'

'What about your wife? What'll she think about it?'

Tim pinked up slightly, as he put a juicy meaning on the *it*. Bugger. The last thing he needed was leading on.

'Oh, we go our separate ways, Dawn, us two do. I thought you knew that. She won't think anything about it at all.'

'I see.'

'It's always a very comfortable one. The room, I mean. It's an upmarket hotel, the Fielding is.'

'So I've been told.'

'What I was wondering was, how about you coming round there sometime this evening, and we'll see what we can make of those old books. We could have a bit of a drinky-poo while we work on them. There's always a well-stocked minibar. I tell you what, after I've given those books of yours a going over, I wouldn't mind betting they'd end up with a smooth surface of their own. I'm a bit of an expert at that type of game.'

He gave her hand a squeeze. She felt suddenly breathless and couldn't speak for a moment. 'Just slip out of here for an hour or two, what you think?' he added.

She whispered (it was all she could do in any case): 'You mean, me come round to your hotel? Just the two of us?'

Now he was looking only the littlest bit below full in the eye to make sure they both remembered that this wasn't about being a pal, just sex. Frank always looked her in the eye, but of course these days that was about as near to party time as they got.

'Two's company, three's a crowd,' Tim said. 'What they say.'

She leaned in towards him, so as to speak directly into his ear. 'You get to do what you want, and we lose the nine hundred. Is that the idea? Or maybe what it is, we find the nine hundred again.' She gave several more breathless breaths into his small pink flap, no trouble given she had less air in her lungs than any time since she had jumped into the sea at Scarborough early one summer, forgetting all about it being like the North Pole.

He sat quite still, trying to work out whether he should gallop ahead or cool it a little. Before he could decide, she added: 'It's a lot of money.'

'Well,' he said, 'it's just technical, isn't it? Sorting out the books.'

'I bet you're a very technical bloke, one way or the other.'

'I been around a bit. Man of the world, you might say.'

'The trouble is,' she whispered as sexily as she could, 'I wouldn't go to bed with a sad little wanker like you in a million years. Or for a million quid.' She thought for a moment. 'Well, maybe for a million quid. But I'd have to count it first.'

As she hoped, it took a second for the penny to drop, all the pennies.

Then Tim said, 'Fuck you,' and got to his feet. He wasn't looking in her direction at all now, just straight forward. He strode over to the bar and rapped on it a couple of times, as if for service. Of course it was just a rap of rage but Dawn had a sudden picture of the trap door in the bar floor opening in response and Frank's lovely round head appearing like it had done this morning when the bread van man was there. She did a laugh that caught her on the hop and came out through her nose as a snort.

Tim turned towards her. 'Fuck you,' he said again, looking at her fully in the eye for the first time, like they both knew where they stood at last.

'You wish,' Dawn said. Bye bye, pub, she thought sadly, though she was still shaking with the laugh and kept on making snorts, or more like it, snores.

'Bitch!' he said, in a much louder voice. It was as if it had sunk in all over again, deeper this time. 'Fucking bitch! What you think you are? God's gift?'

'It was you wanted to bed *me*, as I remember it.'

'Only to show what a slag you are. Slag!' The lines on his face deepened to let his cheeks fold back like a paper fan. His teeth were small ones but white and even. He shook both his fists at her at once then rushed across the room to the fireplace, stopped a couple of feet out from it and caught hold of the mantelshelf with his hands. She saw his right leg go back then swing forward as he kicked the grate.

'Slag!' Kick.

'Slag!' Kick.

'Slag!' Kick.

Then a red river of coals ran out of the gap in the metalwork and landed on his shoe.

He looked blankly down at it. She looked too. '*Slack* is what they call it,' she said. 'Any road, they did up in Bradford. Nutty slack.'

Tim let out a girly shriek, and shook his foot wildly. The coals scattered over the hearth. He turned and ran directionlessly about the room like a panicking animal.

She was just about to call out to him to pull himself together when she realised: his shoe was on fire. There were little flames licking all over it, pale blue ones with yellow points to them like you get on a methylated spirits stove. As he ran they curved backwards, and suddenly she saw they looked like little wings on his heel.

10

'No you're not,' she said.

'What? Not what?' said Thomas.

First reaction to a lie being seen through: ego shrinks to a hard ball, a grenade, you fling it with all your might. Thomas had a moment of blind rage in which he could actually have put his hands around the nurse's thick neck and throttled her. The sheer gratification of that one second could dislodge all the self-abnegation salted down in a lifetime of salting down.

On the tip of his tongue: fuck *you*.

More maddening by far than your adversary being in the wrong is her being right.

Then of course the ego vanishes with a feeble pop and fury rushes back on itself, on yourself. Stupid, pathetic: Romesh was a *Hindu*, for God's sake, for the sake of all those gods, those dancing, many-limbed gods. Presumably he was, at least. Would have put it on some hospital questionnaire, along with dietary requirements and next-of-kin and do not resuscitate, filled in with trembly hand among so many other hospital questionnaires filled in with trembly hand: Religion . . . Hindu.

Romesh's priest would have been a Brahman, if he'd had a priest at all. Thomas was pretending to be a priest but not that sort: he'd somehow ended up lying to the power of two. He had a sense of how lies could slither away as soon as they escaped your mouth, expand and breed, become autonomous and teeming. He squeezed up his eyes, his face, as if he were sucking a lemon or looking into bright light, needing to feel his head was closed now, locked shut. It's not like an ordinary person telling a lie, he thought, it's a serious business for me, because I'm a serious individual. You should have some respect for my lie, for my lies. These are expensive ones.

'He was a great big bloke,' the nurse said.

'Oh yes,' Thomas replied shortly, as if taking merely technical or bureaucratic interest.

'Big fellow.'

What was big from where she stood? She was huge. Not upwards admittedly. She wore a nurse's hat like a shower cap and it seemed to function to keep a lid on things, to wangle her enormousness horizontally like thwarted water.

But all mirrors are trick mirrors. When she looked in her mirror she didn't see that. You don't use your own size to measure the universe with, but an agreed average, like the age of people in heaven.

'Quite a bald guy. Baldish.'

Frank.

Thomas felt a huge weight lift from him. He wasn't alone, Frank had told exactly the same lie, for the same decent reason, with the same element of truth in it: Frank too, landlord of the Old Spring, had a ministering role. No man is an island, Thomas wanted to say to the nurse, suddenly, ridiculously, confident again, and thinking of his connection with Frank rather than his connection with the one for whom the bell tolled. And Frank had no dog collar, so had taken a bigger leap than he had.

'Oh yes,' he said, 'friend of mine.' He paused, then added: 'Colleague.'

'Oh yeah?' she asked. Then she softened it, going for a sudden forgiving sibilance. 'Oh yes?'

It suddenly occurred to Thomas that she had a pretty face, worn like a Venetian mask in the middle of her face. 'We work together,' he said.

'Five minutes,' she said.

'I beg your pardon?'

'Five minutes.'

Dawn ran behind the bar, grabbed a glass, pumped a splash of Buckman's into it, then thought lager would be colder and wetter somehow, and switched to Carlsberg, all the while Tim was hopping round the snug and miaowing like a cat.

She ran up to him, bent down, grabbed him firmly around the thigh to hold his leg still, conscious of the soft weight of his bollocks resting on her knuckles, and poured the lager over his shoe. The flames were nearly invisible, a flicker of blue and a tremble in the air. There was a faint hiss as the liquid put them out, a puff of smoke and steam and the sharp smell of burnt leather.

'Fucking, bloody hell,' Tim said.

Dawn straightened up.

'Cunting, shit-arsed, buggeration.'

'I'm sorry, Tim,' Dawn told him. 'I think it was that polish of yours.'

'You what? You fuckwit, what do you mean it was that polish of mine? It was that bloody fire of yours, that's what it was. Ow ow,' he added self-pityingly as he hopped over to the mantelpiece and glared down at the fireplace. The coals in the grate still glowed red while those that had spilled down into the hearth were already grey and dead-looking.

'No, what I meant was,' Dawn said, 'that polish you put on that doesn't polish them too much, like. It's maybe got some turps in it or white spirit or something that catches alight.'

'I'll tell you something, Dawn,' Tim said. He was so mad and manly that his lower jaw poked out each side of his face wider than his cheek bones. The lines in his cheek showed one after the other like a concertina. 'If I'd bought that other fucking crap they always try to flog you, I'd be on fire now from head to foot like bloody Guy Fawkes, guaranteed.'

'Me and Frank'll replace your shoe, don't fret. Your shoes.'

'You fucking better. It was your fucking fire did it.' He paused for a second, suddenly uneasy, obviously remembering it was him who'd kicked the fucking fire. 'They cost a fucking packet, you know.'

'Oh well, water under the bridge.' There were times in your life when just breathing cost you money. 'Can you get them in town?'

'Might be able to. Might not.' Tim looked grumpy and a bit furtive now.

'Look. Forget what I said just now,' Dawn said. She gathered her courage together. 'I'll come round to the hotel tonight. I was just winding you up. What you said caught me on the hop, you know?' She tried to find her previous whisper again: 'I been waiting for this to happen, something like this. Waiting a long time.'

'Could have fooled me.'

'You got to be hard to get. That's what it's all about.' Think like Shirl does, she thought to herself. Shirl loves playing these sort of games. She recalled the way Shirl managed to squelch up her lips so that they looked like a ripe strawberry. Her lipsticky mouth was like a folded-up kiss, all ready to be unpacked.

Horses for courses. Dawn just didn't have those type of lips. What she did do was put her arms out and fiddle with Tim's tie, pretending to be very interested in the knot. 'We'll have a good time, promise.'

'Sorting out the books,' Tim said, like he wanted to get that cleared up.

'Sorting out all sorts of things.' She dropped her hands from his tie knot and he gave it a pat in turn. 'Tell you what,' she said. 'You take the books with you. I'll let on to Frank I'm off somewhere else.'

Tim looked as if he appreciated the deception. You could see it going through his head: I'm on a promise all right. He stuffed the books in his briefcase.

'I'll see you then, then,' he said. 'About seven?'

Still a whisper: 'See you then.'

Tim went over to the hook where his mac was. He wasn't hopping now. Probably his foot had cooled down. But even though it was only a shoe that got scorched, he walked strangely, like Harry the down-and-out bloke had done earlier that lunchtime, as if the leg that caught fire had ended up a lot shorter than the other one.

Little tiny rain, blown on the wind. It felt like pins and needles on his face. The thing about Rebecca was she was a very bubbly type of person but in between the bubbles, well hard. Getting on the wrong end of her was like being hit by a train. No point arguing with it.

Darren walked up Butler Way and turned right on to Bean Street. It was nearly dark, which made the lit windows of the shops and houses shine bright yellow, with the rain flickering over the front of them like more pins and needles.

He wanted to say *It's a pisser* out loud, but he was just passing the bookshop that had opened at the bottom of Bean Street, and there was a woman going into it, so he waited till he had got beyond and then said it: 'It's a pisser.' He hoped it would bring relief. One of his foster mums had always been on to him about letting it all out, it's good to let it all out when you can. Like you could just crap your feelings and then you'd feel fine again, nice and emptied. She used to let hers out sure enough.

But saying *It's a pisser* out loud made his voice sound like it was a little separate voice all by itself like a dog shut out in the rain, and he suddenly wanted to snivel.

He wiped his eyes with his sleeve, not a good idea being it was made of plasticky leather stuff, and just made his eyes wetter. But it was only rain in any case, a face-full of rain.

That's how Rebecca would be feeling, he suddenly thought. He stopped in his tracks to think about it more: nice and emptied, that's how she'd be feeling now. What she'd done was crap *him* out. She had got a kick out of it, getting shot of him. It made her feel good. She'd been angry sure enough, but she wanted to be angry, she'd enjoyed it.

If I could be angry back, he thought, it would be equals. But he couldn't. He just felt sad.

He shivered in the rain. He didn't want to go back to his flat just yet. He wasn't supposed to be in it this afternoon, he should be in the cancer shop. It was like his flat wasn't expecting him. It wouldn't feel like his at the moment, more like anybody's. Just a cold empty flat with no him about it. No me-ness, he thought, like your personality should be sprinkled all over it like salt on chips. Your things do shifts like everyone else, their job being being yours. Then when you're out at work they can knock off. An ordinary TV in the corner, bog-standard settee, just anyone's, nobody's in particular.

Who cared about the cancer job in any case? They paid you zilch. It was a swizz, like Dawn said. Better out of it. Good old Dawn, she got it right in the first place. Dawn never liked Rebecca, even though she never met her.

Suddenly Darren needed to tell Dawn all about it, then have her tell him what a cow Rebecca was. It was like when you're a kid and somebody is fucking you about, and then along comes your foster mum to meet you at the school gate and it all fades away. In fact he didn't remember that happening, to him anyhow. Not with a foster mum. But one time old Rubber Lips came out of the school office to tell him he was being excluded because of a bit of bother he was into, just at the moment he was being flattened by a great big evil type guy called Greg. As soon as Rubber Lips rolled up, Greg stopped whacking him so suddenly it made Darren think what had been happening was all in his mind, except for bash marks here and there.

The Old Spring came up on the other side of the road and Darren stepped off the kerb to go over to it like being drawn by a magnet. There was a great honk from a car and the skid of tyres, a bloke's voice through the falling rain shouting You stupid fucker, two headlights staring at him like some bastard trying to stare you out, like the car saying What's *your* problem?

Me and that hedgehog, Darren thought, heart pumping. He scrambled back on to the pavement. He felt tears running down his cheeks, no mistaking them for rain this time. First Rebecca, then the car. It went off again with a final fuck-you toot.

He looked up and down the road to see if anyone had seen him but there was nothing about except the rain. He turned back to the road. Just as he was about to put his foot on to it again, he saw the Old Spring door open on the other side and a man step out. The door shut sharply behind him. It wasn't Frank, too small. The man was wearing a dark coat so he looked like a walking shadow. He looked like that black scarecrow that had assembled itself this morning. He turned left from the door, walked along the front of the pub, then turned left up Warren Lane, swinging his legs stiffly as he went.

Darren crossed the road, no cars this time. He climbed up the steps on to the raised pavement, and approached the door of the pub. He raised his fist to knock then thought better of it. He worked here, he didn't need to knock. He had the key.

A shape in the door, she jumped. Tiger Tim hadn't exited after all, was taking a look to see if her mask had slipped, which it had sure enough. Her face underneath would have been blank, she thought, if she could see it. Not expressing yuk, which is what she felt, but nothing at all, having a rest from expressions being on it. Last thing she wanted Tim to see; more of a dead give-away than looking queasy.

'Darren,' she said, putting her hand on her heart. 'That's the second time today. You didn't ought to keep doing this to me. I keep thinking you're somebody you're not.'

'By name of Keith,' Darren said.

Her heart froze. 'You what? What did you say?'

'A ghost by name of Keith.'

Don't move. Don't even breathe. Just be calm and icy. All day long she had heard Keith knocking on her door. 'Darren, I told you before. Frank told you. There's no such thing as ghosts.'

'That's what you called me this morning. Keith.'

That's all it was. She, herself, had put the name in Darren's head. 'I was just remembering somebody. That's all ghosts are, Darren. Nobbut memories.'

'Is that why you can, like, see through them?'

'Yes, Darren, that's why you can see through them.' Suddenly she realised he'd been crying. 'Darren, whatever's the matter?'

'Nothing.' He shrugged his shoulders. 'Nothing's the matter.'

He looked completely lost, standing there soaking in his pitiful plastic jacket. Like he was saying, something was the matter and that something was nothing, that his trouble was he *had* nothing. He had no one.

'What happened to your brolly?'

He looked vaguely round himself, as if he expected it to be hopping along beside him somewhere. 'I dunno. I must have left it at the shop.'

'Come here.'

He came up to her like a shaky little toddler, only tall. She put her arms round his shoulders and gave him a kiss. His long nose poked into her cheek. 'Ooh Darren, you've got a –' She was going to say *Big hooter* but realised he couldn't take a tease at the moment – 'you've got one of them clever noses.'

'Clever?' his voice said beside her left ear. 'How come?'

It was the first thing that had come into her head, or the second thing. Clever nose, she thought, what could I have meant by it? She couldn't explain. Darren wasn't the brightest of the bright but his nose gave his face a sense of direction, like it was a finger to point at things. He wasn't at all like Keith when you looked at him properly. Keith was always a thoughtful lad. He'd had quite a large nose himself, fair enough, but more in proportion.

She gave a quick peck on the tip of Darren's nose to avoid having to answer. Sure enough it felt sharp.

'I been kicked out,' Darren said.

'You what?' She held him at arm's length to inspect what he meant.

'That's why I probably left my umbrella. I had to go pronto. Well, first off Gem showed me her chicken, then I went.'

'Darren, what on earth are you on about?'

'I got the push.'

'From the cancer shop?'

'Yep.'

'They gave you the push?'

'Yep.'

'How can you get the push when they pay you zilch in the first place? You're like a –' She cast round in her mind for what it was like, him being in a shop without being paid for being there – 'a member of the public, for heaven's sake.'

'A big metal vase type thing fell on Rebecca's head. She did her nut. It's like I'm a vortex. When I'm around stuff keeps on going whoosh. I can't help it, Dawn.'

'You're well out of it, Darren. You were doing *them* a favour, not the other way round. The cheek of it, that's what gets me.'

Sky dim and blue as an old tattoo.

Squelch squelch squelch along the canal towpath. Fuckers in their fucking boats lighting their little fucking fires and toasting their fucking chestnuts.

Old Vincy who used to sell copies of the *Big Issue* down by Waitrose, he had one of those fucking narrowboats. He had this bloke what won the lottery come up to him, didn't want to buy a *Big Issue*, said to him, what would make you happy, son? Having a boat of me own on the canal, Vincy said, and Bingo the lottery bloke buys him one, big fucking narrowboat. Didn't want anything in return. Just bought him a whole fucking boat.

So said Vincy, in any case. More likely Vincy just robbed it off of someone, steamed like buggery down the canal, parked it out of sight and painted a new name on.

Vincy said, got my own fucking boat now, light a fire, toast fucking chestnuts on it, all the fuckers on the canal do that. First time he tried: toasted a fucking conker by mistake, fucking thing went off like a bomb, nearly had his eye out.

People sitting in their little dinky boat rooms, having a cup of tea, looking up at the canal bank, like, pairs of legs walking past. Squelch squelch every step of the way, Jake could feel the cold wet mud through his trainers, the exact coldness of the real mud so his feet felt wet even though they were dry and it was just like fucking walking through it barefooted.

Walking into the tunnel. It was like you weren't shutting your own eye, like the daytime was shutting its eye on you. The mud muddier and puddlier in here, coming in through the little lace holes in the trainers, so his feet were getting wet for real now, not just imagining it. Just a little bit of light on the water like it had rowed into the middle of the tunnel of its own self, to remind you your eyes aren't shut at all, even if you can't see a single buggering fucking thing.

Halfway along the tunnel it was like the daytime opened its eye again and Jake could see a dark blue eye at the end of the tunnel, as nearly black as can be but not black.

'Hello there,' Romesh said. His head on the hospital pillow looked fragile as eggshell. 'How nice to see you.'

'Hello,' Thomas said, 'how are you doing?'

'I'm doing very well, thank you. It's quite like a holiday.'

Thomas quickly riffled through all possible holidays: dying in hospital wasn't like any of them. He realised that Romesh's eyes were looking at him while he thought this thought. Like a tooth-filling Jerry had described one evening in the pub that had unexpectedly picked up Radio Four, Romesh had caught exactly what was going through his mind.

'Are they treating you well?'

Romesh's eyes seemed large in his thinned face, and came across contradictorily as both dull and alert, like a cow's when it watches you over its gate with unintelligent curiosity. Romesh's eyes rolled slowly in his head to follow Thomas's gist. Because his face had grown so pale his lips looked strangely definite, the colour of cooked liver.

'Very well indeed, I must say. I will tell you a good wheeze, if you should find yourself in a place like this. Make out you're Hindu. For dietary purposes at least.'

Thomas had an uncomfortable sense of being caught out.

Romesh continued: 'I could equally have said I don't eat red meat but instead I think I've really given them the willies. They keep providing rather nice vegetable curries. I believe they make them especially for me.'

'I've stretched my luck already,' Thomas said, relieved at the admission. 'I told the nurse I was your minister of religion.'

Romesh nodded and smiled vaguely, taking it in his stride. Thomas felt slightly disappointed, as if he should be congratulated or taken to task for stretching the envelope. 'They want to keep me hidden away,' Romesh said, 'I'm not sure why. I'm not contagious.'

'I'm sure you're not.'

'No, it's just a structural problem. Things breaking down.' His big expressive eyes looked inward for a moment, at what it was that had broken down. Then they returned to Thomas. 'Let me tell you why this is like a holiday for me: no carpets.'

'True enough.' Stupidly Thomas looked about to see if he could see any signs of carpeting on the ward. Of course not. The floors were covered in a sort of hard linoleum that would allow efficient mopping up of bodily fluids. That brought back the horror of discovering Julian and he kept his gaze averted from Romesh's antennae for fear the scene would transmit. As a result an old man passing Romesh's cubicle thought he was being looked at and gave him a smile with just one tooth in it.

'You know how carpets smell,' Romesh said, also smiling, but rather ruefully. 'I even prefer the hospital smell for now. You take an interest, of course you do, when it's your job. In pile. In colour. In material. In patterns. Oh my goodness, patterns.' He shook his head at the cascade, the kaleidoscope, of patterns. The action seemed reckless, like shaking a Ming vase. 'But sometimes we stock a few good oriental rugs,' he added judiciously. 'Even occasionally an Indian one. And of course there are the customers. It's very pleasant to meet different people. Well, usually pleasant, I should say. But every now and then I think to myself, is this all my life has in store, these little tufts of wool? Or even worse, of polypropylene?' He repeated the long word slowly, as if it were a Hindu incantation, the name of an arcane deity. 'Day after day, same old carpets.'

'That holds good no matter what line you're in.' Same old religion, Thomas thought, same old daily God. No wonder

Julian had spent so much energy trying to sex it up. Nauseating metaphors entered Thomas's mind: bluebottles buzzing at a pane, a dog trying to fuck a chairleg. Day after day making new forays at something that never responds. 'Same old, same old.'

'I suppose so. But carpets are especially repetitive, I think. It's what makes a carpet a carpet in the first place, more of the same. Forever and ever amen.'

'Well, there you are. You said it.'

'Now now, Thomas, I was not trying to compare God to a carpet.'

'You were talking about the principle of repetition. Perhaps it's the key to both.'

'If you say so,' Romesh said, amused but wary.

'Also there's the matter of flying carpets.'

'Ah well, we have never had many of those in stock. What a pity.' He twisted his head to one side to look at the black window. The bright ward light picked out raindrops on its surface like flaws in the glass. 'The heat of this place and the rain falling all day long have been reminding me of a monsoon, back in India.'

'Ah,' Thomas said. 'So that's where you've been on your flying carpet.'

A note to end on, he thought, as he saw the sister approach, hugely and weightlessly as a low cloud.

As he neared the eye at the end of the tunnel, Jake could see the black figure of a woman standing there in the rain. She had big round hair and a short dress on.

One thing about tattoos: he didn't like meeting women in poor light, in case when they made out what was on his face coming towards them in the dim they thought he was going to do stuff to them. Once one did a jump of shock. She saw him coming towards her along the pavement and just saw him, then she saw his tattoos and did her jump of shock. She

143

jumped up about a fucking foot, and her hair went up on end and her hands like bent into claws, so she looked like she'd had an electric shock, she looked like a cat in mid-air, an electrified cat. Jumping sudden that way she made a space that sucked him in, and for a second he wanted to do stuff to her just to get it done with, like when you nearly jump in the canal because you've got tired of not jumping in it.

But there was a good point about tattoos on your face: no fucker can see you're scared your own fucking self, and looking not scared stops you having to do stuff to get to look not scared again.

Then when Jake squelched a bit closer she suddenly changed into a he, and the big hair was a big hat and the dress was a jacket type of fucker and it was fucking Roof. The black head wasn't the dark it was a black head.

'Fucking hell, Roof,' Jake said.

'Cheers, bruv,' Roof told him.

'Fucking hell.'

'You said that already. What's your problem?'

'I thought you was somebody else.'

'I said meet me here. Who else is it going to be?'

'What you wear that big hat for, that's the point of it.'

'What you wear your fucking war-paint for? It's for *dec-or-ay-shun*, man, is what it's for. Plus it's to stash a afro in.'

'You haven't got a fucking afro,' Jake said, being that Roof had short hard hair.

'It's for my afro what I haven't got. It'll come in handy, man, if the seventies ever come back. I got enough for you and your mates if you want it. If you got any mates.'

'I got a mate painting a shop front down Pomeroy Road. I'm supposed to be helping out.'

'A bit of this'll help you help out more,' Roof said. 'Anyhow, it's too dark now.' He got out a little poly bag and shook it like a nonce shaking a bag of sweets at a kiddie. Jake got his wad from his back pocket and doled notes till Roof nodded.

'Good place to hide,' Roof said. Jake looked round him, at the towpath, at the tunnel behind. 'The rain,' Roof explained.

Jake looked at the rain.

'Look man,' Roof said, lowering his voice like as if the rain might do the dirty on him after all. 'I got some bad news. You was seen that night, outside the Griffin. Know what I mean? He knows *you* know. I think he be comin round sometime, to make sure you're OK, OK? To make sure it's *con-fid-en-shull*.'

'When?'

'Tonight, my man. Tonight's what I think.'

Frank and Pete drove up a muddy track in Norfolk on a dim November afternoon. Two years ago, not raining. The bare hedges and the grass looked grey. Pete pulled into the gateway of a field sloping down to a pond that was surrounded by tall dry sedges. They fizzed softly in the chilly breeze. A couple of ducks bobbed on the dark water.

'We're not going to take a pop at them, surely not?' Frank asked.

Pete gave a little laugh and twisted round to look at him. 'Not squeamish, are you, Frank?'

'No, don't think so. But they're just sitting ducks.'

'The original sitting ducks. Not to worry.' Pete's large hard hand patted Frank's knee. 'We're the sitting ducks. What we're going to do is sit here for a while till the light begins to go. Then fowl will begin flying in from all over. They like to roost by the water. That's when we'll get a bit of sport.'

They sat, perched on the open jeep in the chilly air. It felt strange being side by side in an unmoving car, like kids pretending to drive. Still, they talked, or at least Pete did. He was entertaining company. He'd been in the navy too, senior to Frank, but they hadn't known each other in the service. They met at a weekend seminar for those about to take retirement and had developed one of those high-speed friendships you do when your life is taking a new turn. Frank had the odd sense that they shared a past and didn't, at the same time.

Pete talked about the hunting, shooting, fishing life he'd got into since he left the navy. Frank could almost get the feel of it, screwing yourself hard into the landscape till you couldn't any longer tell the difference. Even Pete's jeep looked as if it had just grown like a battered old cabbage in some field. Frank knew his own attitude was different: countryside was for looking at, not being a part of. That's why he'd always imagined a country pub.

Pete explained all about trout fishing. The flies he'd made, how he cast, places on the river that were good, long summer evenings standing in the water. It was like a speech. When he finished he gave out a sigh and turned forward to look out the windscreen again. You could see he was still thinking about it, fish swimming around in his head like in a bowl.

And then as if it was moving completely of its own accord, Pete's left hand rose from his lap and clamped Frank's groin. Frank gave out a sharp gasp, and Pete breathed deeply in relief. He thought Frank was being appreciative.

Frank moved on the torn old seat, trying to pull away, but Pete thought that meant yes too, that he was just getting himself more comfortable, and gripped him the harder.

'Pete, I don't –' The trouble was his voice was a breathless whisper, it seemed to be saying Yes as well, despite what it was trying to say, yes yes yes, like he was just pretending to draw back.

'How I see it, Frank,' Pete said, turning to face him once more and replacing his left hand with his right, gently kneading him, 'what's the harm in it? Here we are, got some time to kill, all on our lonesomes out in the wilderness. Doesn't mean anything to anyone else. We go back to our lovely womenfolk, what's the odds? No harm done. I'm not suggesting anything soppy. We're just out hunting, it's a bloke thing. Two blokes together: doesn't concern anyone else.'

Frank imagined pushing Pete's hand away. It would be like the start of a fight. He'd always kept away from such stuff in the navy, apart from one horrible experience when he had just joined, and was only a lad. The purser tried it on with all the new boys, and eventually got his bollocks kicked in for his pains, by Frank along with a few others. But apart from that – because of that – Frank had always kept his distance when any blokes looked like they were taking an interest.

Perhaps that had been wrong, he suddenly thought. Perhaps it had been unfriendly. Once someone in his mess had said about him being aloof. The word had sounded like an animal living in some lonely place like Siberia.

I've not been a joiner, Frank thought, kept people at arm's length. And now here he was, at the end of somebody's arm at last.

How do I feel about it, that's the point, he told himself. What *am* I feeling?

Time to be honest. What he was feeling was a certain amount of warmth and pleasure coming from down there, that was all.

What harm could it do? To his surprise Frank found himself placing his own hand on Pete's groin.

'That's the idea,' Pete had said, giving him a harder squeeze. 'Just got an hour and the ducks will be flying over.'

On the bus the old age pensioners had squashed themselves together like a bunch of sheep while Jake sat on his own like a fucking bomb about to go off.

Roof said once upon a time: 'I don't catch no buses, my man. Don't *app-ree-she-ate* no white ladies taking one look at the spare seat beside of me and scampering off to park themselves in another place. Nor the white blokes, neither. Nor the white kiddies neither.'

What Jake thought about that was, What kind of fucking drug dealer wants to catch a fucking bus in the first place?

But the first stop they stopped at, a lady gets on and fucking plonks herself right by Jake, taking no notice of the other seats going spare and the groaning and bleating of the old age pensioners wagging their white heads at her in warning. Maybe she was colour blind. She wasn't old, maybe in her forties. Maybe she couldn't spot the colour blue. Tattoos ought to be fucking red like traffic lights, to signal no-go area.

'What a day,' the lady said.

Jake looked to see who she was talking to. The lady gave a nod of her head in his direction, as to say, you, you fucker. She smelled like lemons and something else.

Jake shrugged his shoulders.

'You've been out in the weather,' the lady said. 'You look like a drowned rat.'

'I been on the towpath. Up by the canal.'

'You look as if you've been *in* the canal.'

He shrugged his shoulders again and looked at the rain specking the windows.

'Make sure you change those clothes of yours, when you get home,' the lady said, 'otherwise you'll get pneumonia.'

'What's all this?' Frank asked from the doorway into the snug. Darren and Dawn were standing near the fire grate, deep in conversation.

'Hello, Frank,' Dawn said.

'Hello, Frank,' said Darren, a bit shiftily, Frank thought. In fact the two of them had that awkward look of a bloke and a woman being come upon.

It's just Darren, for Christ's sake, Frank told himself. 'I thought you'd be head to head with Tim Green,' he told Dawn.

'He went.' There was a pause. It didn't help, the way Darren got his hair to stand on end with some kind of gel. He always looked caught on the hop, whatever was going on. It was like in respect of hair he already had all his shocks and horrors built in. 'Poor old Darren here's got the push,' Dawn added.

'Have you, Darren? How come?'

'He knocked a heavy vase on that Rebecca's head.'

'This vase went flying, Frank. It whacked old Rebecca right on the top of the head.'

'Shame it didn't brain her,' Dawn said darkly.

'Blow me. Things do happen when you're in the vicinity, don't they Darren?' Frank felt cheerful again; Darren had just been being Darren.

'Told you,' Darren said to Dawn. 'It's like I'm a vortex.'

'So she told you to sling your hook?' Frank said. 'I'm sorry about that. But the pay wasn't that good, as I remember. Nothing an hour, or thereabouts.'

'Nothing exactly, Frank. Yep.'

'Round number, anyway.'

Darren nodded as if that was a fair point.

'You can do better than that, I'm sure.' Frank told him. 'So how did *you* get on, Dawn?' he added. 'It might have been an idea to whack Tim Green on the head, and all.'

'He's going to go through the books again, and let us know.'

Frank shook his head. 'Doesn't sound good.'

'You never know,' Dawn told him. 'Look on the bright side.'

'Anyway, I've got to riddle the coals through that grate and let it cool. I've found a bloke who says he can fix it this evening. I'm taking it over to him about half six. With any luck it'll be on the go again by nine.'

'Oh Frank, I've got to nip out about that time too.'

'Hey up, Dawn. You're on to do the early stint and me to come down later. That's what we always do on Thursdays.'

'I forgot. I said I'd go to see poor Romesh. I haven't been since the other day. I can't let him down Frank, not with him going downhill the way he is. I've been summing up my courage and just got enough going for me now. I should have done more for him. I should have spotted he wasn't right as soon as he had that prang.' She looked suddenly shaky and tearful. 'Poor love.'

'That's a nuisance, that is.' He went over to the fire and gave it a kick, not so much to riddle it as relieve his feelings.

'We could give Connie a call,' Dawn suggested.

'She's off out. I know she can't make it tonight. She told me her comings and goings for the week. She's got some boyfriend or other.'

'I could do it,' Darren said.

'Thank you, Darren. It's a nice offer,' Frank told him.

'Thank you, Darren, you're a thoughtful lad,' Dawn said. She turned to Frank. 'See, he's willing to muck in in a crisis, and getting the sack's all the appreciation he got in that place. Cancer shop's the right name for it.'

'I can't tell any difference,' Darren said. 'Rebecca gives me the sack from working in the shop even though she doesn't pay me any pay, and you give me the sack from being a barman even though I never been a barman once. What's the odds on that?'

Dawn looked over at Frank. He drummed his fingers on the mantelpiece. He felt caught out. It wasn't so much that Darren had a point, but the lad spotting what was going on that way seemed to suggest he had it in him to manage better than you might think. Dawn gave a little nod. That was a surprise, Dawn OK to let Darren loose on her precious pub.

'Thing is, Darren,' Frank said, 'when we train up new bar staff, we get them to work alongside us for an evening, to learn the ropes. They've got to learn the cost of the drinks for starters.'

'I know them,' Darren said.

'What do you mean, you know them? You know the price of a pint of Buckman's, I expect.'

'I know them all. I listen to you serving. I know them, Frank.'

It being Darren, plus the tone of his voice, did it for Frank. For Dawn, too. 'He knows them, Frank,' she said. 'We've got a price list anyhow.'

'All right, Darren, if you say so. Gin and tonic?'

'Three forty.'

'Tonic?'

'One twenty.'

'See, Frank?' Dawn said. 'Told you.'

That uneasy feeling he'd had when he walked in came back to Frank. It was almost as if something was going on. Dawn had always liked Darren well enough but she was a hard task-master and was usually ready to spell out his limitations. She always said that everything went in one of his ears and out the other. Now suddenly she was all for leaving her precious pub in his hands. 'All right, Darren, you win,' he said finally.

'Ye-es,' Darren said, shaking his fist in front of his face, as if it was a little private friend he was talking to.

'I'll just riddle the grate,' Frank told him, 'and then we'll practise on the till a while.'

'Tell you what,' Darren said, 'I worked it out when I got fired from the cancer shop. Since I've been cleaning for you I've earned more than nine hundred quid already. Not bad, OK? And now more. Yes!'

'Hearts of gold, we've got,' Frank said.

'Nine hundred quid?' Dawn asked.

II

Rain trickling down Jerry's left ear, wind in his left eye, Petergate Rise stretching down in front of him. One thing I hate, he remembered: having small feet. As he looked down the road past the council estate towards the bowl of the town centre, with the spotlighted priory in the middle, he caught small feet at the bottom of his visual field, poking out of his trousers like a pair of rats.

Alan's house on the right, end terrace side-on to the road, with the front door on what should be the side of the building. It reminded Jerry of one of those flatfish caught in evolutionary transition, with one eye sneaking round from the bottom of the head to the top.

He knocked on Alan's door. Kathy opened it. From the standpoint of the dark and rain she looked as though she was being displayed in a sort of electric box. She still had her power suit on, grey flannel type of thing, almost like a man's, which only showed up how she didn't look like a man at all. She made him feel like a potato, newly dug.

'Hello, Jerry,' she said. 'You're not crying?'

'Me, no. My eye's watering with the wind. It's just the left one.'

'Come in, then. It's horrible out there. When I was driving back from school, my wipers could hardly keep up.'

Jerry remembered Dawn, that charmer, saying to him and Alan: haven't you two got a home to go to? She ought to have a look in here. Alan had a home to go to all right. Blue hall, big enough for little furniture, four wicker chairs for pre-dinner drinks; dining-room beyond in one direction, sitting room beyond that, kitchen to the left, with Rachel sitting at the breakfast table doing her homework; stewy type smell wafting across from the cooker.

'Hello, Jerry,' Rachel said, not looking up.

'Hello, there.'

'Bloody hell, Jerry,' Alan said, coming down the stairs.

'Yeah, I'm sorry. I was just working up Digory Place, so I was walking past anyhow.'

'Go on, Al,' Kathy said. 'Now he's here.'

'Go on, Dad,' said Rachel, still not looking up. In a sing-song voice: 'You know you want to.'

'Just so you can tot it up to use against me in a couple of years time, when you've decided to be a drug addict,' Alan told her.

'I thought a quickie,' Jerry said.

'The famous swift half,' Kathy said, going over to the cooker. She took the lid off a pan. It was like unleashing a stew monster to stop Alan leaving the house.

'It's a naughty night,' Alan said, looking towards his front door as if he had X-ray eyes and could see the rain beyond.

'You're about to eat,' Jerry admitted.

'No we're not. I just wanted to splosh some wine in. Look.' Kathy picked up an opened bottle of red by the cooker and sploshed some in.

Jerry felt a sudden stupid need to prove his credentials. 'Know what I discovered today?' he asked. 'The elephant is the only animal that can change the position of its penis. You've got to hand it to Google.'

'Thank you for that thought, Jerry,' Kathy said.

'Nice one, Jerry,' Alan told him.

'It's all right, Dad,' said Rachel, still bent over her work, 'I have heard of elephants. And penises.'

'More's the pity, that's all I can say,' Alan replied. 'Especially in combination. It can only lead to disappointment later on.'

'It's because they're an awkward shape for getting near to each other,' Jerry explained, feeling an awkward shape himself. They were a good-looking family, even Alan in his lean, stooped, acid fashion.

'Hedgehogs are the ones I feel sorry for,' Kathy said, sploshing some of the wine into a glass.

'It's just bloke hedgehogs who've got to worry,' Alan told her, 'so you'd be OK.'

'Off,' Kathy said, waving her glass dismissively.

'Off,' said Rachel from her books.

'I'll have a bath, in the meantime,' Kathy explained.

Jerry turned to the front door and opened it. 'So will I, by the looks of it,' Alan said.

Jerry had a thick winter coat on, misbuttoned like a badly-wrapped parcel, fudging his large contours.

'I've been putting a network in in this office, Starling and Co.,' Jerry said, 'over towards Glenfield Park.'

'Oh yes.'

'There's a girl working there, she has sort of 1940s type hair. Damn, that's my eye gone again.'

'What you mean, your eye's gone?'

'The wind makes it weep. The left one.'

'Piping your eye.'

'That must be it. Curly hair, with this parting. Coming halfway down her ears.'

'What do they make?'

'Who?'

'Starling and Co.'

'I don't know. I don't think they make anything. They're just an office.'

'God, it's all a charade, isn't it? The economy. Life.' Me, Alan might as well have added. He could hear himself coming round the corner, with that staccato cynicism. 'No wonder the credit crunch crunched.'

'And one of those square shouldered dresses.'

Jerry's attachments were many, shallow and one-sided. He espoused the Dante and Beatrice school of courtship, where the beloved was drooled at across a room or street. He could fall in love with a barmaid at thirty yards. It enabled him to be romantic without the clincher of getting his leg over, his short fat leg.

'I told her I'd be in the Old Spring.'

'Oh yes? Did she tell you where *she*'d be?'

'She like smiled. Non-committal.'

She obviously hadn't smiled as such, she'd *like* smiled, a smile that imitated itself. A memory or reconstruction of a smile. Same look as Mona Lisa, it struck Alan.

They went past the Griffin, pub for the Petergate council estate. A motley group of punters was huddled under its porch, black and white together, puffing their ciggies and drinking their drinks while the rain barrelled down an inch away. One of the black kids was wearing what would have been a flat hat except that it was hugely swollen, plus what looked like a velvet frockcoat. Halfway out of the shelter was a grey-haired white guy, glaring hunched at the others as he tried to remember how to look ready for anything that could be thrown at him, shifting his weight from one grubby trainer to the other and clasping his pint pot close to him like an injury. Tied to the next lamppost, bunches of dead flowers, in memory of a bloke knifed on the pavement a couple of weeks before, after a row in the pub. Allegedly loads of people witnessed it but none dared point the finger.

I can talk, Alan thought, avoiding eye contact as he walked past. He heard Jerry sigh with relief as they cleared the place, which annoyed him the more: it was accurate.

Up a flight of stone steps to a ramped Georgian pavement, climbing clear of social challenge.

There ahead, the Old Spring.

A figure in a dark coat was caught in the light from the windows, collapsing his umbrella before going in. He was speckled immediately by illuminated rain: a sudden pearly king. Then he was gone through the door and Alan felt an urge to hurry up, some atavistic fear of first comers downing all the beer. Podgy Jerry beside him was still spouting about the girl at Starling's. He seemed to have developed density and weight, become a burden to tow along, like Sisyphus's stone.

Then they were at the door themselves, and through.

'Bloody hell,' Alan said out loud, 'all it was was the padre.' Sure enough Father Thomas was just going through the inner doorway into the snug, back in dreary monochrome. 'I thought we were safe from his twaddle this time of day.'

'Thank you very fucking much,' Nick told Jake. 'Just in time to help me pack up.'

'I thought you'd have been long gone,' Jake said. He pointed at the rain, pissing down worse than ever.

'What you come back for, in that case?'

'I said I'd come back so I come back.'

'Mr Reliable. Only snag, you didn't do a hand's turn all afternoon.' Nick turned to look at the shop front. 'I finished off the inside of the window surround,' he said, suddenly not mad for a second. Thinking about how nice he'd painted the window surround must have taken his mind off of it. 'While the weather was poor, like. Have a go at the front tomorrow.' Then he remembered again about Jake letting him down. 'Fucking hell, Jake, you're a useless fucking sod.' He clenched his big teeth together and shook them at Jake's face like some kind of fucking horse. 'What's the good?' he asked, not even opening his teeth to say it. 'What's the fucking good?'

'I'll be here tomorrow,' Jake said. 'That do you?' He remembered Roof's warning. If I haven't been fucking stabbed by then, he said inside.

'What's the fucking good, Jake?' Nick asked. Bloody hell, Jake thought, any moment now, the bum's rush. He'd seen people do like this before, get mad, then forget it, then remember it, then get more mad than ever, then suddenly, two fucking fingers. He couldn't remember who or when or what but he recalled that happening in the past.

'Thank you very much,' Jake said. Here I am, fucking being rained on on the street, clothes soaked through to the skin, shoes like a fucking pair of sunk boats, getting fucking pneumonia like what the lady on the bus said, and here comes the bum's fucking rush.

'Bloke like you,' Nick said. 'One thing you ought to be able to fucking guarantee. You of all people. A bit of commitment when it comes to exterior decoration.' It was like almost a joke. Jake saw it in Nick's face, whether to make a joke of it. 'Not much to ask, is it? A bit of commitment,' he repeated, leaving his option open.

Then decided: no fucking way. He gave a hard look through the pissing rain, eyes screwed up not because of the weather but just to *be* well hard. 'One thing,' he said. He shook his head. 'One *fuck*ing thing.'

It was like he was getting to the point of no return, like he was just one second off giving the bum's rush.

'Got something for you,' Jake said.

'You what?'

'I'll give it you in the van.' Jake nodded his head sideways at where Nick's van was parked on a double yellow outside the shop. It was a horrible van, bashed to buggery, with THE GOLDEN PAINTBRUSH painted on the side and a picture of a paintbrush, done by Nick, with golden drops dripping off of it, like it was just finishing a pee. Fuck fuck fuck, go squelching along that towpath, spend a fucking fortune, get the fear of fucking God put in him by Roof, get soaked like a drowned rat, then first thing that happens, he has to part with some of it for free, just to stop fucking Nick from giving him the fucking push.

I'd rather stick it up your fucking arse, Nick, Jake thought, how would that suit you?

When Thomas walked into the snug he saw the fire wasn't lit. In fact it wasn't even there, a piece of cardboard propped in the aperture instead, like a cubist rendering of flame. He went up to the bar. Darren was standing behind it.

'Darren?' he asked, surprised.

Darren cocked his head to one side and tilted his forefinger in Thomas's direction, the apogee of knowingness. It occurred to Thomas how little experience Darren must have of being knowing. Knowingness, like knowledge, didn't belong to boys like him, but to people like Thomas himself: it went with the territory. One of the things Thomas disliked about wearing a dog-collar was its suggestion of smug authority, like the graduate gowns teachers wore in the old days.

'Buckman's?' Darren asked in return.

Thomas nearly asked him what he was doing there but decided at the last minute not to, take it in his stride instead. He didn't want to make him feel an interloper. 'Please,' he said.

'Fire fucking pending,' came a voice from behind. Jerry.

Thomas looked over his shoulder, but didn't twist his head round far enough to catch Jerry full on. Quid pro quo: Jerry didn't quite look at him either. Thomas then turned the other way, to look at the fireplace again. Sure enough, FIRE PENDING was written in black felt tip on the cardboard. Alan was staring at it with scrunched up eyes, as if trying to decipher Linear B.

'What you doing, Darren?' Jerry asked. 'Helping your-self?'

The pint clonked on to the bar. 'Thanks, Darren,' Thomas said. Darren had coloured up. Jerry laughed.

'Jerry,' Alan said, turning from the fireplace, 'please don't laugh. You always sound as if you've got a punctured lung. It makes me nervous.'

True enough, Jerry was squat and neckless; he laughed as if it was a form of panting, with his shoulders heaving up and down. 'I keep expecting him to deflate like a burst balloon,' Alan told Thomas, eyes unfunny. Thomas had noticed before a kind of malice in Alan that sharpened his powers of observation. Jerry laughed the more.

'Frank's gone off with the fire,' Darren said, taking Thomas's money.

Jerry blinked, wanting to tease out something funny or surreal to say about that.

'It needs welding,' Darren added. He expertly pinged the till. 'Bloke in Silver Street said he'd do it. I'm filling in.'

'Buckman's, in that case,' said Jerry, giving up on a wise crack.

Darren picked a ready-poured pint up from below the level of the bar, as if it had been flicked into existence by Jerry's word. Jerry opened his mouth, impressed, then quickly put a swig of bitter in it to avoid giving Darren the credit. Alan put his lips together to say Buckman's also but his pint arrived in front of him before he could get the word out.

'Service has improved, anyhow,' Alan said. 'Talking of which, what's your mistress up to, then?'

'His mistress is here,' Dawn said, striding in from the back room. Her tough lanky presence was oddly softened round the edges, as if warmed in front of the fire that was now pending. She was wearing a skirt and jacket in raspberry wool, and had her hair up in a complicated knot. 'And I don't want any bother for the lad. He's kindly helping out. Father, don't let these old lags give young Darren any lip while Frank and me are out.'

Thank you, Dawn, Thomas thought sadly, that's done wonders for my credibility. A man of the cloth was always going to be grit in a pub's oyster; the last thing he needed was being classified as class monitor.

'All dressed up,' Alan said. 'What's the plan: invading Poland?'

'I beg your pardon?' Dawn asked.

'Just a compliment.'

'It didn't sound like a compliment where I'm standing.'

'Dressed to kill,' Alan said. He flipped his right hand, like a conjuror showing the queen of spades. 'See? Compliment.'

'Lip,' Dawn said, touching her own narrow pair. Thomas realised she'd put lipstick on them, a pale orange. 'That's just exactly what I'm talking about.' She was also wearing perfume, something nice, with a touch of sourness to it. 'If you must know, I'm visiting poor Romesh,' she continued, relenting.

'Ha,' Alan said. 'True love.'

'You what?' She bristled again immediately. 'What did you say?'

'Hope Frank doesn't clock it.'

Dawn suddenly blushed, a painful scarlet that invaded her pale complexion and clashed with her orange lips.

'Or the Father here,' Jerry added, pleased at the opportunity to join in.

Dawn was stymied for words. Thomas could understand her impasse: the ugly insinuation was true but not ugly, so she didn't know whether to agree with it or deny it. He felt a sudden pity for the elaborate ball of hair on the back of her head.

'Nobody has to hide love from me,' he said. 'The more of it the better, so far as I'm concerned.'

'I hope you're not advocating sin, Father,' Alan said.

'We're not talking about sin, we're talking about love.' OK, be pompous, have the courage of your convictions, such as they are.

'Sometimes one leads to the other,' Alan said.

'I've just come back from Romesh myself,' Thomas said, facing Dawn square on.

Her eyes lit up, vindicated. Love, Thomas thought bitterly, there wasn't a lot of that involved in his own contribution. It had simply been an alibi, to avoid the emotions swirling around at De La Tour House. A denial of love, in point of fact, like Peter denying Christ thrice: he'd just been opting out of the embarrassment of grief.

He'd been happy to make small talk with Romesh on his deathbed, glad at the chance of being whimsical about flying carpets. He hadn't asked the man if he had a flying carpet to take him beyond India, to ferry him all the way to his God or gods or whatever place or space he had in lieu. He hadn't offered to pray with him. He hadn't followed his lie through to its logical conclusion, where it could have redeemed itself and become the truth.

'How was he?' she asked. 'I've not seen him for a day or two, shame on me.'

'All right,' Thomas said automatically, conscious of his rising inflexion that made it sound like a hard-won assertion in the face of doubt. 'We talked about flying carpets.' No, Romesh *hadn't* been all right. Nor had he flown anywhere on a flying carpet. 'No, not really. He looked poorly, Dawn. He had that look about him.'

It was a look he'd glimpsed on Julian's face, too, over the months, but he had deliberately evaded its implications: following Julian's own lead in that respect, creating a little conspiracy between them to deny the inevitable. He'd been dimly aware of the lie, of overlooking pallor, twinges of need and fear in the eyes, droplets of sweat on the upper lip. Somehow he had managed to convince himself it was life-affirming to ignore the insidious onset of death.

Dawn raised a fist to her orange lips. Thomas saw that she'd painted her nails an orangey-red too. They were suddenly shapely and noticeable: he was conscious of the way they lined up in a sequence, like a row of reddish bells or the keys of a clarinet.

'Oh bless,' she said, 'poor chap. He's such a gentleman, Father. I love the way he treats everybody so polite, no matter who.'

It was odd. Alan and Jerry, who didn't treat everybody so polite, who were so urgent in their need to generate enough friction out of people to produce an ironic spark, seemed to dwindle into insignificance for the moment in the presence of Dawn's feelings. They talked to each other, at a distance from the bar.

'Nice man,' Thomas said.

Dawn nodded, teary-eyed.

'I wonder where he was going to,' Thomas asked, trying to keep a prurient edge out of his voice, 'that night.' God, he thought, I'm as bad as the lags. I want to cut him down to size, defuse Dawn's emotion, or diffuse it maybe. It's the same as with Julian, anything to avoid sorrow's raw explicitness. I want to hint that he was up to what he shouldn't be up to, that in some way he deserved what was coming to him, that his story had a moral meaning. To find a touch of spice in that night's event, stumble upon goings on in some brothel in the depths of the countryside.

'Don't you know?' Dawn asked.

'No. Not at all. No. He never told me. I didn't like to ask.'

'He was after owls.'

'It was late, I know that much.'

'No, *owls*.'

'Owls?'

'He was going to the arboretum, to spot owls. He's in an owl club.'

Thomas just looked at her, astonished. He took a pull at his pint, to collect himself.

'They take it in turns, the members, like doing shifts. Watch what the owls get up to in the night-time, I suppose. They have these special things what you look through in the dark, so you can still see. It wasn't just owls. I think they did bats as well. I used to say to Romesh, what about your beauty sleep? But he used to tell me, I've got carpets, carpets, carpets, all day long, I have to leave nature to the night-time. He always went the night before his day off.'

'I had no idea,' Thomas said. 'None at all.'

'Are *you* interested in nature, Father?'

Thomas knew whatever he said would be thrown back at him later, after Dawn had gone. So what? Talking of nature: you might as well be hung for a sheep as for a lamb. 'Yes, I am as a matter of fact. Not so much owls, to tell you the truth. Recently I've been reading a book about dung beetles.'

He sensed sharp intakes of breath from Alan and Jerry, the way their bodies somehow flinched or puckered with suppressed glee. Dawn though looked back at him perfectly straightforwardly, eyes greedy for the titbit, anything that might provide support for Romesh.

'Frank likes shooting ducks,' she said. 'He's got a friend in Norfolk he does it with. I said to him, why can't you just go and look at them, like Romesh does. Do you think he's going to die, Father?'

Thomas almost said: we're all going to do that, Dawn, but remembered his new resolution. You might as well be hung for a sheep as for a lamb. He held her gaze to keep his courage up and fix the lags in the periphery of his sight, two dim gargoyles warming their behinds at a cardboard fire. It was a moment for simple seriousness. 'I think he will, Dawn,' he said.

A tear sprang immediately into each of her eyes. It gave him an odd sense of power, as if he'd said abracadabra. That in turn made him aware of what Alan and Jerry would be thinking: touting for custom, manipulating emotions.

'I wish I'd –' She made a gesture with her hand. Her nails took the light from the little cluster of bulbs above, an amber diminuendo in the brownish air of the snug. It was as if she were trying to catch hold of something, time itself perhaps. She wanted to prevent Romesh from going out after his owls that night, she was trying to hold him back. It was a gesture of yearning. 'There's so much death in the world,' she said. 'Everywhere you look.'

'There's exactly the same amount as life,' Thomas told her. 'That's the deal.'

She shut her eyes, compressed her lips, nodded. Then she turned and went without another word, just a quick flicker of her fingers on his shoulder.

Thomas turned back to the bar. Darren leaned across. 'I got sacked today, Father.'

'Did you?' Thomas felt momentary indignation at the lad's self-concern, but then realised. Darren had been there, listening to every word. He was offering his own small trouble as a present, to take Thomas's mind away from the bigger woe. It was like the pinprick of acupuncture. 'You don't look very sacked from where I'm standing,' Thomas told him. 'Promoted, I would have said.'

The fire got heavier as Frank went along. His arms seemed to elongate with each step, as if they were made of plasticine.

The worst part was it needed both hands, so he couldn't use his umbrella. The fire was like ballast, stopping him from dodging the drops or trying to hurry through them as per Jerry's conundrum.

Medium-sized rain now, medium-heavy, pattering on the poly bag he'd shoved the fire in to stop it getting wet and holding back the welding process. A fire wasn't the sort of thing you could just dab dry.

Images of Dawn jigged into Frank's bouncing head as he went.

Dawn worried sick about the nine hundred quid, her voice hard as stone, hard as those numbers that wouldn't give no matter how much they looked and looked at them: no way out, Frank, what I can see. Dawn grim and moody.

Dawn in a huddle with Shirl, gone girly all of a sudden. Girls did that in his teenage years in Tiverton, whispering together as though boys just existed for them to serve up on toast to their pals later on. Shirl doing her stuff, waving her hands and rolling her eyes and Dawn taking it all in. Then Frank looked across for a moment while he was talking to Katie about her wedding dress and suchlike nonsense and Dawn had become all stiff and teary while Shirl patted her hand and comforted her. What was that about?

Frank felt the rain falling on his beanie as if it was falling right through it and through his skull directly on to his brain, a horrible niggling prickling feeling. No other weather but sex weather wherever you looked, whoever you were, whatever direction you went, dropping on people's heads all day long, soaking all and sundry. Shirl had gone through her conquests and confidences in that whisper of hers and then it was Dawn's turn and she had nothing to offer back, struck dumb. Looking all forlorn for what she didn't have.

Dawn businesslike: doing the books with that greaseball Tim Green.

Dawn mumsy with Darren, determined to get him behind her beloved bar, not worried that he had no experience, not even taking on board the fact that Darren jumped at his own shadow. Dawn had strong views about misfits and oddballs and wobblers. Frank thought of the sad bastards that Dawn didn't want to give house room to, Harry with one shoe off and one shoe on, who didn't even have a house to live in; Jake covered from the top of his head to the soles of his feet in those tattoos. Old Darren fancying himself as a magnet for poltergeists. This afternoon he'd managed to get himself fired from a charity shop, which must be some kind of record in the career disaster stakes. But the first thing Dawn does, she makes him cock of the walk. Though truth be told it was surprising how good he'd turned out to be at the numbers game.

Dawn titivating herself for her visit to Romesh in hospital. She loved that man. She always said as much. Because she was so upfront about it Frank hadn't worried.

But Romesh was so polite, he was too polite to go to bed with another bloke's wife. And in any case he was too ill to go to bed with anybody now. He was stuck in a hospital bed on his own.

Not fair to Darren, Frank thought suddenly, I wasn't being fair to Darren. He's a nice boy, a good cleaner, who's had God-knows-what happen to him in the course of his short life. No excuse to get narky just because Dawn goes soft on him all of a sudden.

Romesh at life's end: how do you compete with that?

But who would want to?

Alan appeared by the bar one side of Thomas, Jerry on the other, a pincer movement. Each clunked his pint on the bar top, like dropping anchor. Alan looked straight in front of him. 'Dung beetles,' he said in a deliberately gloomy tone.

'Yep,' Jerry said from the other side, as if *he*'d brought the subject up, rather than Thomas. 'Interesting animals. They can roll several times their own -'

'Dung bloody beetles,' Alan said. 'What a life.' He shook his head.

'They're not the only ones,' Jerry pointed out. 'There's a blind albino woodlouse that lives its whole life underground, in an ants' nest, eating the ants' crap. That's all it does.'

There was a pause. Then Alan said, 'Imagine being a blind albino woodlouse, lying on your deathbed, thinking: What the hell was *that* all about then?'

'Remembering the halcyon days of youth,' Thomas said, trying to hit the right note. Bugger, he thought immediately, I wish I hadn't said halcyon. Big mistake, to try too hard.

'When the ant crap tasted fresh and full of promise,' Alan said, to his relief. 'What *I* think,' Alan went on, 'whether you're a dung beetle or, on the other hand, an albino woodlouse, what you have to do is avoid the bigger picture. What do *you* think, Father?'

You're basically taking the piss, that's what I think, Thomas thought. There was Romesh, lying on his hospital bed after a lifetime of carpets, with an interest in owls. Were they saying all of that was nothing but ant crap, that Romesh amounted to no more than a woodlouse? An albino one at that. Thomas thought of the pallor that had seeped into Romesh's brown skin. Is that what they were getting at?

Thomas felt himself trying to gauge their antagonism, like running his thumb across the carving knife blade before Sunday lunch, the nicest occasion of the week at De La Tour House. One great bonus of a religious life: going to Sunday mass always felt like a job well done, a good morning's work: a morning's good work. Julian used to insist Paul should carve, out of a kind of culinary modesty on his own part, and he would take the cue, diligently sharpening the knife on its bone, shooting his cuffs before addressing each slice, draping the meat across the blade of his knife to serve it on the plates with a kind of ritual informality. It was hard to imagine doing any of that again.

What was the balance between joke and aggression? Impossible to assess, particularly since Thomas wasn't able to make eye contact, given that there was one on each side of him at the bar, a row of three all facing forward in unison. Their stance felt both intimate and not, like using a urinal.

Julian had ended his life with his head dropping into a pool of his own vomit. Perhaps Alan and Jerry were doing no more than face the facts. After all, they'd homed in exactly on what dung beetles had meant to Thomas: nothing.

Frankie's shop hove into view in the distance. Frank staggered with his fire along the last stretch of gleaming pavement. There were necklaces of Christmas lights strung prematurely across the road and with his head and shoulders forced downwards by the weight he was carrying, Frank could see reflected blobs of pink and green and blue on the wet flags.

Just before he reached the door of the shop he stopped. Time for a rest. The fire was heavy as lead by now, making his legs buckle and his hands go numb. He put it carefully down. Then he took off his beanie and gave it a shake. His fingers had gone clumsy and he dropped it right into a little pool. Thanks a lot, he said out loud, looking round to make sure no one was near enough to hear him, except for God maybe.

12

It's a funny thing, Dawn thought, as the taxi swished her round King's Square. There were strings of white lights strung in the trees in the middle. You have something you have to do, and you put it off and you put it off. But all the putting off has to go somewhere. It's like squashing stuff into a trunk. One day you accidentally open the lid and it all comes flying out at you like a Jack-in-the-box or one of them ghosts rearing up at poor Darren. They reminded her of cobwebs with beads of dew on, the lights.

Visiting Romesh was an alibi. She'd just said it because she couldn't say she was going to a hotel to call on Tim Green. But once she said it she had to do it, so it would come out less of a lie. And as she talked to the Father about it she was filled with panic, as if all the days she hadn't gone to Romesh were flying back at her, filling the air, knocking her sideways. If she didn't get to the hospital at once, if she wasn't there already, yesterday, the day before, poor Romesh would be dead.

I been careless, she thought, I been looking the other way. I've never learned anything from my life, just looked the other way.

In the hospital a fat nurse parked herself in the way.

'Yes,' Dawn said.

'Yes what?'

'I squirted my hands,' Dawn said.

'No,' the nurse told her.

'I beg your pardon?'

'We have to restrict visits to Mr Mehta. Family only.'

'I love the bloke, will that do you?' Dawn said, squeezing past the nurse and hurrying on. She hadn't time to waste; anyhow, it was true.

Then she was there, at his bedside. It was funny, after all her haste, coming to a stop. She almost overbalanced with the sudden stillness.

Romesh was asleep, snuffling in his dreams, brown head very brown on the white pillow.

She tiptoed up close and bent over. She nearly leaned down to kiss him, but theirs wasn't a kissy sort of relationship. What she loved were his cool good manners. When he was in the pub, quietly attentive to those around him but distant too, as if inspecting owls through his night-time binoculars, he made everybody else seemed sketchy and unfinished by comparison. It was like an outline had been drawn around him.

She'd tried to explain to Frank about it. You mean because he's brown, Frank told her. He wagged his finger, as much to say, better watch your words, duck. No, no, she'd said, angry that he didn't cotton on. But actually it *was* because Romesh was brown, in a way. Not just brown-skinned but brown in his personality or his soul or whatever it was you have inside your skin. As if his soul had a definite colour and shape while everybody else's just faded away on the air the way cigarette smoke used to do in the snug when the fan was turned on.

Romesh opened his eyes a tiny amount. They gleamed between his long black lashes. She could almost feel little images of herself entering the pupils.

'How you feeling, Romesh?' she whispered.

He lay still, his eyes still open, peering up at her but not quite full on, as if he couldn't turn his head the last necessary bit.

'How you doing?' she asked, a bit of roughness in her voice this time, wanting to pull him back from wherever he'd gone to.

'Fine,' he whispered at last. 'All the better for seeing you.'

'Oh Romesh,' she said. She felt a horrible big sob gather at the back of her nose and eyes, like a sneeze forming. It would come rushing out and blow away all Romesh's delicate feelings. 'What a kidder,' she added.

'No. You look so nice.' His eyes moved up a little, to show he was really looking. 'All dressed up.'

'I got to look nice for my favourite customer. For my favourite man in the whole world.'

Romesh gave a funny little smile, a tiny one, as if that was a secret between himself and his pillow. He took a long breath, perhaps a sigh. 'Good job my friend Frank isn't here,' he said. 'He might not to be pleased to hear you say that.'

'Don't worry about old Frank. He'll live.'

As soon as she spoke she wanted to put her fist to her mouth and bite her knuckles in sheer pain. How could she? Romesh had sort of shrunk for a moment when she said it, like putting salt on a slug. In panic she cast about in her mind to find a rewind button and call it back. Stupid, stupid. It was as if she had been saying, don't you worry about Frank, he'll win out in the long run. Tears ran down her cheeks. Even as they did she thought: this will make my eyes a mess.

Romesh's hand came out from under the sheets. It crept of its own accord, like a small animal, towards Dawn's arm, and patted it. 'I'm so lucky,' he said.

'I wouldn't say that,' Dawn said. 'Not at the moment, anyhow.' She tried to say the last bit as brightly as possible through her tears, as if she thought Romesh's illness was just a temporary set-back.

'I have such good friends, that's why.'

'I wish you were back home, Romesh.'

'So do I, of course.'

'I mean in the pub. Where you belong.'

'Well, now I can't go to the pub, the pub seems to be coming to me.'

'I wish I could pour you a pint of beer, that's what I wish most. I should have smuggled one in in my handbag.'

There was a long silence. Romesh wasn't looking at her now, just along the surface of the pillow, at something only he could see. Then he seemed to snap himself out of it, giving his head a little shake. He spoke very quietly. 'I don't expect I will ever drink a pint of beer again, Dawn. That makes me a bit sad, after all.'

Dawn stood under the hospital porch thing, waiting for a taxi. She felt exactly as if she'd just failed an important exam. Some chance. She'd never been clever enough in her life to even *take* an important exam.

Made a bloody pig's ear of that, she thought. Every single thing she'd said to Romesh had turned sour. He might just as well have been her worst enemy instead of her best friend. All her visit had done was make the poor man more unhappy and more lonely than he was before. Nice one, Dawn.

As punishment she stepped forward into the rain. If it fell into her eyes and dislodged the mascara a bit more, it might act as a disguise for her tears.

She put a ciggy in her mouth. Straight off somebody jumped out at her from behind. 'Sorry,' he said. He was a porter or something, in white overalls.

'Hang on,' she said. 'You don't want to do that. You nearly gave me a heart attack.' He was Asian like Romesh, quite a scrawny fellow with thick clever-looking specs that caught the light from the hospital entrance. 'Were you hid in a bush?'

'Madam, I'm sorry but smoking is not allowed.'

'I'm outside, if you haven't noticed. I'm standing in the rain.' She raised her hand to show him her cigarette. 'I'm smoking a wet cigarette.'

'Sorry, no.'

'Look, I run a pub. I know the law. Not allowed in public places, that's where it's not allowed. *In*. Public places. That's the word: in.' She used her cigarette to point at the word *in*, hanging in the rainy air just in front of her. 'And we're *out*.'

'Smoking is not permitted anywhere in the grounds. Hospital rule. Health Trust rule. You have to go over there to the public highway.' He pointed in turn, down the driveway to the lights of the road.

She looked in that direction, her eyes half-closed as if she wasn't believing anything she saw, traffic, night-time, rain coming down. Then her shoulders slumped forlornly. 'You win,' she told him after a moment. She shrugged her shoulders, mainly to stop them slumping any more, then got her little portable ashtray out of her handbag and stubbed her ciggy out. It made a bolshy little click as she snapped it shut. She opened it and shut it again, to make sure the porter heard.

He disappeared back inside without another word, and she put her ashtray back in her bag. Stupidly, being told off made her want to cry all over again.

A taxi rolled up. 'Where you after, darling?' the driver asked.

It wasn't one she knew, luckily. 'Fielding Hotel,' she told him.

'Aha,' said Frankie, opening the door. 'The naval person.'

'I brought the fire.' Frank found himself huffing and puffing, so as to show what an effort it was – so as to fix Frankie's attention on the fire, not him.

'I bet you did.'

Impossible to say the slightest thing to Frankie without it going round the wrong corner. Frank shook his head. He tried to shrug his shoulders at the same time, but they were too weighed down. He followed Frankie into the shop, leg-in-each-corner fashion.

'Put it down there,' Frankie told him, pointing at a bit of paved floor. It was dank and damp here in the shop, some of the lights off so there were just patches of illumination. Frank lowered the fire to the ground.

'Cuppa?' Frankie asked.

Frank wanted to say no, I'm in a hurry, but Frankie had already turned away from him and was heading towards a huge old butcher's block that was positioned along the wall, the sort that was worn down in the middle where so much meat had been cleaved over the years. A kettle, along with a teapot and a couple of mugs, were all set out on a flat section at one end. Frank wondered whether the second mug had been placed there with now in mind. Frankie switched the kettle on and turned back to face Frank. 'Here we are then,' Frankie said.

'Yep,' Frank agreed, trying to make it sound business-like. He rubbed his hands together though his fingers were so numb from carrying the fire that he could barely feel them.

'I'd get that wet coat off if I were you,' Frankie said. 'There's a hallstand over there. In fact there's eight or nine hallstands over there. Take your pick.'

'I'm OK,' Frank told him.

'You don't want to catch your death. It'll take a while.'

'Okey-dokey.' Frank said with a sigh. He went over and hung his coat on one of the hooks.

'How's the licensed trade then?' Frankie asked when he came back.

'Oh, it's all right. Do even better, lit by a fire.'

Frankie took no notice of the hint but looked at him expectantly, like he wanted the bigger picture.

'It's a nice pub,' Frank continued. 'I run it with my partner. With my wife.'

A lie, being they'd never got wed. Dawn had shied away from the very idea. I been there once, she said, and I'm in no hurry to repeat the experience.

Frank had wondered at the time whether he'd brought up the subject in too sidelong a fashion. He'd talked about it looking better for them to have the same name on the licensed sign above the door, romantic in one way, not in another, depending on your point of view. He remembered how he couldn't help sounding gruff about it. Some moments you can't give your tone of voice a lift, however hard you try.

Fact was, like he'd told Katie at lunch time, he himself choked at the idea of being pinned down, it wasn't just Dawn who was mithered, as she called it. He'd been a sailor all right, but not the kind Frankie was getting at. Girl in every port, he liked to think, though that wasn't strictly true: he should have been so lucky. A girl from time to time was more like it, and then he'd sail away. A life on the ocean wave.

I like to think of my old pop turning in his grave, Dawn had said. Far as I'm concerned, good as is good enough.

Frankie gave a little grin at the word wife. That's what they all say, he looked as though he was saying. The rim of his hairstyle seemed to gather up the patchy electric light, individual hairs glowing like little gold filaments, a halo effect except it made him look evil more than good.

'Good on you both,' he told Frank.

Bloody cheek, Frank thought, I don't need your blessing, Dawn neither.

But maybe Frankie was on the right track. Certainly those shenanigans with Pete seemed to prove the point. Ever since they started he'd not been able to get intimate with Dawn. Living a lie, that's how it would have seemed if he had. Even though, the times when he went to Norfolk and what happened, happened, out on those flat empty windswept places with twilight about to fall and flying ducks imminent, it was Pete who seemed to be the lie.

Before a trip came round Frank would think, this time I'll cancel. But he never did. For starters, cancelling would have seemed too much like a give-away. Once, he tried to persuade Dawn to go with him. Even if she didn't go out in Pete's jeep, which of course she wouldn't, just knowing she was tucked away in Pete's little house – a modern town house, funnily enough, when it ought to have been some old thatched cottage – just having her sitting there chinwagging with Pete's wife, would calm everything down, stop him and Pete getting up to anything.

'It's too big of an ask,' Dawn had told him, 'us both going off from the pub at the same time. You got your friends and I've got mine,' she added. 'We're not spring chickens. You can go off and shoot things and be lads together to your heart's content.'

Frank had given her a look to see if she meant anything by being lads together, but it didn't seem so.

As each Norfolk trip grew nearer Frank would feel dread and excitement, both at once. Maybe dreading something was exciting in itself, like going to war. When their ship was sailing down to the Falklands one of his mates had said, 'Funny thing, if they called it off now, I'd feel quite let down.' Everybody had jumped down his throat. 'Oh yeah,' one lad said, 'it would be so disappointing not to be killed after all.' None of them were killed in point of fact, being they never engaged with the enemy at close quarters. They came back to a hero's welcome in Portsmouth harbour, feeling like swindlers.

But that wasn't all of it, as far as Norfolk was concerned. Part of Frank did look forward to it, properly, without dread. I know which part too, he told himself. Hardly surprising that it did, that he did, given his long abstinence otherwise.

Maybe it added up to the fact he wasn't what he'd thought he was all his life. Maybe he wasn't *who* he'd thought. When he flattened the long-ago nose of that purser, maybe it was just because he didn't want to admit it to himself.

Frankie poured their tea and handed him a cup.

'Sorry it's chilly in here,' he said. 'It's all this dead furniture. You got chairs without bums to sit on them. Tables nobody eats off. Beds nobody gets to lie in.' He gave Frank a look. 'They don't generate any warmth.' He crossed his arms over his chest to hug himself, and gave out a *brrr* sound. The collar of his boring sports jacket rose up over the lower part of his face. 'Sometimes I think to myself, I ought to put a match to the lot of it.'

'Oh well, we'll have the oxy acetylene to keep us warm in a bit,' Frank said, by way of reminding him about the job in hand.

'Funny thing about that sort of heat. It doesn't carry.'

'Does it not?'

'Just stays exactly where it's directed. It's a very focused type of energy, if you get what I'm saying.'

'Oh yes,' Frank said.

A spluttering noise. 'Bless you,' Alan said to Jerry, leaning across Thomas.

'Thank you,' Jerry said.

'Sorry, Father,' Alan said. 'I suppose that's *your* prerogative.'

Father was God-knew-where. In fact that was no doubt exactly true: God would, God did. Father would be in some incense-flavoured location where things of the spirit could be mulled over. Alan imagined it to be like testing an intricate wine on the palate, discriminating between tannins and sulphides, reaching towards a hint of grapefruit or the whiff of tarmac, gauging quality and style of sin, mortal or minor, bodily or spiritual, omitted or committed. Alan had no time for such subtleties himself: booze was for drinking, God for naming in vain, sin for getting away with.

'You what?' Father said, his eyes slowly coming back to the surface from the deep wherein they were sunken.

'Blessing Jerry's sneeze.'

'Oh, help yourself.' He revolved his glass slowly on the bar top. 'Open season on sneezes.'

'Just for the record,' Jerry said, 'I didn't sneeze in any case.'

'Well, you made a disgusting enough noise. I thought to myself, how on earth does he think he's going to seduce the woman from Starling and Company? You sounded as if your nose exploded.' Alan took a pull of his pint while he paused for thought. 'And only half an hour ago you were piping your eye.' He clicked his tongue and shook his head.

'It was the beer,' Darren said.

'The beer?'

'Pump. The beer pump. The Buckman's just run out. It makes that splurgy noise at the end.' Darren pulled a couple of times at an imaginary pump, to prove the point, then rubbed the back of his hand worriedly across his nose.

'Don't we all,' Alan said. Father opened his mouth to say something but thought better of it.

'Hello, Darren?' came Jason's voice from the back room. His big sporty head was peering round the bar. He always had that rather depressing look of being on a playing field, braced by fresh air. 'What happened to you, my man?'

'Beer run out, Jason. Sorry.' A bright red patch appeared in each of Darren's cheeks. 'I was just halfway through pouring it, and it run out on me.'

'Well, hurry up,' Jason said, and withdrew his head.

'What's he mean, hurry up?' Darren asked the threesome confidentially. 'I told him it run out.'

'It was an unearned blessing,' Father said to Jerry.

'Was it?'

'They're the best sort.' He turned back to his glass and slowly shook his head. He looked quite lugubrious. 'The best sort,' he repeated.

'I think any blessing from Alan's bound to be quite low-grade,' Jerry said.

'What you better do,' Alan told Darren, 'is hop down the cellar and attach a new barrel. Have you ever seen Jason playing rugby?'

'No, I never have, I don't think.'

'I haven't either. Wouldn't waste my time. But I believe they call him Desperate Dan.'

'The mechanics of a hand-pump are quite interesting,' Jerry said. 'Same principle as Isambard Kingdom Brunel used in the Dawlish tunnel. Basically you're creating a vacuum and letting beer fill it.'

'A good definition of my life as a whole,' Alan said. 'Do you know how, Darren?'

'Oh yeah, I know how. I've done it with Frank tons of times. He's always hooking up barrels first thing in the morning, when I'm in to clean.'

'There you go then. Chop chop.'

'But what if people come up to the bar wanting a drink? While I'm gone?'

'I'll serve if you want,' Jerry said. 'Always wanted to get on that side of the counter.'

'Better not, Jerry,' Darren told him in not much more than a whisper. 'I don't think you better. Sorry. Sorry. Frank said me, he didn't say nobody else, me to do the bar. He like tested me out a while, to make sure. Better not. I been sacked once today already.'

'Good point,' said Alan. 'Tell you what. If anybody wants a drink, we'll tell them to hang on till you get back. That do you?'

'Thanks, Alan,' Darren said. He looked about himself uncertainly, as if still wanting another cue to be off.

'Important task,' Father told him glumly. He raised his hand as if to pat Darren on the shoulder but then lowered it again to the bar counter, obviously too self-involved to go through with it. But it did the trick anyhow. Lad had obviously been waiting for a blessing of his own.

Darren walked through the rooms in turn: the public, the snug, the back room. People watched him pass, looking up from their drinks.

In the snug Nigel was just spreading arrowroot on the shove-ha'penny board. Jerry said that if you put a smooth layer of arrowroot on, even though the grains were dead tiny, the ha'pennies travelled over the board without touching it, like they were little hovercrafts. You don't know how many grains, Jerry said: millions, millions upon millions, it's all but a liquid. Darren had run his hand over the arrowrooty board. It was a dry liquid, if so, except it did have the coolness of water. Even Darren's fingers slid like hovercrafts.

Nigel looked up from putting his ha'pennies in a little pile all ready. 'Hey up,' he said. He had nearly a full pint. Practising his shoves, maybe he would drink slow.

'Hey up,' Darren said back.

'Seen Colin?'

'He was in lunch.'

'Was he then?'

'He's going to Hamburg tomorrow. First thing.'

'Hamburg, is he? On the pull, I suppose, being Colin the Coach. I don't expect he'll be in, then. He'll need to bank a bit of beauty sleep.'

In the corner of the snug, Dave and Rene. Dave had a bottle of organic cider. He liked to pour it bit by bit. There was one little drink of it at the bottom of his glass, and about two-thirds waiting in the bottle. Rene had her glass of white wine which she'd only had about one swig of. They would probably go outside soon to have a fag, which would slow them up because they always left their drinks behind when they did. They must not like drinking on the pavement. Dave nodded at Darren. Rene held up her glass like for a toast, then put it down again. Darren touched his nose then pointed at her, to toast back.

Alan once said to Darren: 'You know old Dave's beard is false, don't you? If you look at the back of his ears you can see where it clips on.' Next time he had a chance Darren looked at the back of Dave's ears and sure enough there were earpieces there, sloping over the bit where Dave's ears were fixed to the sides of his head. For a second Darren looked at them in shock. Then he realised they were just the earpieces of Dave's glasses.

He knew Alan was a kidder anyway but the funny thing was, ever since that moment, Dave's beard stopped looking real. It looked just stuck on like a disguise. Darren had looked at it with care but couldn't see it in any other way. That's why now he looked at Rene more than Dave. He just mainly looked at Dave's bottle and glass. He'd seen Dave's nod out of the corner of his eye.

In the back room, Jason and another member of the rugby team, Graham. 'Nice one, Darren,' Jason said. That seemed to make the responsibility worse, like he'd just asked Darren to come on and kick the ball.

'Won't be a tick,' Darren said.

First five or six steps down: stage fright. Darren kept thinking of the people up above his head, waiting for him. What if he made a cock-up of it? He *had* changed a barrel with Frank, really and truly, not just saying it, even though it was only one time, not lots. He knew how to do it in theory, but sometimes it was another story when you had to do something all on your own. Things would look different, more impersonal, like they didn't agree with what you wanted to do with them, like they didn't want to cooperate.

He remembered being at school and the teacher bending over his shoulder, telling him how to do a sum, how easy it seemed while she was standing there, her tit resting friendly on your shoulder. Like as if you were borrowing her brain for the time being, like her brain was sending you signals on broadband. Then she walked off, out of range, and the sum went sort of cold as he looked at it. Cold and hard and impossible. Story of his life.

He would come back to the surface of the pub and have to tell everyone he couldn't do it.

He pictured himself walking back to the bar, across the back room, then the snug, into the public and through the flap. People looking up as he passed, like they had just now.

Them saying, OK, Darren? All right, Darren? And him having to say, no, not, couldn't do it.

He wouldn't be able to bluff his way out of it, because as soon as someone asked him for a pint of Buckman's he'd have to own up in any case. Might as well get it over with straightaway. He would change from being the most important person in the whole pub, the barman, into just a berk that had messed up what he had to do.

It always happens to me, he thought. It's not fucking fair. He would feel like a coward, not brave enough to make something happen right, not strong enough to force things to do what he told them. As he plodded down the stairs he felt wobbly and tearful like he had done a few hours ago on Bean Street. He was getting used to feeling his eyes prickle.

Then he took another step.

It was like a stair could be a different kind of stair from all the other stairs. Like it could be a different temperature from the rest of the room. Darren made himself stand on the stair a moment, feeling the panic bouncing about in his chest, while he tested it out. The stair was cool, dampish. He stepped backwards, up to the stair above. Feel, he told himself.

He wished you could feel like you sniffed, on purpose. Choose when and how much you let the stuff on the outside come inside. *Feel*.

He was sure it was exactly the same. He went down again to the next step. No, it wasn't colder, just different. It was a different step anyhow, but more different than being just that.

He remembered that word: portal. The step was a step into somewhere else. Or into some other time, same thing.

He stopped where he was, not wanting to go any further.

The bare bulb was a little way in front of him, same height as his head, more or less. There was a ball of bright white light round the bulb itself, then the light got yellower as it went further away, and when it got to the low part of the walls it was almost brown, where it had let so much darkness seep into it, and in the corners it was black, because the darkness had taken over.

Nothing was moving, no mice. He said it out loud: no mice. His voice sounded thin in the chill air. Frank had told him: 'I won't tolerate mice in the cellar, simple as that.' He doesn't tolerate mice, Darren said, whispering this time. It wasn't mice that was the trouble, but if something was about to move Darren wanted it to know that there was no way it could pretend to be mice, no way it could do a quick scuttle or scrabble in the dark parts of the floor that you might think was mice, no way it could disguise itself.

Darren stood not even breathing. Well, he said to himself, trying to sound busy, is it or isn't it? Going to move.

The light didn't shake. The barrels stayed put. Put, everywhere. In the brown light of the edges, just put. Black patches in the corners: put.

It was all put. Everywhere was put. If there was a little shiver somewhere it was just in his eyeballs, he was staring through them so hard it made them shake a bit, with the heavy usage.

13

'What dung beetles always make me think of . . .' Father Thomas said abstractedly, then fizzled out.

'Oh yes?' asked Alan. 'What?'

Father didn't reply. He was staring over the rim of his glass at the shelf of whiskies on the other side of the bar and the black, rain-flecked window beyond, his expression glum and lowering.

'What do they remind you of?' Alan prompted.

'What?'

'Dung beetles.'

'Oh yes, they do. They do.' Father Thomas sighed.

Alan took a step backwards so he could raise his eyebrows at Jerry behind the Father's back. Jerry raised one eyebrow in return – the other one, Alan realised, wasn't operative. Only having one that would rise might have been what had made him quizzical, how strange. There he was in infant school, chubby legs dangling from his chair, raising his one available eyebrow at the teacher, and she'd thought, OK, OK, little chap questions life, must be brainier than he looks, better feed him loads of facts. And that's how he'd got addicted. Maybe if both his eyebrows had worked in sync he wouldn't have been the scurrier after bits and pieces of information that he'd ended up as. His whole existence was an exercise in applied curiosity.

Suddenly Father Thomas pinged his beer glass, exactly as if he was calling him and Jerry to order. They stepped smartly back into place, one each side of him. But Father said nothing. Instead, he tensed his forefinger against the ball of his thumb, then pinged his glass again.

'Your pint is half full,' Jerry told him.

'Not that one again,' Alan said. 'There is nothing more depressing than being told your glass is half full.'

'No, no, I'm not talking about as opposed to half empty. It's exactly halfway down the scale from a full pint to an empty one. Notewise, I mean.'

Father turned to give Jerry a look – a blank one, Alan guessed from the stillness of the turned head. But Jerry carried on regardless. 'You get the most muted note from a full pint. That's because the mass of liquid stops the glass vibrating much. Obviously. When it's empty, you have a nice bright note.' His hand made a small gesture in the air over the bar counter, like a conductor extracting a ting from the triangle player. 'Ting,' he said with hoarse brightness.

Father was facing the bar again. He gave a small nod, as oblivious of what it was acknowledging as the full-stop at the end of a sentence.

There was a pause. 'The wren has one of the fastest songs of any British bird,' Jerry continued. 'That's because it's one of the *smallest* British birds. It has to have small notes to fit its little beak.'

'We're talking about dung beetles,' Alan said. 'If you don't mind.'

Julian was born to be Father Christmas, dinner an essay in roundness, the great brown ball of a turkey, the hemisphere of the pudding, as if he extended his own kind contours to what he cooked. He wouldn't let anyone else clear away or stack the dishwasher, claiming they might steal the credit for his show.

Paul had sucked at a cigar he'd accepted from Damien, more fool him, everyone else having politely declined. It was sour and stung his tongue, worse still made him queasy. Suddenly he found himself in a silent battle to assert his authority over it, while the others just chattered peacefully around him, sipping port or brandy, Damien puffing away on his with every sign of relish. For Paul, however, it was as if the smoke were a lean finger reaching in to tweak his uvula. Stupid pride stopped him leaving the cigar on the ashtray to go out.

Then Julian was back with a loaded pillowcase on his shoulder, as triumphant as if he'd just laid an enormous egg. They'd had a draw to decide who each of them would buy a present for, one gift apiece, but that constipated generosity could cut no ice with Julian. He'd bought extra presents for everybody, wrapping each one up in metallic gold and green paper that glittered when he drew it gleefully out and put it on the table.

'You've cheated,' Brother Damien said, taking his cigar out of his mouth and inspecting it narrowly, giving himself an excuse, Paul realised, to furrow his brows in disapproval at Julian's kindness. Julian nodded, unabashed.

'It really isn't fair.' Gregory: stickler for decorum, for a certain just-so-ness even here, in their secluded life. Julian shook his head in agreement: yep, right you are, not fair.

Somehow the Brothers managed to assert their moral superiority even as they unwrapped their parcels, that bleak sort of morality you could get in the monastic context. Julian didn't mind: he watched each of them with a sort of cunning satisfaction.

Paul's present from him had been an old book, a translation of a work by the nineteenth-century French naturalist Henri Fabre on the subject of the dung beetle, the sacred beetle as it was called. Julian's attention must have been caught by the word *sacred*. Paul hadn't known he wanted it till he got it, but as soon as it was in his hand it seemed the most fascinating possibility he could imagine. To actually get to the bottom of something – in a sense, given the subject matter, to get to the bottom of everything. His cigar made him feel large, inclusive. He waved it at Julian. 'Julian, you know me so well,' he said.

Julian blushed a little. That's what he wanted to be told. What he'd done was restate his own faith in religion as alchemy: transforming that motley collection of men into a family, in celebration of the Holy Family.

'It's four or five hundred pages long,' Father said.

'Woo,' Alan said. 'How can beetles be that . . . detailed?'

Thomas thought about it. One of Julian's less likely phrases came into mind: it takes two to tango. 'It's the observer that's detailed, the observing mind. Fabre. Monsieur Fabre. He doesn't miss anything.'

'Sounds a bit dry, if you ask me. Even monotonous. Little blighters trundling balls of shit round the place.'

'Any chance of a drink?' a voice said suddenly between them. She was ladyish, aggrieved, with hair in a grey bun. 'You could die of thirst.' Thomas glanced over her shoulder. There was her husband breathing noisily, marooned at a Britannia table.

'The barman is in the cellar, attaching a new barrel,' Alan told her. 'He shouldn't be a minute.' Thomas noted his oddly pernickety way of speaking, making sure each consonant was correctly enunciated. It gave everything he said a sarcastic edge.

'Ah, thank you.' She turned towards her husband. 'Attaching a new barrel,' she said, mouthed rather, as if it were a secret. He stared back at her uncomprehendingly. 'Thank you,' she said again to Alan in a whisper, then looked embarrassed at how intimately it had come out, maybe at how hard his eyes were, looking back. She hurried over to her table.

'I didn't point out Darren's not the brightest spark in the carburettor,' Alan told Thomas. 'Not wanting her to lose all hope.'

'I'm back,' said Jerry, returning from the Gents.

'Congratulations on your safe return,' Alan said.

'Yes, well,' Jerry said, resuming his place at the bar on Thomas's far side.

'It's odd,' Thomas said. 'Odd, odd.' He shook his head and rubbed a hand over his cheek and chin, noticing the stubble that was poking through. It continues to grow on the dead, he remembered, or thought he remembered. Perhaps Julian would need a final shave. He was one of those men whose stubble tended to be clearly visible, like so many splinters embedded in his shiny translucent skin. Jerry had once pointed out that men whose faces had plumped out would inevitably have thinner beards, given the same number of follicles had to cover a larger area. Perhaps that's why Thomas had been aware of the dark particularity of Julian's. 'Fabre will call a female dung beetle a wife,' he said. 'A housewife. He talks about them eating bread and jam. When he means dung.'

'State of the art, dung beetles,' Jerry said. 'They're breeding them in America nowadays. Very ecological beasts.' He held his hand palm up over the bar counter and let plump fingers unfurl as if to act out a dead beetle, or perhaps to release an invisible one he'd caged in his palm. Or maybe it was an ecological flower flowering.

'It sounds like the pathetic fallacy to me,' Alan said. 'You know, when –'

'I know what the pathetic fallacy is,' Thomas told him. He sensed Alan bridle a little at his knowledge. Alan wasn't a man to relish being out-known.

It struck Thomas that Julian had been a purveyor of the pathetic fallacy. He took those stiff and repressed men (me among them, he reminded himself), took the cool and abstract tenets of religion: somehow managed to impose human warmth upon both.

'Bad thing,' Alan said, shaking his head morosely. 'So they say. Attributing human traits to animals. Both pathetic, and a fallacy. Undervalues our non-human friends. Except they're not our friends. Come to think, they're not non-human either. Even that is a way of defining them in human terms.'

'I don't think it works like that with Fabre,' Thomas told him. 'He lures you in, makes you think you almost understand. And then you realise where your head has got to. And there you are, rolling your ball along backwards with your hind legs. Or squatting down in the darkness of your den with only filth to eat. He lets you in for it, the shock of the strange. When you said about the albino woodlouse on its deathbed, wondering what it was all for, *that*'s the pathetic fallacy. But thinking shit is really bread and jam: that's what dung beetles must actually *do*. That's what they do do. That's what they must think.'

There was a pause.

'So to speak,' Thomas added, to take the sting out.

Alan had the last swig of his beer. 'I stand corrected,' he said grimly.

I'm in for it now, Thomas thought, suddenly nervous. But at that moment, back came Darren.

I got Tim Green right where I want him, Dawn thought. She recalled him rushing round the snug with his foot on fire and laughed silently in the back of the cab. Drops of rain ran upwards on the windows, with their speed. They looked like high-speed snails, leaving trails behind them.

The funny dry sparking of oxy-acetylene, Frankie peering down into it like a toad. He was wearing big rubbery goggles, otherwise still in civvies, sports jacket and tie, which helped the effect of an animal all dressed up. He looked up once, suddenly said 'Boo!'

'Ho yes, boo,' Frank said, not unfriendly but dull as possible. It was his job to make everything that came out of Frankie seem ordinary, to calm down all its possibilities, like you do when you're humouring a kid in a bored grown-up sort of voice.

'Be finished in a mo,' Frankie said, peering down into the fire again. Frank looked too. At the focal point the sparks all joined together into a steady brightness, same as sparklers do when they give you a bright nib to write in the air with. Working with a welding torch must feel like using a pointed tool, some kind of poking or nippled device, only in a place where light is king instead of solid things.

Frankie was welding on an iron rib he'd cannibalised from another fire somewhere in the depths of the chilly building. Funny to be in a place that had so many fires for sale yet stayed bone cold as if it hadn't been heated for years, centuries.

It occurred to Frank to wonder what this might cost. Should have asked in advance. He had a habit of rushing into things, taking people on trust. Not good. He would need to reclaim it from the brewery, but he should really have cleared it with them first. Probably should have got a written estimate. Maybe three written estimates. Especially in view of the nine hundred pound business, which he was deliberately not putting his mind to. Dawn was in enough of a lather for the both of them. Maybe that was why he'd got himself so fixed on having the fire repaired straight off.

But not thinking about the problem wouldn't make it go away. The brewery would probably clamp down on everything he asked for until it was settled.

Mending the fire was skilled work, a rush job. Frankie was liable to want a lot for it. It could be bad news.

Maybe worse news if he only wanted a little after all, if he was doing it for a favour.

'How was the cellar?' Alan asked.

'Cracked it,' Darren told him, then blushed.

Thomas saw Alan give the smallest incline of his head, as if the mechanics of congratulation had to operate against tremendous resistance, in the teeth of a mighty, sceptical wind.

Perhaps it was relief that Darren's arrival had got him off the hook, maybe it was a return of that exuberance born of grief; either way, Thomas suddenly had an insight into what made Alan tick. He wasn't mean exactly, that wasn't it. Rather he had a love affair with disappointment: which was why he'd wanted Fabre to show feet of clay on the subject of dung beetles.

'You make a barrel of Buckman's sound like a bottle of old claret,' Alan told Darren.

'I got to pump it through,' Darren said.

'Hello,' said the woman with a grey bun, leaning through the threesome. 'Can I have a pint of beer for my husband?'

'I just got to pump it through,' Darren told her, in not much more than a whisper. He made vague ingratiating movements with his arms, a funny blend of miming the pumping he was about to do and miming a calming pat for the lady. Tall though he was, he suddenly looked like a small boy floundering in the face of authority, fluttering his arms against whatever might be bearing down on him.

'It won't take a moment,' Thomas told her reassuringly. 'He's having to hold the fort by himself.'

She trembled slightly, compromised by the surrounding maleness but not wanting to retreat for a second time. 'Oh well,' she said, giving up; then, with forced chirpiness: 'I'll be back.' She returned to her table. Thomas glanced over his shoulder at the husband stirring confusedly in his seat at the second non-arrival of his pint, his breath coming across the room more raucously than ever.

Nearly there, Darren thought to himself as he put his hand on the pump. He felt like it was the end of a long journey.

Once he'd been sent to brat camp, as they called it, like a holiday for evil kids where you stayed in a hostel and had to go climbing a mountain and sailing on the sea, like they were trying to get you killed and out of their hair but wanted it to look like an accident.

One of the things they made you do was scuba dive. He had to put on a wetsuit and flippers and a face mask and an oxygen bottle on his back, and have a tube stuck in his gob to suck the air in through. The man who was in charge of the scuba said when they were getting ready: A wetsuit won't keep you dry. He sounded like an American bloke. It lets the water in, he said, then your body heats the water up. You end up wearing a bunch of water like a coat.

Darren flip-flopped down the beach. He had to waddle side by side with another bloke, diving buddy as was called, like in an infant school for penguins: two by two. It was funny still being in the air but breathing his own supply, looking out at the beach through his mask as if it wasn't really there. It made him feel he was watching everything on a telly in another world, especially as his breath sounded like Darth Vader.

Then into the water. That was funny in just the same way, having your own private water in the suit but other water all around. The outside water went up the glass of the mask like lager into a pint pot, only green.

Then he was all the way under. And suddenly he realised it was a place where he didn't belong, had no business to be. The water was a bit foggy but he saw a couple of big dim fish nose by and on the seabed some shellfish were crawling around, strange sight since he'd always thought being dead was all shellfish ever did.

And then suddenly panic came.

He wanted to shout, scream. He wanted to tear off his wetsuit. He wanted to step out of his body. He wanted not to be where he was, even who he was. It was like a ghost or alien had got inside his diving gear, inside his insides, was taking up all the room.

That was when he thought to himself: I've got to do everything on purpose.

The only hope.

It was like: one false move, and you're dead.

If he just scuba-ed along like normal, even though he'd never done it before and it was a hard ask to hit normal first time around, but if he did, then maybe he wouldn't die of fright. But one wobbly move, one tremble: done for.

He felt he was sitting inside his own head like a little bloke sitting in the cockpit of a crane on a building site, pulling knobs and levers to make big things a long way away get to work, pulling a knob to make one flipper flip, then another for the other, just flip slow and normal with not a care in the world, crest his arms in front of him as if they were the front part of a body board, giving him a nice relaxed angle as he pushed through the underwater water, as if he was just another human fish passing by.

His diving buddy swam in front of him, twisted round to look at Darren's face with his one big gleaming eye, swirled both his hands round and round in opposite directions as if each one was polishing a pane of glass, then kicked downwards so he was standing on his hands on the bed like a fat gleaming seaweed tree, the two big leaves of his feet like palm tree leaves, swaying a bit in some type of water wind.

But Darren couldn't join in and do like that. One false move: dead.

All he could do was swim slowly on, keeping his clasped arms steady, not letting a flipper out of line, following the scuba bloke who was swimming on in front. On and on, left flipper right flipper, steady steady, don't let on you're scared to death. Darren did it so methodical even his diving buddy stopped arsing around and started swimming slowly along beside him.

As he stepped down from the step on the cellar stairs, the portal step, Darren had felt as if he was scuba diving under the sea all over again, as if the cellar was rising up his face like the thick green water had, as if he was having to breathe from some invisible bottle on his back.

Keep slow, step by step. Don't make a sudden move, to let the cellar know you're there.

One step after the other, not a creak, letting the old bendy wood get used to your weight each separate time, then when you get to the floor walk slowly slowly across it, walk along as slowly and calmly as if you're not really walking at all, as if you're not really there at all, walking so gently you do nothing to ruffle the cellar about you, make no ripple in the watery light.

Then detach the line from the old barrel, hook it up to the new one. He did each thing as if he wasn't him. If he stumbled or made a sudden movement, if he didn't pay attention for a second, it would let the darkness group together like it had this morning when he was cleaning, make itself into a black scarecrow from all the bits and pieces of black down here, those lumps of it stuffed tight in corners or lying under barrels; the skeleton of blackness in the shadow of the steps, sitting on the floor with its back resting against the wall.

He kept his mouth closed in case it acted as a vortex to suck the night-time out into the middle of the room. Eyes half-closed too, same reason, even though it added to the darkness tendency. Plus, didn't blink, in case in the silence down here his eyelids shut with a clatter and made something drop from the shelving on the opposite wall, a bag of crisps scoop down from side to side like a falling leaf, or a mixer bottle go with a smash, and the movement or the noise got stuff on the move, reminded the poltergeist to *be* a poltergeist.

Don't set an example, the trick.

Darren would have closed his ears if he could. He kept his body as a whole closed, body, as, a, whole, he said to himself, closed. When he walked back towards the steps his thighs and knees were touching each other so there was no gap between his legs plus his arsehole was tight shut. He only worked his legs from the knees down, like when people walk on a tightrope. It was horrible keeping so slow and underwater when really he wanted to run like buggery and get the hell out of there.

He reached the bottom of the steps, and stood still. Don't turn round. Whatever you do. The room bunched up behind him. Maybe it was just the old landlord. Perhaps he'd seen Darren do the beer same as he had done it himself all those years ago. Perhaps he'd come out because he was like a brother to him now. Maybe he was standing right behind Darren this minute, so near he was almost in the same space, like identical twins. Darren could feel faint cool breaths down his neck, dead old landlord maybe just waiting for him to start climbing back up the stairs of doom.

I need to go up backwards, Darren remembered. That's how I go up, making sure of nothing underhand. In case he wants me to join him in doom. Being like, barrels first, then steps second, then the cold step, then break my neck. Like what they say in the kids' card game when the identical one crops up: Snap!

But he couldn't turn round, in case what it was was dark and spectral, not human at all, not even human once upon a time. Some stuff can't be looked at.

Two ghosts, that was the bastard of it. One: had to see. One: had to not-see.

The not-see one was trump. Darren had to go up front-wards.

He lifted one leg, slowly slowly, then lowered it slowly. It reminded him of a dropper he had for allergy in his eyes, you held it up above your open eye and squeezed it and lying there you could see the drop slowly form, like the way a tear does in the corner of an eye, sucking up sadness until it's ready to fall. Darren lowered his front leg down on to the first step as slow and careful as a drop being dropped, then when it was in position shifted his weight forward on to it, and began to raise his back leg in the direction of the next step up. Then the first leg again.

When he got to the step below the step of doom he raised his leg higher, higher, past the next step altogether and dangled it above the one above. It was hard to lower from this angle and he had to hold back a little groan or whimper type noise. Slowly slowly his front leg landed.

Then dragging up the back one. Mustn't touch the step of doom. He bent it so it stuck out behind him like you were just going to take a kick in footie, then sort of curved it sideways so it swung well over the step and then arrived beside the first one.

At this point Darren could have bolted for it: hard part done. But no, don't throw it all away. He speeded up but still tiptoed, feeling like someone dancing on the tips of their feet as he went. Then at last, push on the door, out, quick spin round, shut door, maybe a slight clunk from the far side, maybe not, maybe just the door clunking.

He turned round again. There was the room, people in it drinking and talking; no clapping, no cheering, nobody giving a toss, nobody noticing. Just people yackety-yacking, always somebody laughing somewhere though you never spotted who, like the pub's secret laugher.

Now, behind the bar, the final stage. Darren pumped foamy beer into a bucket. Then into a pint glass. Emptied the glass. Another. Held it up to the light. Inspected it. Then another. Inspected that. Then another, and suddenly it was clear, with a head on top of it like an old bloke's curly hair.

'Cracked it,' he said again.

14

A big potted plant in the hotel foyer, so smart and shapely it could have been plastic, but wasn't. Dawn felt the dripping of the rain from her coat was a give-away, as if the sort of people who belonged in here would be immune to such things as weather.

She went up to the desk. There was a young girl on duty, carefully made up to match the potted plant, with beautiful eyebrows. She was wearing a crisp white blouse and little grey jacket, making Dawn feel all the wetter.

'Got soaked just coming from the taxi,' Dawn told her. 'It started bucketing down.'

The receptionist gave a cool little nod and smile, her mouth a tiny bit agape to show pearly teeth. She looked just like she was saying, Taxi? Pull the other one. Dawn nearly explained about the way the taxi had dropped her off a distance away because the traffic had got itself into a standstill. She opened her mouth to say it but stopped herself. Too much information. She closed her mouth again. Now I look even more like a fish.

'Can I help?' the girl asked, looking her up and down, noting, Dawn suddenly realised, the absence of an overnight bag. I'm undressed without one, she thought, and suddenly wanted to laugh for the second time, but edgily, one of those edgy laughs that are made of similar stuff to a scream. She felt a hot flush hit her cheeks, run down her neck, across her boobs, the first for years.

'I've got an appointment with one of your guests,' Dawn told her, taking a grip on her red face, forcing her voice to be as business-like as possible, all shakiness resisted.

'Oh yes?'

'Mr Green. A Mr Green.' Bugger, why'd I say the *a*, like he could have been Mr Blue or Mr Yellow for all I know – like he was only Mr Green by the skin of his teeth. Give myself away at every turn, trying to be casual. 'I think he's in room . . .' She pushed her hand past the wet lips of her coat pocket and pulled out the bit of paper Tim had written his number on.

'Two-oh-seven,' the girl said.

Dawn adjusted her specs on her nose, then read from the paper as if the girl hadn't spoken: 'Two-oh-seven.' She did it to show she wouldn't be put off her stride, but it misfired like everything else, made her look deaf on top of red.

'Shall I call him for you?' The receptionist rested her hand on her phone.

'No, I'll find my way. He is expecting me.' Dawn smiled firmly at her. You could pack quite a lot of punch in a smile, something you learned in the pub game. She'd smiled big stroppy blokes into submission in her time. The important thing was to keep your smile as fake as possible.

As she got into the groove she felt her hotness evaporate. Stupid to worry about stupid things, like what a girl with eyebrows thinks you're up to. Today's the day my brother Keith died, forty years ago. What does anything else matter?

Even while she thought that, she had a pang of guilt at using Keith. Using him to make herself feel better about being suspected of an assignation.

It wasn't that she was ashamed of getting up to anything, or rather of being thought to be about to get up to something. It was that she was so old to be accused of such shenanigans. Ancient and withered and past it. Even Frank didn't fancy her any more.

The horrible word Tim had used when his foot caught fire came into her mind: slag, old slag.

'Lift's over there,' the girl said, pointing. Dawn walked in the direction of her point. If only your body didn't have a back, she wished. If only your bottom wasn't the last thing you had to show when you walked away: what poor design that was.

Frankie switched off his welding torch. A white glow hovered in the air for a moment, the after-image.

Frankie bent down towards the fire and sniffed it, like you might sniff a newly opened bottle of wine or a meal you'd just cooked. 'That should hold,' he said.

'Nice one,' Frank told him.

Frankie took off his goggles. His hair sprang out all of a sudden, released from the thick strap. He looked like a sunflower with a face in the middle. Frank recalled Little Weed in the old Bill and Ben programmes and grunted out a laugh before he could stop himself.

Frankie gave one of those smiles that ask 'What?'

I keep doing this, Frank thought, give him an excuse to make a pass at me.

Maybe that's what I want him to do?

He always thought what went on with Pete was separate, nothing to do with anything else, except maybe flying ducks. It was a little box in his life he got into from time to time, a box the shape of an old open-top jeep that Pete had parked out on the flat land somewhere, with water close by and the light beginning to fade.

Nothing to do with anything else. With anywhere else. With anybody else.

But perhaps that was wishful thinking. Perhaps he was exactly what Frankie thought he was, a retired sailor-boy, a bit of rough you did a favour for if you were that way inclined, hoping for something back.

And perhaps that was what he, Frank, really wanted to be.

No, surely not. He'd thought about Katie in the pub just today. I can prove it, he thought. He tried to summon a nude Katie back into his head but she wouldn't materialise.

And what about Dawn? He hadn't had sex with her ever since that nonsense with Pete started up. He told himself it was guilt that had put an obstacle in his way, but maybe he was deluding himself, making an excuse so as to seem more of a good guy in his own eyes, or at least not such a bad one. Maybe he just didn't fancy her any more.

He ought to have the honesty to face up to what he'd done, who he'd turned out to be, after all these years. Maybe he'd joined the navy in the first place because he had leanings. Tiverton was a landlocked town, no sea-going tradition there. Then he'd spent his career trying to kid himself.

Frankie was still looking, still smiling.

'All right,' Frank said to him, his voice coming out husky, half because he was unwilling, half the opposite, because he was interested, or believed he might be. 'All right then. What do I owe you?'

He took a step forward.

Frankie held his smile steady, and his gaze.

Frank kept up eye contact in return. It reminded him of arm-wrestling on board ship, one of the old codgers telling him that you didn't win with your arm, you won with your eye, that's why boxers stare each other out at the weigh-in, because that was where the bout could be won or lost. It's your eyes not your arms you're wrestling with, the old codger told him. All the muscle is in the look.

Frankie carried on looking straight back. Bloody hell, Frank thought, here we go.

Frankie said, 'Are you suggesting what I think you're suggesting?'

There was a silence.

'Are you?' Frankie asked again.

'Might be. Don't you want to come on board?' Frank's voice had got a wobble in it now. But he kept his eyes steady.

So did Frankie.

Then Frankie said, 'Know what I like?'

'No. What do you like?'

'What I like, I like oral sex.'

'Do you then?' Frank slowly nodded his head, as much as to say, oral sex, OK, I can cope with that. But he kept his eyes steady, rolling them up to compensate while his face was down, as if his eyeballs were bearings on which his head turned.

'Yes, that's what I like.'

There was a silence. They still looked. Frank had to blink, but he did it extra quick so it wouldn't break his gaze.

'And do you know what oral sex is?' Frankie asked.

Frank felt himself blush. My age, he thought, and he thinks I might never have heard of it. Then he realised that the blush might look like he was turned on at the prospect. So be it, maybe he was. No point any more in holding back. Might as well go for it.

'Yep,' he said. It was almost like the red on his face had drifted outwards, like a pink mist was shimmering in the air between them. Frankie's thin face was peering back through the haze from the middle of its sunflower. 'I know what it is,' Frank said.

'What oral sex is,' Frankie said, 'is not having sex, just talking about it. That's what oral sex is.'

'I'll tell you about breathing,' Alan said.

'Oh yes?' Thomas asked. Leave me alone, he thought, I've got to have time to think. No, not think exactly: emote. Or at least, run through my emotions, work out which ones are churning around inside, what they signify, how they should be dealt with.

Perverse really. Why was he in the Old Spring at all if not for the human voice – even Alan's voice? This was the day Julian died. The day he, Thomas, had seen poor Romesh lying at death's door. Breathing was a good topic for the evening's agenda.

The breathing in question was coming from the man who had been waiting for his pint. His wife had finally received it from Darren, taking it in both hands like a communion cup and bearing it off to her husband. It occurred to Thomas he couldn't recall her buying herself a drink of any kind. He didn't look round but was aware of a snuffling as she arrived at the table, the sort a dog makes while checking up on a new bowl of food.

A high-pitched testy grunt, a moment of silence while a swig was taken. The breathing resumed, slightly faster at first to compensate for the held breath while the drink went down.

'Breathing,' said Alan, shaking his head at the banality and tediousness of the idea. 'In out, in out.'

'Don't knock it,' Jerry said. 'Breathing is good.'

'Breathing is not good, Jerry,' Alan told him. 'Breathing sucks.'

Jerry thought for a moment, retracting his head slightly as if his brain needed to distance itself to get an angle. 'True enough,' he agreed. 'It does. It sucks and it blows, that's the thing about it.' He laughed that wheezy way he always did. 'You know what volume of –'

'I took my daughter to a concert,' Alan told Thomas. 'She was ten at the time, or thereabouts. I thought: I'll give her something to think about.'

Thomas started at the news Alan had a daughter, finished his pint to conceal the recoil. A daughter. Alan. He seemed too dry, too sceptical, too ironic. Thomas was aware of resentment rising inside him like a hiccup. How could a man like that arrive at such an outcome? Why not me, he thought. I'm not sardonic or pessimistic. I don't shake my head at life like Alan does, I say yes to it.

'When you're ready, Darren,' he said by way of proving the point, sliding his pint over the bar.

'Hokey-doke,' Darren said. He'd been full of beans since changing the barrel. 'Tell you what –'

'Make it a jug,' Thomas told him.

'Hokey-doke,' Darren said again. He got a jug and began to fill it. 'You know ghosts?' he asked Thomas.

'Ye-es,' Thomas replied cautiously. From anyone but Darren it could have been a trick question.

'I got a big idea about ghosts when I was down in the cellar.'

'Did you just?'

'Yep.'

'Pint, Darren, please,' said one of the rugby team in the back room, Graham his name, Thomas remembered.

'Just finishing this jug, Gray,' Darren said.

Jake, the blue man, was already standing in the public bar, also waiting to be served, but he said nothing.

'Ghosts, yes,' Darren said. He passed the jug over.

'Thank you, Darren.' Thomas took it and lifted it, offering it to Jerry first.

'Yes, Jake?' Darren asked. 'Be with you in a minute, Gray.' The tattoos had made their silent point.

'Ta,' Jerry said to Thomas, sliding his glass into position. Thomas poured his beer then turned to Alan.

'My poor old liver,' Alan said, as if the offer were just a malicious health threat. Thomas poured.

'First sign of liver problems,' Jerry said, 'the palms of your hands go red.'

'I thought that was the first sign of crucifixion,' Alan said, holding his glass up to toast Thomas and implicate him in the sacrilege.

How can I preen myself on my yes to life, Thomas wondered, when it was me who so manifestly said no, so definitively, so long ago? Poverty, chastity, obedience, words with No built into them. No, no, no. In his head the negatives resounded hollowly, like Mrs Thatcher dismissing Europe or society.

Of course, the other side of those coins was Yes yes yes, yes to spiritual riches, yes to devotion to God, yes to acting out the word. But none of that produces a daughter of one's own. Unless one can perform alchemy like Julian, and transmogrify spirit to flesh and flesh to spirit. By making all things holy, to channel holiness into all things.

Tears rose into Thomas's eyes. It wasn't just that Julian wrote poems on the subject – he personified it, in his large, immediate, warm presence. He showed how the cold abstractions of the life everlasting could become intimate and mortal. And being mortal, he had died.

I can't afford to have lost him, Thomas thought. He took a pull at his beer. I need him so much.

'I wanted her to hear Beethoven's Choral Symphony,' Alan explained. 'So there we were, with the massed ranks of the orchestra, several choirs, and these ten-tonne soloists who had been flown in from all parts. But a couple of rows behind us there was a breather, just like that man there.' He turned and gave a nod towards the table where the man and his wife were sitting. Thomas turned too, as discreetly as possible, feeling it was rude to do so, rude not to. The couple weren't conversing. The woman with a bun was just sitting watching her husband drink his beer as if he was a television programme. His face looked loose and veiny, entropic.

'I could hear him rasping in and out during the first three movements,' Alan went on, turning back to the bar, 'in out, in out. Sucking and blowing, as Jerry so gracefully put it.'

'Alan doesn't like to face facts,' Jerry told Thomas.

'I faced facts that night, sure enough,' Alan said. 'Or at least I had my back to them. Suck, blow, for half an hour solid. I consoled myself with the thought that when we got to the final movement it would be drowned out. The most sublime sound known to man. I wanted my daughter to hear what human beings were capable of.'

'Beethoven was stone deaf when he wrote that piece,' Jerry said.

'Lucky old him,' Alan remarked. 'Anyway, there they were, going all out, the fat lady singing her butt off, the brasses going hell for leather, the conductor nearly giving himself apoplexy, and there, rising above the whole concatenation: hee haw hee haw, the perishing breather carried on with his breathing. That's what filled my ears. That's what my daughter heard.'

'Tertiary emphysema, it sounds like,' Jerry said.

'I'll tell you something,' Alan said, 'tertiary emphysema can drown out the music of the spheres any day of the week.'

Jake passed a pint to Nick. How come, he thought, I give him twenty fucking quid's worth of dope then have to buy his fucking beer for him on top?

'Cheers,' Nick said.

Fuck your fucking job, Jake thought. 'Cheers,' he said back, and swigged some pint. 'Nice pint,' he said, it being a new barrel of Buckman's.

'Beer I like is Davenport's,' Nick said. 'Midlands beer, brewed in Birmingham. That's my idea of a nice light pint.' He took a pull of his beer and pulled a face like it was some fucking medicine he had to get down.

If you don't fucking like what I got you, why don't you fucking give it me back? Jake asked him in his head. You must be the only bloke in the whole sodding country who thinks Birmingham's the best place to brew beer.

'So,' Nick said. He did a small burp on to the back of his hand, then inspected where it had been like it might have left a trace. 'The job. Tomorrow.'

So I'm not sacked, big bloody deal, Jake thought, inspecting his pint. He switched it from his love hand to his hate hand, but Nick took no notice. I must have spent more on not getting the bum's rush, Jake realised, than what the job is paying me in the first fucking place.

'You can do the main walloping,' Nick said.

'The main walloping?'

'Yep. You can do the main walloping. While you're doing that I'll be getting on with the signage. I give the board a quick coat this afternoon, while the rain wasn't coming down too bad, so I can get straight on with it tomorrow. It's going to be a similar job like what I done on the side of my van. I got to write Pie-Eyed, plus a picture of a pie.'

'Pie-Eyed? What is it when it's home, a fucking boozer?'

'No, pie shop. It's like a joke. The gaffer bloke, he comes from up north, Manchester way. He had this pie shop up there, so he thought he'd start one down here. Pies and cold meat, and sandwiches and whatnot. He said I could choose my pie. What pie I paint on the shop front.'

'You want to paint a pasty on it, down this area.'

'But that's the thing. They're all pasties here, in't they? That's why he's gone for pie. Makes it a bit different. I mean he's still going to sell pasties, along with the other stuff, but he's not going to emphasise it. "You come in the shop and want a pasty, a pasty you can have," he said to me. "That's my standpoint on the subject," he said. So I give it some thought and I thought I'd go for pork, a pork pie. I mean, to paint. Maybe seen partly from above, like tilted a bit.'

Jake visualised it for a moment. 'You could paint a pair of eyes on the top of it,' he suddenly said. 'A pair of eyes going boss-eyed. That would do the trick.'

Nick gave him a look as much as to say, don't muscle in on my painting, mate.

*

Dawn got into the lift. It was quite a small one – licensed for three persons, it said on the plate. Eyebrows, pah! she told the receptionist (told her in her head). Also: potted plant, pah! as well. A three-person lift, what's that about? A piddling little metal box was all it was.

One good thing, it had the same carpeting on the floor as the rest of the hotel reception, one of those hardworking oatmeal types, Berber maybe. Maybe bought from Romesh, who knows?

Quick, before anyone else comes along, especially a fat bloke, press the button for level 2.

Just as the doors began to close, a peculiar thought came into Dawn's head. This little bit of hall carpet she was stood on was a flying carpet in its own right. Father Thomas had told her about Romesh flying up from his hospital bed. That must have been a lovely event for a man who'd been in the business his whole life long, a bit like a railway worker getting complimentary train tickets. But he'd come back down to earth with a bang by the time she visited, poor man. From what the Father had said about Romesh's state, his carpet must have nose-dived more or less straight off. First crashes his car, then his carpet, poor Romesh.

As the lift began to rise Dawn had a picture in her head of this square of carpet, detached from the rest like a turf cut from a lawn, flying up up up through the floors, and then down down down again to join up to all the rest of the carpeting once more. And here I am, flying with it, she thought, here I am standing on it while it flies. She felt like one of those surfers she'd seen at the Cornish seaside once upon a time, balanced on the waves and standing for the duration of their ride more or less in mid-air, in a nowhere place. In the solitude of the lift box Dawn raised her arms each side, though they would only go up part way because of the narrow width.

She had it all prepared what she was going to tell Tiger Tim. Get stuffed, it boiled down to. The nine hundred pounds had been found.

They'd been paying Darren from the main till, but budgeted for him from the filled roll money. The other staff wages came out of the main till anyhow, which was then recompensed from Dawn and Frank's income automatically because of written IOUs put in with the takings, but they'd decided young Darren was an extra, on trial, and as such they'd pay him from their private stash. Then they'd forgotten. It was Frank who'd got into the habit of taking the cash from the till to give him, but she'd seen him do it and not reminded him, so it was her fault too. They'd remembered just enough to not put in IOUs, which would have solved the whole problem.

True enough, it was their mistake, the two of them. But the important thing was they could account for the money, every penny of it. None had gone astray. All they had to do to make it right was switch between budgets.

They had what they needed: a logical explanation. To all intents and purposes, they were in the clear. No one could accuse them of siphoning off the till.

Frank didn't even know as yet: she hadn't had time to tell him. But anyhow he didn't take things so hard, Frank didn't. He hadn't got his knickers in a twist about Tim Green or Mr Banks. He coped with what life threw at him, which was the nature of the man.

Tim was a little worm: that was her mindset when she got into the lift. In point of fact it was her mindset when she got out of it again, but there was one important difference.

She had intended to tell him so. She had looked forward to giving him a horrible shock. She had imagined him coming creepily towards her across the carpeting of his bedroom, probably in stockinged feet given the disaster that had happened to his shoe, but still smooth and dapper, which was his style, all ready for action; and then her saying: stop right there, sonny boy.

Better still, giving him a come-on for a moment or two, before saying it. Pointing her mouth at him, opening her arms, just as if.

Getting the timing right in that respect had actually turned her on. To catch him out for the second time in succession, that would prove something. That would prove she could wrap a bloke round her little finger, even at her age. The thought of letting him be all worked up, then puncturing it, made her heart thump. The shock of power.

But somehow, in her ride in the lift, a new idea came into her head.

15

When Tim opened the door of his room he was a different Tim from what Dawn expected. Specs part way down his nose. Little stoop. Tie loosened, collar opened, but not in a sexy way, more like getting down to business.

How can you loosen your tie one way and not another, Dawn wondered. Well, Tim could. He was an expert at wearing clothes, could put any woman to shame.

Behind him there was a light on at a little desk that sure enough had the pub's books on it. She got an impression of a big dim bed beyond the pool of light, like a great big huge ostrich egg that wasn't yet ready to hatch, biding its time.

Even Tim's face looked the part. Those fine lines round his eyes, on his cheeks and forehead, looked as if they had been caused by concentration. You would think he spent ten hours a day with his face squinched up over figures. Come to think of it he probably did.

You clever old sod, Dawn thought admiringly. You know exactly what you're up to. Everything serious, grown up, responsible: a world away from any notion of hanky-panky. Let's address your problem, Dawn. Let's get the books sorted.

Make me trust him. Get me grateful. Take it from there.

She glanced down, very quickly so he wouldn't think she was inspecting his crotch. Sure enough, stockinged feet. Of course he would have, after that shoe went up in flames. He clocked her downward look. What he was thinking was: she looked down and up so fast because she wanted to look at my crotch without letting on she was looking at my crotch.

The fact that she could see exactly what was in his mind made a tide of sexiness rise up in her so fast her head span, and she nearly let out a sigh or groan on the spot. She could feel the sudden heat around her eyes, her ears. It was like he had every reason to think he was in charge, that he was playing her like a fish on a line. But really she was on top, she was playing games with *him*, with more games in store, up her sleeve. The effect of knowing that made her feel wild and free.

'Come in, come in,' he said, 'and welcome.'

'Thank you, Tim.' As she went past him through the door, she sensed him looking up and down the corridor, an automatic look to check unwanted passers-by, and her heart fluttered even more.

He shut the door. 'The good news, Dawn, is I reckon I can see a way for us through all this.'

'Me coat's sodden,' Dawn told him.

'Oh. Take it off. Of course.'

'Good-oh. I'd put it on the bed, but don't want to get it wet.' Said it, said bed. Gotcha, she thought, that puts me in front.

'I'll take it, not to worry.'

She handed it over to him, brushed her hands down the front of her skirt. 'Nice room,' she said. She turned full circle on the spot to take it all in, bed included. 'Very nice, like you said it would be.'

He hung her coat up on a hook behind the door, and looked round the room himself. 'Yes,' he said, 'they always do me well.'

'Glad to hear it.'

'Well, I do them a few favours from time to time. You know how it works.'

Yep, thought Dawn, a nod is as good as a wink. I know how it works.

'I thought,' Tim said, suddenly brisk, wanting to cut through all the suggestiveness, show he was a serious customer, 'we'd get down to work then treat ourselves to a drink a bit later, when we've got it sorted.'

Dawn gave him a cool look, giving nothing away.

'Just a little bit of finesse, as they call it,' he said. 'Then all your troubles will be over. Take my word.' She still just looked at him, saying nowt. 'Unless you want one now,' he finished awkwardly. 'A drink, I mean. Got wet. Come in out of the weather. Might need a warmer.' Like as if he was correcting himself: 'A *winter* warmer. Yes.' He nodded his head as if he was agreeing with that. 'I got a nice minibar. All ready to go.'

'Tell you what,' Dawn said, 'I think I've got it licked.'

Tim did a little jolt at the word. 'What? What have you got? Licked?'

'The nine hundred pound. I know where it went.'

He stood rigid, as if someone had dropped an ice cube down his neck. Slowly the expression on his face changed. Dawn had the hang of those thin creases of his now, what they were for. They were there so chunks of his face could sort of fold over and reassemble, like when you did one of those Rubik's cubes. A new expression appeared, this one younger than ever, a schoolboy's expression, all petulant and fed up, one of those schoolboys that gets the worst of it but won't hit back, just chunters to himself.

I'm thinking of my Keith again, Dawn thought, him and his friends. Those are the only schoolboys I knew, except those that've come into the pubs I've run over the years and tried to order a drink. But I know enough about schoolboys to know there's always one in every bunch of them that gets put upon and looks all sullen and hurt, also mutters to himself.

Keith hadn't been that sort of boy at all, Keith would do his best to fight back, skin and bones but what he was.

Tim here isn't Keith come back. Nor a messenger from Keith. Tim is just a tit from the brewery whose number I've got. Simple as that.

And what I'm going to get up to in this hotel room has nothing to do with Keith. For once in my life I'm going to stay free of him. Nor has it got anything to do with Frank, bless his heart. Except him not giving me any gives me the right to get some somewhere else, far as I can see.

For once in my life what I'm going to get up to is on my own behalf, not tied to anybody else.

It seemed the wickedest and most exciting idea she'd ever had.

'Bloody hell,' Jerry said in a hoarse voice.

'I beg your pardon?' Thomas asked.

'Sorry Father,' Jerry said, nodding through him, so to speak, in Alan's direction. 'Look who's just walked in,' he asked Alan.

Alan looked round. 'Bloody Colin the Coach,' he said glumly, turning back to his pint.

'What you mean?' Jerry asked. 'Oh, bloody hell, not Colin the Coach.'

'Sorry to tell you,' Alan replied. 'It's him all right.'

Thomas looked over his shoulder. Yes, it was Colin sure enough, extraordinarily spick and span in his blazer, his hair brushed flat, looking as if he'd just been belched out of some Colin-machine somewhere, brand-new.

'No, what I mean, that's not who I meant. What bloody use is bloody Colin?'

'Fair point,' Alan said.

'Hello, Colin,' said Nigel from the shove-ha'penny board. 'Didn't expect you in tonight.' He sounded pleased.

'Her,' Jerry whispered urgently. 'Bloody *her*.' He pointed bluntly, with a nod of his head. Thomas was aware that his own head and Alan's turned in sync to see. A couple of women were arriving at a table in the corner, pink-faced with air and rain, taking their outer clothes off in a flurry.

'Oh, *her*,' Alan said. He paused, just long enough. 'Which one?' A specialist in lethal timing: Thomas could imagine him clinching lectures.

'Bloody hell,' Jerry said. He seemed to bury his face in his beer.

'Well, I'm not psychic.'

'I described her to you on the way.' Jerry suddenly looked disorganised, unravelling.

'Oh yes, you did. Telephones, wasn't it?' Alan glanced back vaguely as if hoping to spot telephones.

'*Telephones*? What the bloody hell you on about?'

'Forties hairdo, didn't you say?' He cupped each ear. 'Telephones.'

'I did not say bloody telephones. I said she had curly hair with a parting and a dress with padded shoulders.'

Alan looked. 'They both have curly hair,' he said.

The two women had hung their coats on nearby pegs and were settling themselves at the table. They seemed slightly large to Thomas, both of them, but that might have been due to the bustle of coming into the pub. One had blonde hair, cut nicely at jaw length, the other dark, nearly black, just down to the base of her ears.

'Fuck me,' Jerry said. He was vibrating with tension.

'Blonde or brunette?'

'Bloody blonde, what you think?'

'OK, OK, you better go over to meet and greet. She came at your invitation, after all.'

'No, she didn't.'

'Yes, she did.'

'No she didn't.'

'What do you mean? Do you think it's just coincidence?' Again Thomas noticed the care with which Alan handled his words, making sure each retained a cutting edge.

'There's two of them.'

'Yes. Well?'

'So she didn't come to see me.'

'She came with her friend for protection, that's all.' Alan now scratched his head, and then resumed as if talking to a child: 'You go over and sit with them. If all goes well, girl number one will give girl number two a secret nod, unbeknownst to you. When things have been ticking over for twenty minutes or so, and you've nearly got to the end of your first drink. Then girl number two will remember she's got to be off somewhere, and bingo.'

There was a pause, as if this information was too complex for Jerry to digest straightaway.

'Women, really,' Thomas said, to fill the gap.

'Yep. Women,' Alan replied with some satisfaction. It obviously gave him pleasure, how predictable people were.

'No, I didn't mean women in that sense.'

This time it was Alan who paused, reflected. 'How many senses are there?'

'I meant, not girls. They're not really girls.'

Jerry glanced nervously across at them, as if to check. It had been the wrong point to make, Thomas realised. Women were an even more challenging proposition for him than girls would be. You could see it on his face, what a difficult word that was, women.

'Go,' Alan said. 'Before one of them gets up to buy the drinks. Get over there and ask them what they're having.'

'I'm just finish –'

'Go.'

Jerry went. Thomas watched him go. Despite his unwillingness he was oddly light on his feet, as if on tiptoe. Thomas almost expected him to do that deft flick of the legs, the skip you almost don't see, that happens in one of the ballroom dances, foxtrot possibly, noted while he and the Brothers watched *Strictly Come Dancing* on a Saturday evening, Julian avidly egging on the winners and losers.

'Good,' Alan said. 'Now I've nursemaided him, I can bugger off.'

Immediately, Thomas felt disappointed, and then, as if that sensation opened some crevice in the dam, panic. What choice would he have, but to go too? Back to De La Tour House in the night-time rain, concocting some excuse for his long absence while the others had been grieving. Back to a sudden space where Julian used to be.

'There's more beer in the jug,' he said.

Alan shook his head, shrugged his shoulders, held his glass out. 'All right then. But I've got a wife and kids waiting for me at home.' Perhaps in lieu of emotions, Alan needed to enrich his own every move with contradiction. He breathed irony in and out with each breath: irony of the world, in; irony of his own take on that world, out. Suck and blow, that was what he'd said he resented, the naivety of that process; obviously he had to complicate it in order to achieve sufficient challenge or dignity.

Even rank untruth would fit the bill. 'Well, one kid, to be exact,' he added, sighing. He could whimsy a second daughter into brief existence, as if to show how undemanding reproduction essentially was, how an intelligent man hardly needed to concentrate, could lose count, even on a count of one.

Thomas poured. 'One more than I have,' he said ruefully.

'I don't know about that, Father,' Alan said, emphasising the word Father, as if, at some cunning level of his cunning brain, he intuited Thomas's own lie. Thomas felt the injustice of it swell in his chest. It was Alan, it was all of them, who had refused to take on board he was a lay-brother, not a priest, it was Alan and co. who had discarded that distinction as a mere technicality. He felt he'd fallen into a trap.

'Blow me,' Frank said, walking in with his revamped fire in his arms. 'What you doing here, Colin?'

Claire just sat and watched while Daniel harrumphed his beer. Even though he didn't have a moustache she was reminded, as his eyes focused on the rising glass and his lips lined up on the rim, of a walrus about to catch a flung cod.

The looseness of his face, the looseness his face now had, maybe that was it. Small eyes peering greedily out.

Perhaps walruses had loose faces. She tried to visualise one but all she could recall was a seal, elegant in its tight black DJ. But it was a walrus that came to mind. Maybe just the word.

She couldn't have a drink herself nowadays, when she brought him out for one. It felt like meanness, like not being able to kiss back after an argument, but she simply couldn't bring herself to. The chink of glasses, the simultaneous sipping: that was to do with being equals, husband and wife. It implied something that was now no longer true. And any kiss she gave him would be a motherly peck on his flabby cheek. That was the point, motherly was how she felt. To drink with him would be like a parent eating jelly and cake at a toddlers' party.

Frank fixed his attention straight on to Colin. Reason: he didn't want to inspect Darren, who he could see out of the corner of his eye more or less standing to attention. It wasn't fair on the lad to call him to account straight off.

Not that Frank trusted him, exactly. It was more that he *didn't* trust him, in point of fact, didn't trust him to have handled everything smoothly. Darren wasn't a smooth type of a boy. Said himself he was a bit of a vortex, whatever that was when it was at home. Frank visualised a buffeting wind, blowing things headlong.

Also, Frank had remembered that the Buckman's was getting low in the barrel. It had seeped into the back of his mind while Frankie was doing his spot welding, just at the very moment Frank was fearing the worst, waiting for Frankie to finish what he was doing and say, 'What now?'

It had almost been a consolation, to have something usual to worry about. It was like a tale Pete had told him. One of his Traveller friends, over in Norfolk, was a pig-killer on demand. People called him in from time to time to do the business, people who had maybe just the one animal of their own: a freezer pig. One day something went a bit wrong and the pig being done slithered out of the Traveller bloke's hands just when its throat was halfway cut, and rushed madly about the yard squealing and bleeding. Then in the middle of all its woe it suddenly noticed a tuft of grass growing in among the cobbles and trotted over to have a nibble.

'Don't let anyone tell you pigs are clever,' Pete had said. But Frank thought there *was* something clever about it, the way the animal remembered that it needed to eat to live, remembered what life was like even in its death-throes. Same about pub-worries: even the blumming nine hundred quid had the benefit of familiarity, also was like a dry worry, the sort you just had in your head.

The point was, as far as the barrel was concerned, that Darren might have tried to change it, or that he might not have. Less than ideal, either way. Could be a mess in the cellar, or a load of edgy customers. No bigger sin in the licensed trade, withholding booze from punters who want it. Dawn had a story about her old man, opened his pub the evening her poor brother got himself killed on his bicycle, for fear he would lose trade if not.

The funny thing was Frank didn't want to catch Darren out. In the navy he'd never understood the satisfaction some of the officers got from finding out what one poor old dopey rating or other had cocked up, going through his actions with a fine-tooth comb, bringing every half-witted thing to light. Frank preferred to gloss things over a little. That's what got on Dawn's nerves about him. Anything for an easy life, you, she'd told him more than once. Ride with the punches, was his way of putting it.

Colin looked up like as if he'd been caught out doing something he shouldn't be doing. 'Just going to play a game of shove-ha'penny with Nigel here,' he said, putting his hand on Nigel's shoulder.

'That's right,' Nigel said. Nigel was a pale complexioned middle-aged bloke, silver hair, well-worn business-type suit. He looked strange nodding his head like a schoolboy trying to convince his teacher. 'We're just going to have ourselves a game.'

'No,' Frank said. He stepped over to the grate and put the fire basket down. Frankie stepped up towards the grate as well. Frank had the awkward sensation of people looking at the two of them, wondering who his new pal was. Nothing to hide, Frank told himself. Nothing whatsoever. 'What I meant,' he explained to Colin, 'I thought you would be home tucked up in bed, getting your beauty sleep. Haven't you got to catch your plane to Hamburg first off? Crack of dawn, like?'

Colin sniffed twice, loudly, as if buying time.

Suddenly Jerry piped up, catching Frank on the hop. He wasn't standing at the bar with his old buddy Alan, but was sitting at the corner table with a couple of women Frank didn't know. 'Home of fast food,' Jerry said. He turned to the two women. 'A hamburger isn't a burger made of ham,' he told them, 'like people think.' The women looked politely interested. 'They imagine there's been some kind of misunderstanding, and change it to beefburger.'

Jerry laughed in that way of his and shook his head at the folly of it. 'It's a common fallacy,' he went on. The women nodded politely, like to say, oh yes, we suffered from that common fallacy ourselves. Thing about Jerry, he was a bloke who knew so much he couldn't guess any longer what other people knew and what they didn't know.

'Maybe ham *is* the German word for beef,' Nigel suggested. He went suddenly paler still, as if his brain had been turned up to maximum.

Jerry turned back towards him and Colin. 'What hamburgers are is a kind of beef patty that originated in Hamburg,' he told them sternly, along with everybody else. It was odd to see him taking command of the whole room, as though he was conducting an orchestra. Nothing like having women to impress.

Colin stuck his bottom lip out and nodded, like the women had done.

Over at the bar, Alan said in a bored voice: 'And hot dogs are a sausage sandwich that originated on the Isle of Dogs during the sweltering summer of 1976.'

Colin looked round at him and nodded again. Nigel looked too, and nodded also.

'Piss off, Alan,' Jerry said. One of the women sitting with him giggled.

'You want to go to the Isle of Dogs,' Nigel told Colin, 'when you've done Hamburg.'

'Yes,' Alan added, 'and after that you could take a trip to the leaning tower of Pizza.' He had a way of saying a word as if he'd just taken the wrapping off it. That's how he said *Pizza*.

'Hello Father,' Frank said, noticing him standing beyond Alan. 'Still here then?'

'Hello,' Father said. 'Yes,' he replied. He gave a sheepish smile. Stupid, Frank told himself, making a punter feel bad just for being a punter. 'This is Frankie,' he said to the Father, but loud enough for the bar as a whole to hear. Father welcoming Frankie would make him above board, the point. 'Frankie welded the fire for me. He's come in for a drink.'

'Hello Frankie,' Father said. 'Job well done. A fire makes a pub.' There were murmurs of agreement from round the room. 'Specially on a day like this.'

Frankie opened his hands out and shrugged his shoulders, like he was Tommy Cooper saying, Just like that.

'I thought what a fire made was the place where bad folks go,' Alan said.

'Hey there, Darren,' Frank said at last. 'How's it going?'

'It's going good,' Darren told him.

'How's the Buckman's going then?'

'Went.'

'Thought it would.'

'Stuck a new barrel on.'

'Did you now?'

'Yep.'

'And?'

'Try it.' Darren passed over a little sample glass ready poured.

'On the ball, Darren,' Frank said, surprised at his speed of service. He held the shot glass up to the light. Clear as crystal. Then swigged it in one. 'Nice,' he said.

'Top hole,' Alan said.

'Good lad,' Frank told Darren. Darren trotted to the end of the bar and back again, as if praise was something you had to burn off. He shook his fists back and forth like he was shaking invisible maracas.

Frank put the grate down on the hearth, and Frankie helped him push it into place.

'Tell me about the lad behind the bar,' Frankie asked, while their heads were close together.

'Darren?'

'He looks so young, yet on top of his brief. I like that combination. Does he have a you-know-what?'

'Darren?'

'Nuff said.'

Frank pushed the fire into its place as noisily as possible, hoping the noise would be rough and annoying enough to cover up the words Frankie had already said, just in case anyone had been listening. Luckily Alan didn't look like he'd picked up anything.

Alan turned back to face the bar. Thomas turned back too. Alan leaned his head sideways towards him. It was odd to feel intimacy from such a difficult man.

Come to think, it was odd to feel intimacy from anybody. Even Julian hadn't been intimate, just exuberant in his commendations of it.

It struck Thomas that when you were near enough, you could detect waves or ripples from another person's body, as a sensitive enough seismograph might register the tiniest or deepest of earthquakes.

'Brought his toyboy with him,' Alan said *sotto voce*.

'What?' Thomas asked.

'Frank. His toyboy.'

Thomas took half a step sideways. So much for recording the ripples of intimacy, he thought, it was just Alan leaning in to confide something spiteful. Frank had gone into the public so he could get through the bar flap and pour Frankie a drink. Behind the partition he was asking Jake how he did.

'What on earth are you saying?' Thomas asked Alan.

'Don't you think?' Alan asked back. 'What about the way he calls men "m'dear"? Probably not you, of course, being a man of the cloth.'

In fact Frank did call Thomas that. It was one of the things Thomas liked about the Old Spring, part of its warmth. It had always struck him as just quaint, a component of Frank's west country accent. Even Jake was m'dear.

'No,' Thomas said. Then, impatiently: 'No!'

'Suit yourself,' Alan said coolly. Then he leaned over again. 'But how come his little friend has a hairstyle like his whole head's being flambéed.'

Thomas couldn't stop a sudden guilty laugh.

Frank rolled up on the other side of the bar, right in front of them. 'What'll you have then?' he asked in a carrying voice, looking between them. Thomas glanced over to follow his gaze. Frankie was testing the spars of the fire to see if his welding had taken. 'Buckman's?'

'No thank you,' Frankie said. 'Jimmy Beam, if that's OK.'

'On the rocks?'

'Just one rock.'

'So,' Alan said in a normal voice, as if continuing an earlier conversation. 'I started to compose recipes in honour of famous figures of history.'

'Did you then?' Despite himself Thomas liked the sense of being a conspirator. What a thought – perhaps the easiest communion to achieve was of bad faith, of badness in point of fact.

'My masterpiece was *truite à la Marie Antoinette*.'

'Oh yes?'

Just in front of Thomas, Frank plinked the one cube into Frankie's drink.

'Simple enough recipe.' Alan said. 'Trout with its head cut off, stuffed with cake.'

'Dawn not back yet?' Frank asked Darren.

'Not yet.'

'I'm going to get the fire going.'

'Oh.'

'So you carry on behind the bar for the time being, OK?'

'Oh, right.'

First off when Frank said about getting the fire going, Darren was disappointed, wanting to do it himself. Then when Frank said carry on behind the bar, he was chuffed as hell but made his face carry on remembering being disappointed a couple of seconds before so it wouldn't show. He felt like if he let on how pleased he was, Frank would change his mind. He might think there was something dodgy about him liking doing it so much.

Katie came in. 'How do, Darren?' she said. She didn't seem surprised he was behind the bar. Maybe I'm getting a barman type look on me, Darren thought. There was a swirl of scent hanging pinkly in the air round her. She was wearing a jumper that made her tits look soft and woollen. 'Is that arsehole in?' she asked Darren.

'Yep,' Darren told her. 'He's in the lounge.'

'With the other arseholes, I suppose.'

'Yep.'

'I think the collective noun is a congeries,' Alan told her.

'That so?' She looked at Alan like he was something the cat coughed up. 'Hello Frank,' she suddenly said very loudly, as though she had eyes in the back of her head. Frank was over by the fireplace, handing the Jim Beam to the fire bloke, Frankie, and he nearly dropped it in surprise. He looked back towards Katie's back like she was a ghost. 'Hello Katie,' he said in a small voice.

'Like for a pub rugby team?' Darren asked Alan.

'M'dear,' Frank added in Katie's direction, like delayed action, like he felt it wasn't enough just saying *Hello Katie*, especially as her voice had been so loud. He did a sort of wave in her direction but Katie still didn't turn to look at him. Frank's face had gone bright red, like he'd lit his fire already. The Frankie bloke did a little smile as he took a swig of his Jim Beam.

'No,' Alan told Darren, 'like for a bunch of arseholes.'

Jerry came over to buy drinks for himself and his lady friends.

'I went diving once upon a time,' Darren told Alan, getting Jerry's drinks. 'This instructor bloke warned us about the danger of conger eels. I know they're not the same thing as a bunch of arseholes but I just remembered about them. Before we went into the water, he warned us.'

'Dangerous beasts, conger eels,' Jerry said. He looked all pleased with himself, like a blown up balloon, like as if the women at his table could hear what he was saying. 'They have their teeth cantilevered backwards so once they bite you, you stay bit.' He held up his hand so it looked like a conger eel's mouth biting, with his fingers and thumb bent inwards towards the palm. He opened and shut it a couple of times, like it was an eel champing at you. 'They can't let you go even if they want to. You have to get them surgically removed.'

Now Katie did quickly glance over her shoulder in Frank's direction. Just at that moment he got on his knees and started laying the fire. Katie turned back. 'Glad to see him kneeling down, anyhow,' she said. 'Excuse me, Father.'

'You're welcome,' Father said.

'I'll have a –' Katie told Darren.

'Dry white wine,' Darren told her.

'I'll get that,' Gray said, coming in from the lounge.

'I'd rather buy my own, thank you very much.'

'Oh, come on, Katie.'

'You stood me up at lunchtime,' Katie told him. 'You sod.'

'No, I just –'

'*And* you got Frank to cover for you.'

Gray was just going to argue, then lowered his hands. 'Who told you?'

'I thought Frank was better than that. I didn't think you were better than that. But I thought Frank was better than that. I thought he was kind and sympathetic.'

'He *is* kind and sympathetic.'

'He is to you. I hope his poxy fire goes out. *Nobody* told me, if you must know. I guessed. I sat at work this arvo, and worked it out. I ticked it off on my fingers till I got to the truth. I even ticked it off on this finger.' She raised her hand and pointed her ring finger at him, with her engagement ring on it. 'More fool me. I worked it out by a process of elimination, just like Sherlock Holmes.'

'More like *Murder, She Wrote*,' Alan said to Father.

Katie gave Alan a harsh look, like he was another thing the cat coughed up, then turned back to Gray. 'And who I eliminated, was you. I wish.'

'Look, Katie, I just –'

'It'll cost you six hundred quid.'

'What will? Will it?'

'For the wedding dress. I was going to discuss it with you. I was going to go all through the finances of our whole wedding day. But being you didn't show, I discussed it with myself. I chose one. The one I wanted. The one I might look quite nice in, even if I *am* marrying a slimy toad. Six hundred. That's what we're spending on it. Agreed?'

Gray went suddenly a bit relaxed, like people do when they've been shot. He looked at Darren as much as to say, get it? Get it? Funny thing was, Darren did get it, as if working behind the bar gave you a pair of X-ray eyes so you could see what the customers were thinking. Gray had gone a bit relaxed because he realised Katie was still going to marry him, that's why, even though he'd been buggering her about, and had fucked off at lunchtime.

'Agreed,' Gray said.

'Good. Darren, that slimy toad there owes you for my wine.'

Darren held his hand out. 'Tell you what, Father,' he said while the slimy toad was getting his money out, 'while I was down in the cellar I –'

Then just at that exact second, of all the people in the whole wide world, into the pub walked Gemma.

Darren stared at her. He'd never seen her outside of the cancer shop before.

The funny thing, the first thing he noticed, apart from her being her, was she didn't have a chicken on top of her head.

16

'What I'm doing here,' Gemma told Darren, 'is seeing you.'

Darren's heart pounded. He'd expected her to say she'd come in here to meet her boyfriend.

Perhaps that's what she *was* saying?

Getting out of the taxi, in front of the Old Spring, Dawn's whole body felt as if it was opened up to the outside world.

The rain was still coming down, a very small type of one. As it touched her cheeks she was reminded of cool lips kissing her, just that light brushing kind of way, and the memory made her feel trembly again.

Stand out here for a moment and have a quick smoke, she thought. Luckily no punters were doing the same, for the time being.

She remembered some words of Shirl's as she lit up: there is nothing in the world like having a completely meaningless shag. Wish I'd discovered that before, Dawn thought. No nine hundred pounds involved, no feeling of guilt about Keith never having had a shag in his short life. Just getting on with it.

Her cigarette made her feel worldy-wise, like she was smoking that way actresses used to do in films, as if smoking wasn't just smoking but a way of thinking about life. Each inhale, narrow your eyes and give a tiny nod of your head, as much as to say, now I've understood that particular thing. Then puff out and wave it away, like you're moving on to another idea.

The rain was lit up by the pub lights and looked like teeming shoals of silver fishes swimming downwards towards the pavement, except where they swam through her puffs of smoke and turned the palest blue. She remembered catching tiddlers, her and Keith as kids, the way they'd be transparent with their little guts showing through.

Not Keith, not now. Not after she'd been up to what she'd been up to. This is now, that was then. Forty years ago exactly he was already dead. Forty years ago exactly she even knew he was dead.

She waved her puff away. Inhaled again so hard she all but swallowed the fag, and then suddenly she seemed to contract down below, and got a tingling shivery feeling as if it was raining inside her, as if little silvery fishes were nibbling her in there. Blimey she thought, I never had an orgasm from pulling on a cigarette before, because that was what it was like, not full-blown but one of those little aftershocks you can get when you've had a good one to start with.

She leaned back against the lintel of the door. If anyone came out she could just say she was having a bit of a turn. Then she chucked her cigarette into the big ashtray her and Frank had installed out there. It fizzed as it hit the water.

She brushed her hands down her coat. That had been a good idea. The wet and the cold and the smoke might have shooshed away the fug of bed she'd probably carried along with her, also the smell of sex. She needed to walk in fresh.

And that's exactly how she felt, now she did walk in, just the damp night air around her like a shawl.

First thing she saw, as she walked into the public: Darren leaning across the bar. Talking to a girl who was perched on a stool, and was talking back in a loud posh voice.

Dawn stopped in her tracks. There was Darren, the last boy on earth able to get himself a girlfriend, with a girlfriend.

No mistaking it: you could tell. He was trembling slightly with excitement as he talked to her. On her stool the girl was a bit higher than him, and that made his eyes, pointing up at her, look like eyes at prayer. His sharp nose poked up towards the girl's face like an arrow waiting to be fired.

Soon as my back is turned, Dawn thought, it changes.

Stupid: what's the matter with me? Am I jealous? Just because I had it away this evening, doesn't mean poor old Darren shouldn't have a bit of romance in his life. I should be glad for him.

On the bench that ran along the outside wall of the public, Jake, drinking his pint, not couth enough to say hello, looking like a stilton that had hung around too long.

Across the bar, beyond the partition in the snug area, Alan and the Father. Father sort of jerked as he clocked her, wanting to speak, but she passed on, into the snug itself, so the two of them would have their backs to her and she'd have a second to get a purchase.

Along the snug wall the shove-ha'penny board was down, with Nigel and Colin playing at it. In the corner, Jerry sitting with a woman. The two of them laughing away.

Jerry?

If you were going to have a pecking order of no-hopers where females were concerned, Jerry would be second to Darren, maybe a dead heat. And yet here he was, fixed up as well. And Dawn had only been away from the place three hours. What was going on? Jerry's lady-friend was a big bonny girl with shoulder pads. You could tell they were clicking. When they laughed it was like one laugh shared between the two of them, like one of them deaths by chocolate you eat with a spoon apiece.

Then suddenly Dawn clocked Frank bending over the fire. And just beyond his large pink head, a flash of blonde curls.

Dawn's mouth dropped open. Rage bubbled up inside her chest. There was something about the way they were stood together in the fire place, some kind of electricity in the atmosphere between them, that told her something was going on. It was having a sixth sense, a woman's sense, for when the dirty was being done.

The sheer brass nerve of it took her breath away. She, Dawn, goes off and has a bit on the side for once in her life, and Frank straight off takes the opportunity to get fixed up himself.

Let me breathe, Dawn wanted to shout. Don't spoil *every*thing for me. You haven't fancied me once for the last couple of years. At least let me commit adultery in peace.

It wasn't adultery because she and Frank had never got wed. But when she was doing the deed she had needed it to be adultery after all. That was the only way to shut the bedroom door against the big wide world beyond.

The Father turned round, away from the bar. Alan followed suit, to see what he was looking at.

The old witch was back, staring over at Frank as if pole-axed. Frank was bent over, fiddling with his blessed fire. Suddenly she raised the flat of her hand to her mouth and sniggered against it. Then she turned and stepped over towards him and Thomas as if she was stepping on tiptoe, hand still muffling her cackles.

'Bloody hell, gents,' she said when she got close, as near *sotto voce* as her Viking voice would permit. 'I saw old Goldilocks over there and thought Frank had found himself a new woman.'

'You know how the poem goes,' Alan told her. '"When all at once I saw a crowd, a host of golden daffodils." Or words to that effect.'

'He's got big hair, right enough,' Dawn agreed.

'I just popped in on the off-chance,' Gemma told Darren. 'My dad was coming into town and gave me a lift. I thought you might be drowning your sorrows after getting the push like you did. I remember you told me this is your pub where you do cleaning in the morning time. I didn't know you were working behind the bar as well.'

Cracked it, Darren thought. First day ever I work behind the bar and at the exact right moment in comes the one girl I want to come in and see me. Got to take it in my stride. 'I help out a bit,' he said. 'How the chickens getting on?'

'Tucked up in bed.'

'Do they go to bed? I thought they must sleep standing up, like horses.'

Gemma laughed. Her laugh was high-pitched, silvery. Darren felt his heart pound. She'd come here to see him. Then he'd made her laugh.

'Chickens are nothing like a horse,' Gemma said. 'You're not going to catch a horse laying an egg, are you?'

She thought he was an idiot. 'I only meant sleepwise,' he said.

'What they do, chickens, they go into their house so the foxes won't eat them. They climb up a ladder. They sort of jump, then give their wings a quick flutter, and land on the next rung up. One thing foxes are no good at doing is climbing up a ladder. They put their feet into the holes all the time. Then the chickens go to sleep on their perches. They like lower their bodies on to their feet, so they can rest their legs a bit.'

There was a pause. 'How's old Rebecca getting on then?' Darren asked.

'Oh, like this.' Gemma put a hand on her head and sort of looked out at everything like she was in a cave, or was a rabbit at the entrance to its burrow, peering. 'Ooh, ooh, what a headache.'

'Oh fuck,' Darren said.

'She just feels guilty, in my opinion. She knows she'll have to tell like the cancer bosses about giving you the push.'

'Funny thing is, I went down to the cellar just now, and changed the barrel nice as pie.'

'It was an accident, Darren. These things happen. What you got to realise, she's a right bitch. If I'd a dropped a vase on her head I would've done it on purpose. Only *you* would do it like, completely innocent.'

Funny thing was, Gemma's praise made Darren more embarrassed than when she laughed at him. 'What you don't know about chickens,' he said, 'isn't worth knowing.'

The moment, the exact moment, Frank put match to scrunched newspaper, he was aware that Dawn had come into the room.

He stopped where he was for a moment, pinning his attention on the paper's edge curling in the cool transparent flame, as if by staring hard enough he could make the fire fill his whole head and keep old Dawn out of it.

He needed a pause to collect his ideas. He felt he was caught red-handed, with Frankie crouching down beside him.

It's worse being accused of something you didn't do. If you're guilty you can lie or own up. If you're not, you just look guilty.

'Think it will be all right?' he asked Frankie, just because it seemed best to be in a conversation. Nothing more awkward than silence. He'd never been one of them silent kinds of landlord. He'd rather talk nonsense than not talk at all.

'I don't see why not,' Frankie said, turning from the fire to look at him, a tad puzzled. 'Why wouldn't it?'

'You never know till you put it to the test.'

'Tell you what,' Frankie said, getting to his feet, 'you got to fill me in.'

'Oh yes?' Frank replied.

'The three at the bar. The dismal pair who look like they've both of them just swallowed a lemon. Father Ted and the other one. Now a woman's over with them. Tall thin woman. But she looks like a happier bunny altogether.'

Frank glanced round from his all-fours position. Yep. He got to his feet too, feeling bulky. 'She's my missus, that's who she is.'

'Whoops.' Frankie pointed a finger pistol at his head and fired it with his thumb. 'The thing of it is, I just said bunny in the sense of happy. Like people are quite often not a happy bunny, at least in this life. But from here she looks like she *is* a happy bunny. Compared to the face-aches she's standing next to, anyhow.'

'I brought you something,' Gemma said.

'Oh yes?' Darren asked.

'I got it in here.' She scrabbled in her handbag, one of those big bucket type of ones. Then she pulled out a little padded envelope, the sort you send CDs or DVDs in. It was bulging. She passed it across the bar to him.

'What is it?'

'That's for you to find out.'

Suddenly Darren felt himself blush right to his earlobes. What she said made him remember that time this afternoon when she got him to come into the cubicle at the cancer shop and he thought she was going to show him her tits, or at least a photograph of them. The bag had been sellotaped shut. He opened it hoping she wouldn't see his hand shaking a bit: it shook anyhow, even in normal conditions.

Inside was a little cardboard box, also sellotaped shut. He opened that too. Inside, straw.

'Careful,' Gemma said. 'Careful getting that out.'

He pulled out the straw, which was pressed together like a little nest. In the middle of it was a brown egg. It was smooth, pinky brown with little freckles on. Sure enough it looked like a tiny tit. The intimacy of it took his breath away. He felt like he might cry any moment. If he spoke his voice would come out all broken up, like crazy paving.

'How is he?' Thomas asked.

'Same old prat as usual, by the looks of it,' Dawn replied. Frank had got to his feet. 'He's probably too long in the tooth to be any different.'

Seeing him rise slowly and ponderously made her remember the way his head had appeared from the trap door when the Half a Loaf man was here this morning. 'He looks like he's yabbering nineteen to the dozen with that bloke with all the hair.'

'Probably got a lot to talk about,' Alan said in that dry sarky way of his. Could pick holes in anything. What made Frank into a good landlord was his way of being nice to any Tom, Dick or Harry, which a dried up old so-and-so like Alan was would never get his head round.

He's got a lovely round pink head, she thought, Frank has, one that rises up like the sun. He's even nice to people you didn't ought to be nice to, like Jake.

But better that than the other way, especially being Dawn herself was a bit the other way, with a tendency to resist, go flat on people instead of welcoming.

Not that anyone would know that from her behaviour the last hour or so. Not much resisting then. She felt a laugh coming on and clamped her mouth shut against it.

'Not Frank,' Thomas said quietly. 'I meant Romesh.'

Dawn froze. She'd forgotten clean about him. It had totally slipped her mind that Romesh was her alibi.

Something febrile about Dawn, Thomas noted, a brittle gaiety. She'd come in determined to put a brave face on where she'd been, what she'd witnessed: the decline towards death of a man for whom she obviously felt love.

He remembered what he, Thomas, had said about love before she went off to the hospital, in the face of Alan's cynicism, and felt pleased that he'd said it – as well he might, given it applied to him too, to his love for Julian. If you didn't believe that love could be innocent and uncomplicated, you might as well not believe anything.

Just as she was about to reply, Jerry came over to buy drinks for himself and his lady-friend.

'Told you,' Alan said to Jerry.

'What?'

'That the other one would hop it when you got your feet under the table.'

'She said she had to meet someone,' Jerry said.

'Not good,' Dawn told the three of them, shaking her head. 'Not at all good.'

'What?' Jerry asked. He looked like a little boy worried his sweets were going to be taken off him. He glanced back to check his woman was still there. She sat with her eyes downcast, modestly avoiding his gaze.

As he had earlier on, Thomas felt a pang at the complicated manoeuvrings of courtship. All the strategy of shifts and evasions and sudden takings of ground, all the details of conquest, all of it, missed out on. The nearest he'd got in his own life was in the comings and goings of spiritual commitment, performing a life-long mating dance with the great blank absent presence of Almighty God, so bright with glory he couldn't be seen at all.

What if Julian's sexual analogies weren't analogies after all, but wistful yearnings for the pleasures of the flesh? What if religion itself was the analogy? My God, what if God were nothing more than a sexual simile, a means of emphasis?

'What?' Jerry asked again.

'Dawn's talking about Romesh,' Alan explained.

'Oh,' said Jerry. '*I* was telling Karen about Outer Mongolia.'

He still hadn't got the point. Now he knew he wasn't being challenged he'd simply decided that they were swapping conversational topics.

Suddenly Thomas lost his temper. 'A man's dying, if you don't mind,' he said harshly.

To give him credit, Jerry looked stung. Hurt even.

'I went there last year,' he said feebly, by way of explanation. For a moment Thomas thought he meant death, before cottoning on.

'Oh he was bad,' Dawn said. 'Bad, bad.' Her voice was shaky with the sudden horror of it, as Romesh's plight rose to the forefront of her consciousness. 'It was a bad place to visit, that bed. With poor Romesh lying on it. A terrible place.'

A familiar darkness began to seep into Thomas's mind.

'Mongolia wasn't that great either,' Jerry said. 'I was saying to Karen.'

'You know what I said to him?' Dawn said, talking directly at Thomas. 'I said, how I wish I could pour you a pint of beer. How I wish I could have smuggled it in in my handbag.' Her lower lip trembled.

Darren leaned over from where he was talking to his young lady. 'The beer's bang on, as well. I got an egg.'

'Your taste buds go all funny when you're ill,' Jerry said. 'It's a well-known fact.' One of Jerry's eyes had started watering, as though he was half in sympathy with Dawn's sorrow.

'When I had flu,' Alan said, 'everything I ate tasted of tin. And drank. Liquid tin, in the latter case.' He picked up his pint. 'But I persevered.'

'I had fermented yak milk in Mongolia,' Jerry said. 'You didn't need to be ill to taste the horribleness of that.' He took his drinks back to his table and to Karen, tripping along on small deft feet beneath his boxy frame.

Dawn looked longingly at Thomas, her eyes bright with tears. She needs me to be her minister, he realised. But how could he, with the darkness sifting down upon him, settling like a thin demonic snow upon his hair and lips and eyes, upon his very soul?

'You did all you could,' he told himself, but out loud, so Dawn could make use of it too.

I was in the mood to be bad, Dawn thought. And now I am being. Here I am blarting my eyes out because I feel guilty at shagging Tiger Tim straight after visiting the hospital, and I'm letting them all think it's because I feel sorrow for Romesh, poor blighter.

'I think I'll go upstairs for a couple of minutes, gents,' she said. She pointed at her eyes. 'Sort out my eyes.'

'You can't die another person's death for them,' Thomas said gently. 'Only Jesus can do that.'

Another aphorism for general use, Thomas decided.

He'd been trying to convince himself of the truth of it all afternoon. But Jesus's death on everyone's behalf missed the very point, really: it confronted the wrong definition of death.

The one that counted involved the loss of detail, the loss of the whole mortal intricate particularity of somebody. What was left behind was like one of those eighteenth century gravestones that soberly listed a few bland virtues. You were left with nothing more than a spiritual tendency, like the faintest aftertaste of wine or food. It was hard to care whether that thin residue ended up in heaven or the other place, though even when he'd believed he believed, Thomas had never believed in hell.

What you wanted for yourself, when you woke up on Judgement Day, was not the approbation of the Almighty, or a seat on a puffy white cloud. You wanted to walk into the Old Spring again, and have another pint. What you wanted for your dead friend was that one day he would go back into the kitchen of the De La Tour house and set about making cheese on toast with onions and tomatoes buried in the cheese. What possible conception of life everlasting could equal that?

All Dawn longed for was for her dying love to come up to the bar and order another pint.

'Maybe when I come down again,' Dawn said, 'that Colin chappie will have buggered off. I thought he was going to Germany, anyhow.'

'Colin?' Thomas asked, surprised.

'He does my head in. Some days you can take only so much.'

'He seems harmless enough to me. He's certainly wearing a smart blazer.'

'Listen to him.'

Thomas listened, looking over his shoulder at Colin playing shove-ha'penny with Nigel. They were concentrating on the game, hardly speaking.

'I would say he's being pretty quiet.'

'It's his sniffing. That's what bugs me. That's what gets me down.'

Thomas listened again. Sure enough, Colin gave out a couple of loud sniffs. 'Oh,' Thomas said, registering.

'It's like his nostrils are too narrow,' Dawn said. 'It makes me feel panicky.'

'*My* problem is that old halfwit over there,' Alan said, nodding towards the couple where the wife had had to wait for the husband's pint and seemed to drink nothing herself. 'He breathes as if his life depended on it.'

How strange. Thomas had not heard Colin's sniffs until Dawn mentioned them. And now he suddenly tuned back in to the huffing and puffing of the man whose wife was acting as a sort of handmaiden to him. In fact, he realised, he was able to hear them both, the breath breath of the old man, followed by the sniff sniff of Colin leaning over the shove-ha'penny board, the two noises strangely fitting together and creating a rhythm of their own.

'I'm off,' Dawn said. 'I'll be down in a bit.'

17

Gav came in and sat down on the bench beside Jake.
'You took your fucking time,' Jake said.

'I poked my head round earlier on. You were with some bloke.'

'Was I? No, I wasn't.'

'Yes, you fucking was.'

'That was Nick. Fucker I'm on a job with.'

'There you go then. That's a bloke in it? Nick's a bloke, in it?'

Jake shook his head, not to say no, to say fuck off. It was like Gav always had to have the last word.

'I don't need him knowing all our business,' Gav said.

'The only business what he knows, what Nick knows –' Jake said Nick sarcastic, like saying *Nick*, not a *bloke*, thank you very much – 'is bumming off of me and painting his fucking pork pie.'

Gav shut up for a minute. Then asked: 'You seen Roof then?'

'I seen him. I got sodding wet through seeing him. I got some gear.'

'Yeah, well.'

'What you fucking mean, yeah well? You got to take your share.'

'Time and place, man,' Gav said. 'Time and place, in it?'

Always on the edge, fucking Gav. Like his whole head was an edge. Roof said one time, your pal Gav, he looks like his head got squashed in a door. You look at him side on, head like everybody else. Look from in front, where the fuck's it gone? According to Roof. Which *he* could fucking talk, with his hat.

But still, fact was Gav had a way of sliding himself away from any stuff that was going down. Sort of being half wherever he was, half not. Like the time Jake was getting totalled, Gav just had tattoos put on where his clothes go, under his shirt and whatnot. Not even one on his neck except a little dotted line across at the back, like as to say, cut head off here.

Any chance to bottle out, consider Gav bottled. He, Jake, sploshes around in the muck on the canal bank, Gav stays warm and dry. Same as when that bloke got dropped, outside of the Griffin. Gav had shot off at just the exact right moment to get himself a kebab, come back when it was over. Never come back at all, saw the police cars and buggered off. Just left Jake to eyeball the whole sorry business.

When you look at Gav, all you clock is whatever he's standing in front of, Roof said.

'I been told,' Gav said, 'that you might be getting a visitor.'

'Oh yes?'

'Coming to make sure there's no way . . .'

Gav tailed off as some girl on a stool at the bar, talking to Darren, sort of flicked her head round and looked at them.

'No way what?' Jake asked.

'Liable to speak out,' Gav said in a whisper.

The girl flicked back. 'I thought it was Daddy coming in,' she told Darren, dead hoity-toity. She had one of those voices that was loud even though she didn't speak loud. She said Daddy like it was dah-dee. No fucker was coming in except Jason back from the gents still zipping his knob back in. Big bloke but three pints he got dead wobbly.

'Fat chance,' Jake said.

'You know what I mean. Blab.'

'I know what you fucking mean.'

'Well, fuck you too.' Gav looked at him out of his one side-on eye. 'Fuck you, too,' he said again.

'I never blabbed in my whole life, so fuck you.'

'I never said you did. But it's not like you're one of that bunch, in it? You're like an outsider. It's gone and give him the fidgets.'

Just at the word, Jake felt his own leg begin to vibrate, as it did sometimes, like it was saying, time to blow, time to fuck off out of here.

'You stay in the mind,' Gav said, 'that's the thing of it.'

'Fuck.'

'All I'm saying: coming round. That's all I'm saying.'

'You got to take your share.'

'Yeah, yeah. I know I got to take my share. Just not this minute, OK? OK? This exact minute?'

'What you want to do then, this minute? Buy yourself another fucking kebab?'

'You don't want to do it in here, do you? Divvy up, like? Like this is a place for that sort of business?'

'We could step outside, what I'm saying.'

'We don't know who's waiting outside, what *I'm* saying.'

'Fuck,' said Jake.

Darren thought: she gave me an egg, in a little box.

Plus she showed me a picture of herself with a chicken standing on her head.

Plus she came in here to see how I was getting on, being I got fired for clonking Rebecca.

Time to do something back.

Not wear a dress. She would have to forget that one.

The good thing was, the one time she came in was the one time in his whole life he was working behind the bar, plus had replaced the barrel and kept the punters happy.

She was getting twitchy because her dad was due any minute. She kept looking round.

'He'll do his nut,' she whispered, 'if he sees that tattooed man there.'

She had a carrying type whisper but luckily Jake was busy doing his business with Gav.

'I can't chuck him out,' Darren whispered back. 'He's not done anything wrong. He's a good bloke really, except swearing a lot.'

'I heard him fucking swearing,' Gemma said. She whispered *fucking* so poshly it made his heart thump. She said the *g* right at the end of it, like a little bell ringing, like the word had become rude all over again. 'I think, the best thing is for me to wait outside. Pops'll be along right away.'

'Cool. I'll wait outside with you.'

'Nice one, Darren.'

'Won't he think, what's she doing in the wet when she could be in a warm pub? Pops, I mean. Your old man.' Darren looked over at the fire, blazing away. Frank and his pal with the big hair were standing by it, talking with Colin the Coach and Nigel.

'He'll just think, there she is, how convenient. He'll just say, hop in.' Gemma looked right in Darren's eyes. 'I'm a big girl now, Darren. I don't have to explain. All he did, he just gave me a lift in. All he's going to do, give me a lift back again.'

'Yip. *Big girl*. Got you.' Darren loved the words big girl, the sweet way she said them. Talk of a portal, they were a portal, like two gates swinging open, letting him through. The trouble was, there was another portal, the bar flap, and when he went through that one he'd just be an ordinary punter again, no longer in charge of the whole shebang. 'Tell you what I'm going to do,' he said.

'What are you going to do, Darren?'

Before he'd opened his mouth to say it, he hadn't any idea what it was he was going to do. It was like he was relying on another voice to speak through him. He made his mouth not move too fast to give it time to make up the words. 'What I'm going to do.' Sure enough, the voice began to speak. 'See those two-pint thingies?'

'What two-pint thingies? Oh those.'

They had plastic two-pint containers on the shelf, so people could take home some draught bitter when they left the pub.

'I'm going to fill one up and take it off with me to the hospital. One of the regulars is in there, Romesh by name.'

'Romesh,' said Gemma. 'Is he Welsh?'

'He's ill, what he is. He was in a car crash a month or two back and got buggered inside.'

'Oh, yak.'

'Yep, inside his insides. Somewhere very deep. It don't look good for him, Gemma. He said to Dawn, lying on his bed over there in the hospital, what he wanted most in the world was a pint of beer. He said, he thought he would never drink a pint of beer again in this life. Dawn was telling about it just now. Never in this life, how sad is that? Like when I leaned over to tell about the egg, Dawn was saying about it. So I thought, I know what I'll do, I'll take him one.'

'But I only had the one egg,' Gemma said. 'And I gave it to you.'

'No, no, not an egg, silly. Nobody's going to have my egg.' Gemma sort of wiggled with pleasure at being called silly, and Darren felt himself flush up. Got away with that one. 'You know what I'm going to do with my egg? I'm going to keep it.'

'Are you? But it'll go bad. Silly boy!' It was like playing table tennis: he pinged the word *silly* over to her, she hit it with her little bat and pinged it right back again.

'I'm going to make a hole with a pin each end of the egg, and blow it out into a bowl. Then I'm going to stir it all up and make scrambled egg for myself. Then I'll have the eggshell intact, to keep on my mantelpiece. That's what I decided to do with my egg. What I'm going to take Romesh is a couple of pints of beer.'

'Oh Darren? That's so nice of you, Darren.' Quick as a bird pecking bread off a bird table, Gemma leaned over the bar and gave him a kiss. He could feel her lip-prints on his cheek.

Yes yes yes, Darren thought. Plus it means, I go through the bar flap and the bar sort of comes through with me, it's like my own bar-type life-support system. I'll still be a barman on the other side of the portal, couple of pints of beer under my arm, off to serve a customer. Like I'm not just doing the job, the job's coming with me.

'We're off to grab a curry,' Jerry said.

'You don't owe us an explanation,' Alan said coolly.

'Hiya,' said Jerry's young lady. She gave a girly wave from the far side of Jerry's shoulder, exactly as if she were waving an imaginary handkerchief at an imaginary train. In reply Alan gave out a sort of disgruntled grunt. Thomas contented himself with what felt, even from the inside, like a beery smile.

Thomas had picked up on the *us*. He felt a flicker of pride, even though by most standards Alan's orbit should be an arid enough place to find oneself.

'I postponed a stew to come out with that young man,' Alan told Thomas, as Jerry and his friend left. 'And now he's stood me up for a curry.'

'I think he's stood you up for a woman, in point of fact.'

Alan thought it over. 'Fair enough,' he said.

'I missed out on a Welsh rarebit when I came in at lunchtime,' Thomas agreed glumly.

'He always likes to make a speedy exit,' Alan said. 'Though not as a rule with a female on his arm.'

They stood in silence for a while. At any moment Alan would take his leave and go off to be reconciled with his stew. Thomas cast about in his mind for something to say. 'And I was hoping to ask him about Outer Mongolia,' was what came up in the end.

'Were you then? Why?'

'Why not?'

'Well, it's not the first topic that springs to mind.'

'He went there, didn't he say?'

'He did go there, a year or two back. That's true. On one of those adventure camping expeditions. It wasn't a happy experience for him.'

'I gathered not, no.'

'I can't imagine one of those camping holidays would ever be a happy experience for anyone.' Alan shuddered. 'What he said was, Mongolia is extremely blank.'

'Is that so?'

'I suppose you always think of every place as equally full. If it lacks people, it compensates with landscape. Etcetera. *Ad infinitum*. You don't expect to go to a place and find it isn't there.'

'I suppose not.'

'Well, Outer Mongolia isn't, at least according to Jerry. Miles of tundra. No trees. As far as I can gather Outer Mongolia is simply a sort of gap in the continuum. When he woke up in the morning wanting to relieve himself, there was nothing to go behind. Perhaps that's the best way of testing whether a place is a place or not. See if there is any opportunity to take a dump. He just had to wander away from the campsite until he dwindled. Luckily the laws of perspective still worked even though they didn't have a lot to work *with*.'

'I don't think you can have a gap in a continuum,' Thomas said. 'It wouldn't be a continuum.'

'But you haven't been to Outer Mongolia.'
'True enough.' Or maybe not.

It wasn't a three-dimensional dream. It was thin and sketchy. When he thought about it, Thomas realised that having Alzheimer's must be similar. Events take place in front of you but you don't quite pick them up. You don't remember them even as they are happening. Even the present needs to be woven from the thread of memory. You have to remember from one second to the next.

Drabness and claustrophobia, that was what he'd been aware of. And something niggling, neurotic, repetitive, an overwhelming sense that life lacked possibility. That he couldn't go anywhere, that there was nowhere to go.

But words couldn't evoke it. Words weren't available there, wherever he was.

There may or may not have been other beings present, but that wasn't relevant. The point was that he was trapped within the confines of himself, and that was a lonely place to be. He felt like a broken record, clattering through an endless, meaningless rhythm, a rhythm that had become meaningless simply because it *was* endless. Anything you say or sing or do *for ever*, loses all its point, becomes mere noise.

He woke up, needing to go to the lavatory, but he didn't escape the dream because the dream wasn't so much a dream in any case, but a way of perceiving himself. A way of seeing that he was trapped in a life of no value, from which there was no escape. A way of seeing that there was nothing to see.

As he walked along the dim landing he saw Brother Julian, who was just coming out of the bathroom himself. Paul spoke. He didn't know what words he said.

Over breakfast the next morning Julian told him what he'd said: 'I've been in such a dark place.' Those were the words.

That wasn't exactly the truth of course. As he spoke Paul was in the dark place still. To an extent he'd been in it ever since. But there was panic prowling about his chest and to admit the truth of where he was, to say, I am in the dark place, would have let it free. It was an experience you had to pretend you were looking back at, that you were seeing from the outside.

Julian asked him more about it, of course. Eventually Paul owned up: 'I think I dreamed I was a dung beetle.'

It wasn't exactly the case. What he had discovered in his dream was that he might just as *well* have been a dung beetle, that his life had no more meaning than theirs did, that we all live in a dark place; that from cradle to grave we use our back legs to pedal our dung along.

'I caught myself on the hop,' Colin the Coach said.

'I don't get you,' Frank told him.

'Tell you what,' Frankie said, 'that Darren of yours has got a fine nose. Aquiline, I would call it. It's a shame he's wearing the nastiest shirt in the whole universe.'

'He's not *my* Darren,' Frank said testily. 'He just works here.'

'I expect he bought it in a charity shop.' Frankie shook his head. 'Horrible shirt. Throwing himself away on a bit of a girl. It all adds up. What a waste.' He ran his hand through his hair, which bent over and then sprang up again.

'What you mean, hop?' Frank asked Colin.

'Taking myself by surprise.'

'I take myself by surprise all the time,' Nigel said.

'I was walking past the travel agent's and I just sort of swerved in,' Colin explained. 'Before I knew what I was doing. The girl behind the desk said she had a cheap overnight in Hamburg going, I said yes, it was a done deal. I was out the shop before I even knew I'd gone in.'

'I do that kind of stuff,' Nigel put in. 'Then I think to myself, whoa!'

'And now I'm stuck with it.'

'You'll enjoy it, I'm sure,' Frank told him. 'New place to see. And you'll only be there the blink of an eye.'

'The thought of it makes me feel really depressed.' Colin looked shaky.

'But you go places all the time,' Frank reminded him. 'You're a coach driver, for goodness' sake.'

'I know. I know. But that's work. That's just what I do. Water off a duck's back. This is different. This is me, going there voluntary, to foreign parts. For what?'

Colin saying, *This is me*, rang a sudden bell for Frank. Small Colin, big Hamburg. Frank thought: this is just what gets me about Norfolk. I feel like I'm not at home. Not where I belong. He hadn't been sure anything got him about Norfolk. Sometimes it seemed it did, sometimes it seemed it didn't. Now it suddenly seemed obvious. The whole place edged him out. At some deep level it filled him with dread. Maybe that was what was attractive about it.

Flying ducks, Frank thought, big sky, being with Pete in that open jeep of his: where's *me* in all this?

'It's one of the world's biggest ports, so I hear,' Frankie said. 'That not so, Frank?'

'I never went there,' Frank told him gruffly.

'It's better to travel than arrive,' Nigel said.

'I don't want to do either.' Colin shook his head despairingly. 'I can't think of anything I want to do less.'

'Where do you *want* to go?' Nigel asked. 'That's what we need to clear up.'

'I don't want to go anywhere. I just want to stay here and play shove-ha'penny.'

There was a moment of silence. Colin sniffed loudly, as if sniffing back tears: hard to tell, being he sniffed anyway.

'Why don't you then?' Frankie said finally.

'What you mean?' Colin asked.

'Not go. Stay.'

'I can't do that.'

'Why not?'

'I bought the ticket.'

'You could make out you broke your leg,' Nigel said.

'So what?' Frankie asked Colin.

'It would be a waste.'

'You said yourself, it didn't cost a lot.'

'Water under the bridge,' Frank put in.

Colin shook his head, obviously baffled by the very idea. You bought a ticket, you went, that was obviously the way his mind worked.

'Of course,' Nigel said, 'you'd have to get a medical note. Maybe you could forge one.'

'Shall I tell you my philosophy of life?' Frankie asked.

Colin looked at him nervously. 'I suppose so,' he said in a grudging voice, like a child being egged on.

Uh oh, Frank thought, what now?

'Everything is how you look at it. Simple as that.'

Colin nodded cautiously.

'Get it?' Frankie asked. He looked at them all in turn, Frank, Nigel, Colin. Frank gave him a hard look back, hoping it sent the message *Don't let this get personal*. Nigel just looked away, at the fire. Colin nodded his head like he'd got it, then changed his mind and shook it instead.

'Look,' Frankie said. 'You got yourself a booking for Hamburg. Let's say, it cost a hundred pounds.' Colin flinched. Impossible to tell whether it was because the amount was more, or less, or bang on. 'OK,' Frankie went on. 'You wake up tomorrow and you think to yourself, I'm not on duty today or tomorrow. How do I want to spend my time? How I want to spend my time is wander down the Old Spring, have a pint or two, play some shove-ha'penny. That's what you think.'

'But –'

'But then you remember that for reasons best known to himself, Frank here has put a price on the door. Fifty pounds entrance a day. One hundred the two days. You think to yourself, that's a lot.'

'It is a bloody lot,' Nigel said indignantly. 'What you want to do that for, Frank?'

'So,' Frankie told Colin, 'you're taken aback for a moment or two. Quite disappointed. Then you think to yourself, Blow it, I'll go anyway. I'm on holiday after all. I'll treat myself.'

For a moment Colin looked struck by the idea. Then his face fell. 'Trouble is, my booking's for Hamburg, isn't it, not for the Old Spring?'

'In my opinion it's a rip-off, all ends up,' Nigel said. 'I know some pubs charge at New Year's, but I never heard anything the likes of that.'

'That's all right,' Frank said.

'That's all right,' Frankie said. 'Frank here accepts Hamburg bookings in lieu, don't you, Frank?'

'Fat lot of use that is to me,' Nigel pointed out. 'I haven't got one.'

'Yes, I do,' Frank said.

'So,' said Frankie, 'that's your money accounted for. Nothing wasted. You just spent it differently than you originally intended.'

Bloody hell, Frank thought, maybe Dawn and me could get up to that sort of game with our nine hundred quid we haven't got. Colin was shaking his head admiringly, as if it was a pleasure to see a skilled con man at work. Nigel was still giving Frank the fish eye, angry at his prices.

'Hang on,' Frankie said, 'look at young Darren over there. He's got his hand up like some little schoolboy who wants a pee. Poor little chap. How about I go over?'

Sure enough, Darren had raised his hand, and was looking over in Frank's direction.

'Oh *Darren*,' Frank said, feeling as if he was just remembering the word *Darren*. 'No. Don't worry. I'll deal with it.'

'If I wanted to go to Outer Mongolia,' Alan said, 'I wouldn't.'

'Well, no,' Thomas replied.

'What I mean is, I would go to Patagonia.'

'Ah,' Thomas said carefully. 'I see.' Alan turned sideways to give him a long sceptical look. 'I think I see,' Thomas amended awkwardly.

'If I wanted to go *nowhere*,' Alan explained, 'Patagonia's the place I'd choose. Tierra del Fuego to be precise. The end of the world. I always thought I'd like to stand on the tip of Tierra del Fuego, facing south, looking right into the howling elements. I just have a feeling that the wind that would blow ashore would blow away all the bullshit.'

'Darwin thought, as I remember, that the savages who lived there were the most backward people in the whole world.'

'I didn't think you would be into Darwin, being a man of the cloth.'

Thomas shrugged his shoulders by way of saying, Well, there you go.

'Anyhow,' Alan said, 'what Darwin saw as backward, I might see as just lacking in bullshit.'

'I think they lacked clothes,' said Thomas, 'that was what they lacked. Which seems a bit odd, considering the climate they must have had to put up with.'

'Sorry, Darren,' Frank said. 'You're doing such a good job, I forgot all about you. That's the trouble when people do a good job. They become invisible.'

Darren flushed up, pleased.

'You should have flagged me down before,' Frank added.

'No worries,' Darren said. 'I saw you were busy with your pal.'

'My pal?' Frank glanced over at Frankie, still talking with Colin the Coach. 'Oh, him.' He glanced back at Darren, to see if he meant anything by the way he said *pal*. There he was, all set up and lovey-dovey with his girlfriend sitting on the bar-stool the other side of the flap. Meanwhile there was old Frankie by the fireplace, impossible to shift. It was like he was stuck with him for life. My pal. Frankie's blond hairstyle bobbing away at poor old Colin, Colin waving his arms slowly back at him like an upside down beetle. Dawn, he thought, what you up to up there? Come down and save me. 'He fixed the fire nice, though, didn't he?'

'The thing is, Gemma's got to go now.'

'Hello, Gemma,' Frank said.

'Hello,' Gemma said. She sort of poked her head forward then pulled it back again, like a cuckoo popping out of a cuckoo-clock.

'Off you trot,' Frank told Darren, who opened the bar flap and came through. He was carrying a two pint carry-out.

'I put the money in the till for this,' Darren said, waving it at him.

'You shouldn't have. You're one of us now.'

Dawn looked at herself naked in the mirror. No marks, that was what she was checking. No love bites in the wrong place. In any place.

He was a dirty-minded little so and so, Tim. He got her to take off her clothes while he lay on the bed and watched. Her idea had been sneak into the bathroom to do it, and come back in wearing a towel, like they do on TV, but no such luck. She nearly refused but stopped herself.

I'm not here to refuse, she told herself. I'm here to do the lot, whatever's going down. This is not like it would have been in payment for fixing the books, giving him just enough and no more. This isn't what I owe him. This is what I owe me. I want to go for it, for once in my life.

'Slow down, slow down,' Tim said. 'One at a time. No hurry.'

He'd gone into the bathroom and put a pair of pyjamas on, funnily enough, the sort with a t-shirt and shorts. One law for him, one law for her. Fair dos, it wouldn't have done anything for her to see him wiggle out of his boxers. His legs were quite hairy. Frank had smooth legs. She looked to see whether his foot had got scorched but it seemed white enough. His face was flushed dark as he watched her. The lines on his face looked now like old orgasms, stuck there like the marks of past high tides.

Dirty bastard, she thought.

She could feel her breath wavery in her chest. Her nipples had got so hard they ached. She'd never done anything like this in her whole life. It was funny, she let herself be right under his thumb, obeyed every instruction, yet all the time she was in charge, this was all for her own benefit, she was just using him for what she wanted.

When she began to pull her pants down he made her turn round, so he could see her bum come into view. She kept her back straight while she pressed down on the sides of her knickers so as not to let her bum poke out, then bent her knees to keep upright until she'd worked them far enough down her thighs that they fell free. All right, she thought, my bum is fine still. Still lean; hadn't started to prune. I'm doing all this rigmarole just in the nick of time, she thought.

As she faced away she could feel his gaze on her bum cheeks, as if there was a different sensation for your bum being looked at from it not being looked at.

Then she had to turn round again so he could clock the front of her.

'I told you to take everything off,' he said. He spoke it in a hard rough voice, as if he was only just keeping anger back.

'I have took everything off,' she answered. She could feel the warm air of the bedroom circulating round her body, as if she was suspended in very thin, gentle water.

'Think about it,' he said.

She glanced up and down her body, suddenly wondering if she'd overlooked anything. No, what could there be? No bra, no knickers, no tights. Her heart pounded in her chest. She could see her tits throbbing with the beat of it. That word he'd licked round his lips earlier on today came back to her: sheer. That's how I am now, she thought, sheer. Sheer sheer.

'I haven't got a stitch on,' she told him.

'No?' he said. 'No?'

'Not a stitch.'

'What about that then?' he said pointing.

'What about what?'

'Your plaster.'

'My plaster?' She suddenly remembered it. She raised her hand. 'My *plast*er?'

'Take it off. I said naked. I meant naked.'

For a moment she wanted to laugh. No, don't go there, she thought. It would break the spell. One thing about sex, sheer sex: no sense of humour. She clamped her mouth shut. Somewhere inside herself the giggle did a quick flip and turned into more randiness. She actually heard a little gasp or groan seep through her shut teeth.

She gripped the edge of her plaster and gave it a quick pull. As it came off, she could feel a shot of moisture come between her legs. She thought to herself, panting as quietly as she could, this is the sexiest thing I ever done in my whole life, the sexiest thing anybody's ever done, the sexiest thing there is to do.

'Bring it over here,' Tim said, just like as if her gouged finger was separate from her and had to be carried. She held it in front of her as she approached the bed exactly as if that was the case. Tim grabbed her hand and pulled it to his mouth, licking greedily at the wound. It had begun to heal over but was still moist: she could taste what he tasted, the stickiness of blood and salt.

18

It was still raining. 'I like looking at the rain,' Gemma said. 'What you like about it, Gem?'

'How it looks like a haircut, all over the street.'

When her dad rolled up in a big 4x4, Darren understood what she was thinking of. Her dad leaned over to unlock the passenger door and Darren saw his head was covered in silver bristles, just like he had built-in rain falling on him right there inside the car. He was a big, hard-looking kind of guy. He made Darren feel he was caught red-handed being where he shouldn't be, just being here on the pavement side-by-side with Gemma, as if he had no right even to be standing on the wet slabs, and was liable for a bollocking.

Darren opened his mouth to say Hi but just made a noise instead.

Gemma's dad looked up right in his face. 'Beg pardon?' he said.

'Just saying hello,' Darren told him. This time he got the words out but it was like when you've taken a drag of a fag and your voice goes inside out.

'Wotcher cock,' Gemma's dad said, but dead poshly, the same way Gemma said stuff.

'Guess what, Pops?' Gemma asked him.

'What, Gem?'

Darren clocked that Gemma's dad called her Gem same as what he did. Got that one right, he thought.

'Darren's going to the hospital, to give this Welsh bloke some beer.'

Her dad looked from Gem to Darren. Darren held his breath. It was one of those things that could go either way. Could make him seem like a hooligan, that was the danger. 'No kidding,' Gem's dad said.

'It's true, isn't it, Darren?'

'Yep.'

'You're Darren, then?' asked the dad.

'Yep, that's me.' For a second Darren wondered if there was some way he could make himself look like a Darren, to prove his point, more like a Darren than any other name. He couldn't think of how, so just nodded as if he'd convinced himself of it, for one: like saying, a Darren, that's me all right.

'How do you do, Darren?' Gemma's dad poked a great huge paw up at him. Darren grasped it as best he could. It was funny how you knew a guy like that, with a huge fuck-off vehicle and a daughter and chickens and whatnot, would have to have big hands. Maybe the blokes who started off with big hands were the ones who got to grab everything.

'How do,' Darren said.

'You and Gem worked in the charity shop together, right?'

Darren's heart sank. Yes, or no? 'I got the push,' he said huskily.

Gem's dad nodded. 'She told me,' he said. 'She was quite upset about it.'

'I was upset,' Gem agreed.

'She's only there herself on a temporary basis, in any case,' he said. It was almost like he was saying sorry for her *not* being sacked. 'She's just getting experience to fill out her CV, aren't you, Gem? She wants to go into retail.'

'I want to work in a farm shop. Or maybe a boutique,' Gemma said.

'I'm a barman now,' Darren said.

'I see. That why you're on a beer run?'

'He got flattened in an incident, didn't he, Darren?' asked Gemma. 'This bloke.'

Darren nearly said, not exactly flattened. He thought Gemma's dad would think he was exaggerating. Plus it wouldn't be much use anybody in a flattened state trying to drink beer. But he didn't want to give Gem the lie. We got to sing from the same hymn sheet, he thought.

'Smuggling it in,' Darren said, wagging the take-out container.

'Nice one,' Gemma's dad said. 'Hop in. I'll drop you off.'

'What I want to know,' Alan said, 'what's the backward reach?'

'What do you mean?' Thomas asked. He could tell it was a loaded question. All Alan's questions were loaded. He loaded them like a cowboy would load his gun. They'd gone from the voyage of the *Beagle* to deep time. There was something inexorable about that progression, something geological about it.

'Well, you've got Jesus putting in his guest appearance a couple of thousand years ago. Waving his magic wand.'

'Well, if you want to put it like that,' Thomas said, knowing he sounded pompous. That was the trick, of course, Alan's way of making every belief except non-belief, every ism save nihilism, sound pompous.

'But the human race has been going for a couple of million years,' Alan said. 'How far back can a redeemer redeem, that's what I want to know? Where does he draw the line?'

'I don't think there's any end to redemption.' Thomas took a big pull on his beer as a way of saying, I like to do this too, as well as spout on about religion. 'Any limit on it.'

'Look there,' Alan said. He pointed at the dark riffled grain of the bar surface. 'Rolling savannah. Blazing sun. Couple of apes wandering about scraping their hands on the ground, villainous low foreheads.'

'And nowhere to take a dump,' Thomas said.

'Exactly,' Alan said, pleased.

Thing about me, Thomas thought, I can't be ironic even if I want to be. Everything I say comes out straight, comes out cooperative.

'And there's this redemption thing coming over the horizon,' Alan went on. 'I don't quite know what to call it. The good news.'

'How about the Holy Ghost?'

'OK, the Holy Ghost. Sorry, the Holy Ghost says, you pair can't come to the party. The apes look stunned. They look disappointed. Jesus didn't die for you, the Holy Ghost says. Or rather, Jesus won't die for you, in a few million years' time. You won't be on his agenda. He's got to draw the line somewhere. If he dies for you, then he also dies for the triceratops. And the jellyfish. And the AIDS virus. So you aren't invited. But never mind, your children will be welcome. They've evolved just enough.' Alan looked testy and upset, as if he were one of the uninvited apes in question.

Thomas could feel beer sloshing about in his brain. It made him suddenly want to be eloquent. He wanted to open his mouth and let the words flow. Mustn't, he thought. I'm still capable of knowing better. I've drunk a fair amount but even now I'm the hither side of yon. Keep it terse. 'You know what it says in the book,' he said, almost grumpy himself with the effort of restraint. 'In the beginning was the word.'

'It says a lot of things in the book.'

'Well, that's to its credit, isn't it?'

'Hum,' Alan said.

'Personally I don't believe that it means God made things happen just by giving out orders. In the beginning was the

258

word: I think it means you don't have God until you find a way to *say* God.'

'Ah. Right.' Alan nodded. He even managed to nod sarcastically. He had a bitter little smile on his thin lips. Why do I want to ingratiate myself with this man, Thomas wondered. His lips looked like precision instruments, cutting out each word that passed through them so it was sharp and faceted as a diamond. 'So,' the lips said, 'it's when the little perishers stop grunting and *say* something that they get invited. Like kids from working class backgrounds getting into university and leaving their poor old mums and dads on the council estate.'

'Yes. I suppose so. Kind of.'

'Big thinks,' Alan said. He nodded, in grudging praise of their bigness. 'Have another pint.'

Good God, thought Thomas, I'm talking about final things, and first things, just so I can stay side-by-side at the bar with Alan, and carry on boozing.

Jake thought: I'm fucked. He could see it in Gav's eye, the way it looked at him from the side of his face. It was looking back at him like he was dead or bashed up already. It was like Gav wasn't here to be pals-y, he was here to keep an eye on him, with that eye of his.

Sometime tonight I'm going to be fucking nobbled, Jake thought, and fucking Gav here knows all about it.

I'm fucking fucked.

He pictured tomorrow, that fuckhead Nick perched on a ladder painting a picture of a pork pie above the window of the Pie-Eyed shop. What he couldn't picture was himself, painting away at the window surround. I won't be fucking there, he thought. God knows where I'll be.

Funny the way Frank had thought of Frankie like he was dangerous. Like he knew the ropes somehow, like he could suss Frank out. Like he had some sort of sex detector, that could amplify any little buzzes you might give out. Perhaps it was seeing him using that welder. Made him look in charge, made him look like action man.

Now he seemed more like a puppy dog that had no home to go to. Colin and Nigel were playing shove-ha'penny. Frankie had cracked that one, to give him credit. Little Colin was at the top of his game, full of beans, now he didn't have to go off to Hamburg first thing tomorrow. His ha'pennies were whizzing over the board like guided missiles.

Frankie had watched them play for a minute or two, then got bored and come over to the bar. He'd stayed on the edge of the Father's conversation with Alan but it was too high-brow to break into, so now he was just drumming his fingers on the bar surface and making small talk with Frank whenever he got the chance.

But funnily enough the fact that Frankie was at loose ends made him even more awkward to have around. It was like he was making clear to all and sundry that he was only in the pub for one reason. At least, now that the fire was up and running. (Give him that too, Frank thought, feeling the warmth and radiance right across the room.) That reason being being a buddy of Frank.

It made Frank feel twitchy. When the hell is Dawn coming down? he wondered. She must have been upstairs half an hour at least.

He'd just turned away to wash a few glasses when there was a roar like an animal, from the snug. Frank turned back so fast a soapy goblet flew out of his hand and smashed on the floor.

The elderly gent who was sitting with his wife at the small table in the middle of the room had his head back and was howling like a wolf. His face was red as a traffic light and his eyes were watery. Frank hadn't noticed them before but they looked strangely pale now, as if the blue had faded out of them, staring up at the ceiling with the damp bluish whiteness of a pair of small oysters while the mouth was a big roaring circle below.

Everyone was gawping, people peering in from the public and the back room to check out what the hell was going on. Over at the shove-ha'penny board, Colin's arm was stopped in mid-shove while he looked back. After a moment or two the noise died away, and the man lowered his head, blinked his eyes, smacked his lips a few times, sort of grunted to himself, and then just sat there at his table as if nothing had happened.

'Blumming hell,' Frank said. 'What the devil's the matter?'

The man's wife twisted round to face up to him. 'I'm so sorry,' she said.

'Is he OK? Do you want me to call an ambulance? Or a taxi?'

She shook her head. 'No, no, it's all right. I'll take him home.'

'What is it? Angina?'

'No, no, nothing like that. It's just he's finished his pint of beer.'

There was a stunned silence, then a sudden shuffle, high-pitched sniggering from the rugby team in the back room. Hear, hear, someone said.

'Oh,' Frank said. 'Is that it?'

'Yes, that's it. He gets a bit emotional. That's all it is. We keep getting thrown out of pubs, to tell the truth.'

'I expect you do.'

'Yes, well.' She rose to her feet.

'He's welcome to have another one. If it won't do him any harm.'

'Oh. Oh, that's very good of you.' She looked back at her husband quickly and expertly, as if checking him out. 'Yes, that would be nice. Lovely. That would be lovely, wouldn't it, Daniel? He's only had the one so far. He takes forever to drink it down. I don't think he swallows very well.'

Daniel, having got the roar out of his system, didn't seem interested in what was going on one way or the other, moving his head slightly from side to side but not looking at anything in particular.

'I'll bring it over,' Frank said. 'Can I get *you* anything?'

'No, thank you. Oh yes, why not? I'll have a small glass of dry white wine.' She opened her handbag and took out her purse. 'And you must let me pay for the broken glass.'

'Don't worry about it,' Frank told her. 'Any of it. This is on the house.'

It was like saying the magic words. That exact moment, in comes Dawn.

Darren went up to the reception.

'Can you tell me what ward Romesh Mehta is on?' he asked.

'It's gone half nine,' the woman said. 'Visiting hours are just over.'

Stall for time a sec. 'What?'

'Over,' she repeated.

'What?'

'Vis-it-ing hours.'

'Oh yes. I know they're *over*.'

'Well then.'

'That's why I'm here. *Because* they're over.'

'I beg pardon?'

'I come to collect a lady what's been visiting him. This Romesh bloke.'

'I see. Can't she make her way to the exit herself?'

'She's pretty old,' Darren said. 'She's called Dawn.' Getting together with Gem and being given a lift by her old man made him feel on top of his game. Plus it comes in useful, he thought, being a bad boy when young, gives you stuff to fall back on. Just like you have a blank cheque which you can put whatever amount of money on it you want, you can have blank lies stored up that you stashed away in earlier days, for when you didn't do your homework or missed school or got in a spot of bother with the law, and you can fill them out how you choose, given the need. 'She'll probably get lost. You don't want her wandering round the hospital at all hours of the night. She'll frighten the patients.'

It was funny, being bad again made him feel like a different person, made him feel up for it. Being a good guy, like he mostly was these days, always made him feel slow and hampered.

The corridors were quite dark. Darren didn't know whether they were saving on the electric or it was just a way of saying *bugger off public, it's lights out time*. He walked fast, like he knew exactly where he was and where he was going. When he saw a porter or nurse coming along he gave them a quick nod as he went past, like we're all friends together. He sent mental rays down to the container of beer he was carrying, telling it to act like it was a flask of spare blood or a bottle of medicine if anybody asked.

Then he got to the ward door. He stood outside for a moment, took a breath, then pushed it open.

On the right hand side, little partitioned-off bedrooms, each with a window you could look into. Immediately in front, a little table, with a dispenser of hand cleaner on. Beyond, on the left, an office area, with a nurse sitting there, looking at a computer screen.

Darren took a deep breath, walked up to the table, put the beer down, picked up the dispenser and gave his hands a good squirt. Do everything slow, he told himself, show how you can be calm. He made himself think of a calm thing. The bar, when he'd given it its clean, before it was open to the punters. When he'd got it near as he could to what Dawn wanted it to be, a brown diamond. Having to clean his hands must have made the connection.

A brown diamond, he said under his breath while he rubbed his hands against each other till the blob of stuff was gone. He pictured the woodwork glowing dimly in the electric light, with pink flickers from the firelight catching its surface.

While he was doing it, the nurse got up from her desk and stood in front of him.

Brown diamond, brown diamond, he said in his brain a couple of times more, like it was a spell to keep evil things at bay.

She was a big woman with a very wide uniform. 'Can I help you?' she asked.

'Oh, yes please.'

She waited.

'Thing is,' Darren said, then ran out of steam. She stayed how she was, just waiting. Being big makes people good at just waiting without blabbing off or raising their eyebrows or scratching their noses or anything, like by being big they've got a bit of boulder or mountain in them and don't feel the need to shift.

'My name's Keith,' Darren said.

It came out just like that. What I've got to do, he realised, I got to tell the truth. Sometimes there's no choice. I got a carry-out of beer to give Romesh, can't pretend it's anything else. Making out it's like blood or something's OK for scuttling along the corridors, but this is crunch-time here.

But the thing of it was, if he had to tell the truth, he wanted it to come out with a bit of life in it, come out convincing, like it would if he was making it up in bad boy mode. So he was just going to say Darren, because why not?, but at the last second swerved into Keith.

It was all the same to the nurse, Keith or Darren, what's the odds?, it wasn't like when he was grilled by Gemma's dad and he needed to be Darren just to convince him he was who he was, so her dad knew Gemma would be OK. That everything was *sound*.

Saying he was Keith flipped everything else over that he had to say, made it a lie even while it was the truth, made it easier to handle.

Got to believe I'm Keith, Darren told himself, then I'll believe all the rest of it too.

'Oh yes, Keith?' the nurse said.

'I'm a barman in the Old Spring.'

'That so?'

'Romesh is one of our customers. Romesh Mehta. He's like a regular.'

'I see.'

'I mean, he comes in every day after work, has a drink. I don't mean a lot. Just one or two.'

'Ah ha.'

'I brought him some beer,' Keith said. 'That's what's in here. Two pints of beer.'

'*Two* pints?' she said, like one might have been OK but two pints was stretching it a bit.

'Two,' Keith said. 'To keep him going, like.'

'Keith, Mr Mehta is very ill indeed. That's why he's in this ward. The people in this ward have little bedrooms to themselves, because they're too ill to be on the general wards. They might pick up something catching and go out like a light. He's far too ill to drink any beer.'

'I got to give it to him. He said he'll never have a drink of beer again in this life. I got to turn it around.'

'He just can't, Keith. I'm sorry.'

'Look, you're a nurse, right?'

She looked like she'd sucked a lemon. 'What's your point?'

'What you do, you nurse people?'

'That's true enough.'

'Well, I'm a barman. What *I* do is give people their beer. Right?'

She gave him another long look. She had brown eyes glistening in the dim light. Keith suddenly had a stupid desire to fling his arms round her neck just to break the tension. Got to watch it, he told himself, striking lucky with old Gem is going to my head.

'Tell you what,' she said at last. 'If you're quiet, we can go and have a look at Mr Mehta. I think he's probably fast asleep. But you can leave your beer in his room and when he wakes up in the morning he'll know you've been in to deliver it.'

Keith tiptoed after the nurse into Romesh's bedroom. He was lying flat on his back, keeping completely quiet. There was no sound of breathing. He had a little smile on his face, the sort of smile you might give off when dead. In fact he probably *was* dead, as far as Keith could make out.

'You can put the beer on his side table, there,' the nurse whispered.

'OK,' Keith whispered back. 'Tell you what. I'll just pour a little bit out into this glass type thing.'

There were a couple of plastic glasses on the bedside table, one of them empty. Keith picked it up. The nurse immediately put her hand over the top. 'I told you, Keith, he can't drink it.'

'I'll just put a drop in. Then he can see it, at least. Maybe he can smell it, if he like breathes at all.'

The hand stayed where it was for a moment, then lifted. 'All right,' she said. 'Just a drop. Perhaps the doctors will think it's Lucozade.'

Keith poured a glug into the glass. Romesh didn't budge, stayed as dead as a doornail. 'Cheers,' Keith whispered.

They tiptoed back out again.

'Thanks a bunch, nurse,' Keith said.

'I'm a sister, if you want to know,' the nurse replied. She sounded a bit sharpish now they were out of the cubicle and she could raise her voice again. It was like Keith had noticed with people before, they let you get away with something and then they go all hoity-toity, like they regret cutting you the bit of slack in the first place.

'Oh. OK. Sister.' Keith nodded his head. 'Well, thank *you*, sister,' he said.

Dawn had put the black dress on she wore at the New Year's party, quite low cut but she'd checked no bite marks were on show. High heels, a necklace of freshwater mussels Frank had bought her in the early days. She'd done her hair up again, like it had been earlier this evening, only more so.

'Hello, then,' Frank said. He looked at her like she was someone he hadn't seen before.

'Yes, Frank,' she said.

'I thought you were changing.'

'I have changed.' Perhaps because his head was so round, Frank had one of them smiley faces when glad, and a frowny one when not. Now, frowny. 'I have changed,' Dawn said again. 'Blimey, are you blind or what?'

'I thought you were going to change down. For work, like. You went and changed *up*.' He thought for a moment. 'You off out again?'

'No, Frank.'

'Thank goodness for that.'

Her heart thumped. She remembered when it did that before, when she didn't have a stitch on, her breasts throbbing with the beat of it, Tiger Tim watching with those hot mean eyes of his. Even with the scoop neck of her dress she felt similar, like her nerves were being broadcast across the room. It was Frank sounding so heartfelt, as if her going out before had been a trouble to him, as if he guessed somehow something of what had gone on. She recalled a little edge in his voice when she'd said she was going to visit Romesh, like as if he felt a touch of jealousy.

267

'Dawn, you look splendid,' the Father said.

'Thank you, Father.'

Alan leaned over to the Father and said something. It sounded like 'sucking up'.

'I beg your pardon, Alan?' Dawn asked.

'I was just saying to Father here, in your game you shouldn't notice beautiful women,' Alan said. 'But how could he help? How could you help, Father?'

'How could I help?' Father said, looking up at her. Of course, the difference being *he* said it like he meant it.

'There you go, then,' Alan said. He gave Dawn a long look. 'Tell you what it is, you look like a . . . a new dawn.'

'Thank you very much,' Dawn said. 'I never heard that one before. How many of them have you had?' She nodded her head towards his pint. 'What I want to know.'

'Oh dear,' Alan said, nodding in agreement. 'You have a point. Still, remember our conversation earlier, on the subject of Wordsworth's great poem?

> As oft upon my couch I lie
> In vacant and in pensive mood
> I think about the booze I've drunk
> And wonder, was I very rude?'

Dawn gave him a long look. 'You said it,' she said.

To her surprise the Father suddenly started shaking with laughter. He wasn't used to doing it, she could tell, so his face went all scrunched up, almost as if in pain. Talk about throbbings in the chest: she could see little tsunamis running across his jacket and over that black shirt type of thing below his dog collar.

Dawn turned to Frank. 'I need to have a word with you,' she said. She glanced back at Alan and the Father, who was just calming down. 'Out of earshot of this pair of reprobates. In private.'

'We can't do that, Dawn.' Frank looked all of a fluster. 'There's just the two of us here. Old Darren's done his bit. He went.'

'Well, let's go behind the bar then.'

They stood right by the far wall of the bar. Dawn came up close to Frank, so her face was inches from his. He could smell perfume she'd put on, and toothpaste on her breath. He was aware of the pale pink of the lipstick on her lips. He could even get a faint boiled sweets sort of smell off of that. He couldn't recall when he'd last been so close to her.

'First off,' she whispered, 'what you doing giving drinks away? To them pair at the table. They're not even regulars.'

'It's a long story,' Frank whispered back.

'We've got to watch our finances. You know that. We're nine hundred quid worse off than we thought we were.'

Frank nodded.

'But I got some good news about that business. I worked out what happened.'

'Did you, Dawn?'

'We been paying Darren out of the till. We planned to take his wages out of the roll money. That's what we planned. We sort of forgot.'

Frank thought for a moment, trying to take it in.

'We're in the clear, Frank,' Dawn said triumphantly. He could feel her breath on his face as she spoke: it was like her words were landing on him.

'We still got to find the money,' he pointed out.

'But it's all accounted for, that's the thing of it. We've not done owt wrong.'

'I never thought we had.'

'No more did I. But now nobody can. Think we did. Nobody can say a dickey-bird. I'll get Tim to bring our books back.'

'I don't see what odds it makes.'

'Because we've got it sorted. Because we've got a story to tell. We can make it make sense. *Them* are the odds.'

'If you say so.'

Suddenly she gave him a smacker on the lips.

'Hey up,' said Gray, peering round the partition in search of a pint.

Dawn moved her head slightly back. 'I say so,' she said. 'It's all all right, Frank, promise.'

The next thing he knew his arms were round her and he was kissing her back. There was a ripple of applause from the pub. He felt her, tightly hugged against him, her lips, slightly sticky with her lipstick, pressed against his own. It seemed so easy all of a sudden.

When they'd separated, Frank saw Katie had come up beside Gray. 'Oh blow,' she said to Dawn. 'I thought I had old Frank in the bag.'

19

'Seeing the happy couple,' Alan said, 'reminds me I'd better go home to my stew.'

'I had a friend died today,' Thomas told him abruptly.

'Ha,' said Alan. Thomas knew what his *ha* meant: that explains all the beer. Which of course it did. That was the problem with Alan's knowingness.

'He believed in transformation,' Thomas said. 'In transubstantiation, in fact.'

'Don't *you*? I thought it went with the territory.'

'He celebrated it in hymns. In verse. I think it can happen there. In the words. I'm not sure any more whether it happens anywhere else.'

'Well, the Bible's nothing *but* words,' Alan pointed out. 'A church service is made of words.'

I have to get this said, Thomas realised. If I don't, I'll lapse back into all the beer I've drunk. I'm like someone taking their clothes off at a party, got to carry on or we'll all pause for thought and I'll feel such a fool. 'I mean,' he said, trying to fix on his point, 'in a hymn you can make things rhyme that don't rhyme in the real world.'

'As in my Wordsworth tribute,' Alan agreed. 'Though I think the only transformation I accomplished there was changing gold into base metal.'

'He left me a message, of sorts, my friend did. It was: Song title, dung beetle. He'd written it in his notebook. I think he meant even a dung beetle can be turned into melody. Which I suppose it can. But it doesn't stop it being just a dung beetle, when all's said and done.'

'You and your dung beetles,' Alan said, shaking his head. 'Do you remember young Darren getting his knickers in a twist that time about the noise that hedgehog made getting flattened? And Jerry telling him it was only the sound of air being forced out of its backside, sensitive soul that he is? Jerry, I mean. That would be an unearthly melody, wouldn't it just? Music scored for a hedgehog's bum.'

I finish my fucking beer. I stand up. And little fucking Gav stands up too. He says I got to go now, and off he fucks. Straight off to go to Kev fucking Perry or Kev fucking Perry's mates, and tell them, Jake's on his fucking way.

And then when I get out of here, I'm fair game. No point in telling them I won't say nothing. They won't fucking believe me till they've done stuff to me. Maybe not even then.

Jake stood up.

Fucking Gav stood up too.

Fuck.

'I got to go,' fucking Gav said.

'Hang on a tick,' Jake told him. He gave him like a swing of the head, like as to say, come this way that my head is going. Follow my fucking head.

Claire took a sip of her white wine, watching over the rim as Daniel raised his glass of beer, poised it at his lips, took a short pull. He lowered the glass again, careful to hold it level all the way down to the table top, raised his hand to his lips and used the back of it to rub them dry, then made his walrus noise once more, that repulsive harrumph.

It was funny: he seemed so awkward and clumsy, yet every move he made was carefully calculated. He generated the intricate unwanted detail a bluebottle does when using thin arms to wash its bulbous face. Daniel's limbs had gone thin during his decline, and his face was bulbous, true enough, with protuberant eyes.

A shadow seemed to fall over Claire and she put her own glass down. Funny that, the way you can feel it, as though a shadow possesses its own tiny weight.

She twisted round to see who it was, expecting the kindly landlord again, and almost cried out with shock.

A shadow was standing there. A solid three-dimensional one.

A blue man, entirely blue. Tall, big-built, in a cheap blue tracksuit with a white line down the arms and legs. His face looked as if it had been scribbled out, deprived of meaning. Claire noticed pink rims to the man's eyelids, no tattooing needles narrow enough to tackle them, presumably. They made his eyes look sore.

A small rodent-like man was standing beside him, making slightly apologetic noises, little grunts and groans, hums and has, presumably by way of saying sorry for the way they'd approached unannounced and given her a shock. She knew the word for his noises. It was a phrase she'd learned since Daniel stopped speaking: paralinguistic gestures. She clung to its solidity so as not to go under.

'Your name Angina?' the tattooed man asked.

'I beg your pardon?'

'You called Angina?'

The rodent made whoops and twitters, little scraps of sound to buffer the raw questions.

'No, I'm not called that. No.'

'Oh.' The blue face stared down at her, expressionless. What expression *could* it have? 'Oh. I thought old Frank called you Angina.'

'No, no. My name is Claire.' She was aware of saying it in a sweet all-friends-together way, as you might to a class of infants, afraid of offending him by not being called Angina.

The face continued to look. Perhaps disbelieving. 'Frank doesn't know my name,' she explained. 'We've not been in here before.'

'*My* name is Jake,' the man said.

'Oh. Right. Hello, Jake.'

'I want to tell you something.' He glanced across the table at Daniel.

'I want to tell you both something.'

'Oh yes?'

'A couple of weeks ago I saw a bloke called Kev Perry stick a knife in a bloke called Billy West. Outside the Griffin. Pub called the Griffin.'

'Oh. How horrible.'

The rodent was looking up at the tattooed man in shock. 'Hang on, Jake,' he said.

'You got to remember that,' Jake told Claire. 'In case anybody wants to know. Have you got it?'

'Yes, I think so. Kev Perry. And Billy West. Did he, this Billy . . . ?'

'Yep,' Jake said. 'He did.'

'Oh dear. Dear oh dear.'

'You got to remember too,' Jake said across the table at Daniel.

'Right-oh,' Daniel said.

It was the first word he'd spoken in more than a year. Claire looked at him in amazement. Then she looked up at the tattooed man again. 'You must be on his wave-length,' she said. Jake nodded his head slowly, then moved away, the rodent gibbering in his wake.

'What the hell are they doing?' Frank asked. Jake and Gav had gone over to where Colin the Coach and Nigel were still playing shove-ha'penny. Little Colin looked up as he sensed Jake looming over him and immediately snapped to attention. In his blazer he looked like a newly demobbed squaddie. Nigel peered over his shoulder, like at the first hint of danger he'd duck down into the lee of it. Frankie stood slightly to one side. His golden head began to bob in time with what Jake said.

'Asking to be chucked out, that's what they're doing,' Dawn said. 'Pestering everybody.'

Having said their piece, Jake and Gav walked over towards the bar.

'Out,' Dawn told them.

'You heard the lady,' Gav said to Jake.

'Just two minutes,' Jake said. 'You know the Griffin? I saw Kev Perry drop Billy West on the pavement outside, the other day. That's all I'm saying.'

Alan did one of those silent whistles. 'Did you just?'

'Why don't you go to the police?' the Father asked.

'Out,' Dawn said again.

'*You* can go to the police if you want,' Jake said. 'Anyone can, like.'

He set off towards the back room, Gav bobbing like a tug boat in his wake.

'Hey, wrong way,' Frank said. 'Door's other direction.'

'One more minute,' Jake said.

'I'm off, anyhow,' Gav said, suddenly turning tail and heading for the exit.

'Night!' Frank called after him. '*He* took me serious, at least,' he told Dawn.

'Good night?' Dawn asked. 'What you mean, good night? What planet are you on?'

'Hang on,' Frank told her. 'Wait your hurry. Let's get this over with.' He followed Jake into the snug. 'Quiet a moment, everybody,' Frank called out. A hush descended. 'Jake here's got something he wants to say to you all.'

'I suppose it's like an act of confession,' Thomas said.

Alan looked acidly back at him. 'What's he got to confess? He hasn't done anything.'

'Well, you can confess that too. I have, in my time.'

'Speak for yourself, then.' Alan shook his head. 'I nearly said he's not as green as he is cabbage-looking, but I suppose that's the wrong vegetable. I don't think it would work with an aubergine. But did you see the artful dodger scuttling out of the pub as fast as his little legs would carry him? I bet he's off to have a word with the king of crime. Telling him what Jake's been up to. It puts that Mr Perry in a bit of a cleft stick, doesn't it? He's probably some teenage psychopath. But he'll have to rub out a whole pub-full of people if he wants to suppress that bit of information. It's a question of logistics.'

As Jake left the pub, in walked Darren. His hair was soaking wet and he looked puffed out.

'You just missed the fun,' Frank told him.

'Funny idea of fun,' Dawn said. 'It was old Jake telling everyone who killed that bloke outside the Griffin last week. That Billy Whizz.'

'Oh,' Darren said. He looked over towards the doorway as if to catch Jake's outline lingering there, like when Desperate Dan runs through a wall and leaves a Desperate Dan-shaped hole behind him.

'Anyhow, you're drenched through,' Dawn told him.

'It's barrelling down again,' Darren said. 'I run all the way back from the hospital.'

'Ha,' Frank said. 'Do you think you got less wet than if

you'd *walked* back through the same amount of rain? Instead of running, like?'

'Who was it?' Darren asked. 'What killed him?'

'It was Kev –' Frank began.

'You don't want to know,' Dawn said firmly. 'Ho, Darren, did you say the *hos*pital?'

'Yep. Hospital.'

'What were you doing at the hospital? Are you not feeling well?'

'I been visiting Romesh,' Darren said.

Frank watched as pink slid over Dawn's cheek bones. She *is* keen on that poor bugger, he thought.

Why not? There's enough and to spare. He felt he could afford to be generous. With her, with himself.

Talking of which, Frankie chose that exact moment to walk over.

'Think I'd better be off now,' he said. 'I've had enough excitement for one evening.'

'Hang on a minute, mate,' Frank said. He flipped the hatch, came through the public and into the snug, up to Frankie at the bar. 'Nice one, m'dear. You done me a good turn. I'm really grateful.'

'You're welcome,' Frankie said.

Frank put his hands on Frankie's shoulders and pulled him in for a blokey hug. Why not? he asked himself once again. Nothing to hide, now he and Dawn were dancing hand in hand again.

'You're very welcome,' Frankie said again as they unclinched. 'Any time, eh?'

Frank looked across the snug. 'Fire roaring away,' he said.

'That's the ticket,' Frankie agreed. He punched him lightly on the shoulder. 'See you, friend.' He gave a quick general nod at the room. 'See you,' he said in a louder voice.

There was a murmur of goodbyes as Frankie walked out. Dawn didn't join in. She was looking intently at Darren.

'How was he, then?' she asked.

'I took him a drink of beer,' Darren said.

Dawn's whole body seemed to give a little spasm as the information went in. 'Beer?'

'Yep. One of them two-pint take-outs.'

'You took him beer?'

'Well, you said he said he would never have a glass of beer again. Like when I was talking to Gem I heard you say it. Gem's the girl I was talking to earlier on. She has a bunch of chickens. So I thought, better put that right. Being I'm a barman now, type thing. Her dad give me a lift to the hospital. Gem's dad.'

Dawn raised her fist to her mouth and sort of sniffed it, like she had a flower clutched between her fingers.

'Hey, Dawn,' Frank said. 'That finger of yours looks quite nasty.'

'What?' Dawn looked testily over at Frank. 'What you on about?'

'That finger of yours. You lost your plaster. It looks like it needs another one.'

She moved her fist away from her mouth and inspected her finger. 'Oh that,' she said. 'I think it'll do better with a bit of air on it.' She turned back towards Darren. 'How'd he take it, then? Romesh?'

'He had this lovely smile on his face,' Darren said. 'He kept on smiling the whole time I was there.'

'I must go,' Alan said. 'I shall have to trot past the Griffin with my head averted. Just as well it's still tipping it down. Maybe it will blur my features a bit.'

'I must go too,' Thomas said. 'When I've finished my pint.'

Alan stepped back from the bar. 'Thanks for the chat,' he said.

'Likewise.'

'I'm sorry you lost your friend.'

'Thank you.' Thomas paused a moment as Julian's face suddenly came into his mind, pale and shiny like a full moon. 'Gone to God,' he added.

'No offence, but I think I'd rather go to my wife, for the time being.'

'To be frank, I don't blame you.'

'If she'll let me through the door, that is.'

'Blame it on me.'

'Thank you very much. Nothing like using a man of God as your alibi.'

'Good point,' Thomas said, wincing.

When Alan had gone, Darren sidled up, clutching a pint of beer. He looked a bit anti-climactic now he'd done his good deed for the day.

'How's it going then?' Thomas asked.

'Dawn give me this beer,' Darren told him. 'You know she never gives anyone a free beer.'

'That's gratitude, I imagine, because of what you did for Romesh.'

'No big deal,' Darren said, brusquely confident all of a sudden. 'Remember I wanted to ask you something before? When I'd just gone down the cellar to put a new barrel on?'

'Oh yes, I remember. What was it, Darren?'

'Well, the thing of it was, earlier this afternoon, I saw this like shape, like a man, hurrying out of the pub. I wondered if it was the ghost what lives in the cellar sort of exorcising itself.'

'Could have been, I suppose,' Thomas said judiciously. He pressed his hands together and put them against his lips, as if in thought. 'Could have been,' he repeated.

'Only thing was, the bloke shape what was leaving was black. Like in a black coat. And the bloke I saw in the cellar was this beigey colour. I got the idea when I went down this evening there might be two sorts of ghosts living down there.'

'Ah,' said Thomas. He felt he'd been caught out. Here I am, agreeing myself to death and destruction, he thought. 'Tell you what, Darren, I believe you might be right. I think there *are* two sorts of ghosts.'

'Are there?' Darren asked. The expression on his face could only be described as literal, as if he wanted to gobble up everything Thomas was going to say to him.

'There's dark ones. And more . . . beigey-coloured ones.'

'What's the difference?'

Suddenly the beer kicked in. Should have discovered it earlier in my life, Thomas thought. It would have been an adjunct to my teaching. 'They're all ghosts of us. They all come from inside. The dark ones are ghosts of us from before we became human. We still have that memory somewhere. Of being something that doesn't speak. Of when we were just animals. Like a dung beetle. Or maybe a hedgehog. They make us afraid because they remind us of dying. Because animals just die, when it comes down to it. When they're gone, they're gone.'

'In actual fact,' Darren said, 'apes. Which are the ones we are actually descended from.'

'Apes, yes.'

'This bloke what was leaving the pub. He was more like an ape than a dung beetle.'

'Good point, Darren. I suppose he was. So the dark ghosts are the ones that frighten us. The paler sort are just ghosts of people as people. People don't die in the same way. They don't cease to exist. I had a friend who died today. I was thinking about him just now. That's like a ghost.'

'That's what Dawn told me, earlier on. Like it's a memory.'

'Yes, that's what it is. It's a ghost of his life, not his death. Like when you leave a room, you leave a bit of yourself behind. A sort of atmosphere. Look around. Look around here. What do you see?'

'People boozing.'

'And what else are they doing?'

Darren shrugged his shoulders. 'Talking, that's what they're doing,' Thomas explained. 'Talking their heads off, for hour after hour.'

'That lady sitting at the table with her husband, they're not talking,' Darren said.

'Well, apart from them. There's always an exception that proves the rule. What I'm trying to say, words are the bits of ourselves that we leave behind.'

'You mean, ghosts are words, like?'

'In a manner of speaking, yes.'

'If the bloke that left the pub was really the ghost of an ape, I suppose that leaves the dead landlord still down there in the cellar?'

'I wouldn't worry about him, Darren. You're working behind the bar yourself now. His old bar. You're doing his job. Carrying on where he left off. He's not likely to bother you now.'

'Oh right. Like it.'

'This pub holds all the words that everybody who has ever drunk in here has said. They just swill around.' Thomas swilled his beer round its glass to demonstrate. 'New people come and inherit the words. And add to them themselves.'

'Tell you what, though,' Darren said. 'This two types of ghost theory doesn't explain how come I'm like a vortex for poltergeists.'

Thomas had another swig of his pint, hoping to drink in the answer, but it wasn't necessary.

'The fire's burning down a bit,' Darren said. 'I better liven it up.'

Thomas stayed where he was and finished his beer. Behind him, sitting at the table with his wife, the breather was breathing, and over by the shove-ha'penny board Colin the Coach was sniffing, the pair of them chuntering together in out in out, as if the old building itself was raspily drawing breath, the sound oddly penetrative through the pub's general hubbub.

Acknowledgements

Thanks to the following for reading the manuscript: Lucy Atkins, Nick Boyle, Tessa Hadley, Julia Green, Richard Kerridge, Ashley Pharoah and Tricia Wastvedt; to the late Cy Meyer for the gift of J. Henri Fabre's magnificent work *The Sacred Beetle and Others*, translated by Alexander Teixera de Mattos; to Russian John for an anecdote; to Will for a vital intervention and to him and Helen for all their advice, support and help; to my agent Caroline Dawnay; to Luke Brown and Alan Mahar of Tindal Street Press.

To Jo, who has always done the research with me. And to that great and beleaguered British institution, the pub.